Praise for

Dog
Sitters

"The frolicking fun in Rozsa Gaston's *Dog Sitters* evokes a blend of Kay Thompson's old-world, New York elegance with its scenes at the Stanhope and Algonquin, and Pulitzer-winning novelist Teresa Carpenter's sultry romance sagas."

—Lee Daniels

"A lighthearted romantic journey featuring two very opposite characters and a cheeky pup. The search for Percy keeps us on the edge of our seats, especially as his intrepid dog sitters become aware that their adventure may not only be to find their misplaced charge. You will root for all three of them to find what they're looking for by story's end."

—Nicki Piercy Coddington, Big Dog Design

"An addictive page turner with a compelling plot and a sweet love story, *Dog Sitters* makes for an exceptionally well written poolside read. The playful tension between Hint and Jack alludes to the complex issues in love and life. Delightful."

—Helene Furst, author of *Morning Beans Blog*

Dog Sitters

A Man, a Woman, and a Schnoodle

ROZSA GASTON

Renaissance Editions

New York

Cover design by Tugboat Design

Back cover photo by Rozsa Gaston

Author photo by Classic Kids Photography

Gaston, Rozsa.
Dog Sitters/ Rozsa Gaston.
p. cm.
ISBN-13: 9781479221455

ISBN-10: 1479221457

Library of Congress Control Number: 2012916299

Renaissance Editions
New York
www.renaissanceeditions.com

Contents

For the best dog in the world

You know who you are

1

PERCY

"Percy—come back!" Hint frantically rushed after the black and gray Schnoodle, stumbling through twigs, branches and brush. On her next to last day of dog sitting her best friend's pet she had taken him for an extra long walk.

But Percy paid her no mind, intent on pursuing the small animal he'd spotted in the undergrowth. He'd rushed to investigate, pulling unexpectedly on his leash. Before she could tighten her grip, it had slipped from her hand.

"Percy, get back here now," she commanded. She might as well be shouting at the wind. Her stern tone made no impact. He continued to dash madly after his prey.

She ran faster, but the small dog moved quickly. After a minute, he was gone from sight. She shouted and called, hysteria raising her voice higher and higher. If she lost the dog, what would Nicole and Tom think? How could she explain it to them? But worse, how could she live with herself?

She almost couldn't bear the thought of handing Percy off to Tom's friend the next evening, but her flight to Punta Cana was at 2:15 p.m. the afternoon after that. If all went well, she'd check into the illustrators' conference, confirm her meeting with the artistic director of Story Tales Press, then go watch the sunset on the beach with her cousin Kim and girlfriend Nina. She'd been excited but also sad at the thought of saying good-bye to her canine friend. Now she'd give anything just to catch him so she could turn him over to her replacement.

But shouting to the dog to come back wasn't having the right effect. She sat down on a log. *Calm down, then decide what to do next.* She could call the police. But did police respond to lost dog emergencies? She could go back to the dog run and ask the other dog owners for help locating him. It would be the sensible thing to do. But her intuition told her to try one more time to find him all on her own. She sat still, taking even, long, deep breaths.

Don't let your emotions get in the way, Hint. The voice of her father came into her head as clearly as if he were sitting next to her. When she'd had a problem as a child, he'd always told her to break it down and parse it into manageable pieces. She thought through why Percy had run off. He'd been attracted to the motion of some small animal ahead of them. He'd taken off after it. 'A small animal,' 'ahead of them,' 'attracted to'— she couldn't do much about any of those pieces, could she?

She went back over it again. 'Attracted to . . .' Percy had run off because he was attracted to something. If that were the case, then he could be attracted back to her. He loved her min-istrations, as well as the tone of her voice when she called him

'Snuggle Boy' and other terms. But he hadn't responded to her cries. Could this be because the tone of voice she'd used hadn't attracted him? Perhaps it had scared him off farther.

She would try something different. She would be the object of Percy's next attraction. By now he'd either found the small animal, or more likely, lost it and was looking around for something else to catch his attention.

"Percy is my Snuggle Boy," she began to sing softly to herself. "He's the cutest Snuggle Boy I know. Boy, I've known some Snuggle Boys in my day but none cuter than Percy." She sang the song again, swaying back and forth on the dead tree limb she sat on.

The woods grew quiet. She listened briefly then sang the ditty again. Something rustled in the brush. Motionless, she held her breath. *Whatever it is, pay it no mind.*

Singing calmed her, so she started up again, closing her eyes. Halfway through her song, a joyful bark interrupted her.

"Percy! You came back. You're my smart boy," she called out, careful to remain seated.

The dog ran to her, putting his front paws on her knees. They snuggled as she groped for his leash, hooking it firmly around her wrist. She wasn't taking any more chances, at least not for the remaining time she was guardian of the adorable eighteen-pound Schnauzer/Poodle mix now trying to lick her face.

Walking home briskly, the dog at her side, she marveled at how effective her final strategy had been. Wasn't there a saying, "you attract more flies with honey than with vinegar"? She'd been the honey. Somehow she'd known the dog would be there when she opened her eyes. Then she hadn't lunged for him. She'd felt empowered by simply sitting there and letting him come to her.

An aphorism she had once heard but never fully understood popped into her head. Billy Wilder, the movie director, had purportedly counseled Marilyn Monroe for a scene they were filming, telling her, "Don't just do something—stand there." Now she understood what he had meant. Luring back Percy had given her an epiphany. She hadn't gone after him. She'd made him want to come to her. It was a lesson she planned to apply in other areas of life.

THAT AFTERNOON JACK Whitby left work fifteen minutes early. He would get off the train in Bronxville shortly before six then take his time walking over to Hint Daniel's place to pick up Muttsly. Percy. Whatever.

He hoped his best friend's dog wouldn't try to sleep on his bed. Had Tom left one of his smelly running shirts for Percy to sleep on? Probably not. He would have, if he'd passed the dog off directly to Jack. But Tom's wife's friend had offered to dog sit the first five days, which was fine with Jack, since he knew next to nothing about how to look after an animal himself. Unfortunately Nicole's friend was leaving town the following day, so Tom had asked Jack to take Percy the final five days of their cruise. He'd explained that the year before when they'd vacationed, they'd left the dog in a kennel and the Schnoodle had acted depressed and standoffish on their return. Jack had hesitated, but when Tom told him small dogs were welcome on Metro-North commuter trains, so he could just pick him up on his way home from work, he'd caved in. He'd call in the favor next time Tom had a few U.S. Open tickets left over from his firm's client freebies slush fund.

The trip to Bronxville was over in less than half an hour. He exited the train in the company of dozens of prosperous looking commuters, many of whom were being met by spouses with children, or drivers.

He eyed the crowd. Not a bad place to live. But for a single person? Just what kind of social life did Nicole's girlfriend have? It looked as if they were all married in a place like this.

He strolled down Pondfield Road, Bronxville's main street. The number of high-end consumer goods in shop windows told him the town was populated with plenty of affluent females. They were either making good money themselves or sending their spouses off to bring home the bacon so they could fry it. Only they weren't frying bacon around here. They were buying expensive antiques, fancy lamps, and designer labels. The linen baby clothes in one store window all looked as if they needed to be ironed. Who in the world would do that?

When his niece Marguerite had been a newborn, he'd babysat her a few times. She'd thrown up, pooped, drooled and wet all over him at least once every thirty minutes. He couldn't figure out why people wanted to have babies. They were disgusting.

But Marguerite's smile had been so adorable after he'd burped her and she'd spit up all over his shirt. He didn't really care about messes anyway, and her satisfied expression had been worth it.

Spying the hand-painted sign for Meadow Lane, he turned into it, passing a few comfortably large, clapboard-framed houses after which stood a charming, three-story apartment building with an Italianate tile roof. The plaque over the entryway read number fifteen—the address Hint Daniels had given him.

Inside the marble-floored foyer, he pressed the buzzer marked H. Daniels.

After a long pause, he buzzed again. No answer.

Annoyed, he glanced at his watch. Hadn't they said after six on the twentieth? He pushed the button again, this time longer. The sound echoed through the empty foyer. Looking around, he spied some catalogues and magazines on the polished black granite counter. Examining them revealed that H. Daniels subscribed to *Other Worlds* magazine. He leafed through the periodical, perusing fantastical illustrations of what looked like sci-fi and mythological creatures. Weird. Something one might expect a person with a name like Hint to subscribe to.

He pressed her buzzer again, laying on it for several seconds. An elderly woman popped her head out of a door on the first floor. She gave him a dyspeptic look then slammed her door shut.

Jack ripped off a page from the back of a catalogue and scribbled a short note: *Hint Daniels – I was here. Where were you? I thought we had agreed I'd pick up Percy this evening. – Jack Whitby 917-916-5758 cell.*

The missive wasn't particularly polite, but he wasn't pleased to be inconvenienced like this. He walked rapidly back to the train station, not at all certain when the next train came through that would get him back to Pleasantville. As he waited on the platform, he wondered if Nicole's friend was some sort of ditsy artist. How could she blow off something as important as a pre-arranged pick up of their friends' dog? Hadn't he specifically said the twentieth? Tom had told him she was going to the Caribbean on the twenty-first. How would she get the dog to him in time to make her flight the following day now that she'd screwed up the dog pickup? What a nitwit.

According to the posted schedule the train was due to arrive at 6:45 P.M. He looked at his watch. It was 6:43, two minutes to go. Something about the watch face unsettled him. He checked it again: 6:44 now. Why was an alarm signal going off in his head? He studied his watch. Something didn't seem right.

Then he noticed the date marker.

The nineteenth? He blinked, swallowing hard. He'd thought it was the twentieth. It had been his own mistake. Heat from embarrassment leapt up his neck then flamed into his face.

Sprinting down the steps of the platform, he raced back to Hint Daniel's apartment. If she arrived home and read the note before he retrieved it, she'd think he was not only a nitwit, but a half-wit. Surely she'd tell Nicole about his mistake. And if she spoke with either Tom or Nicole before they got back, Tom would never let him live down the mistake. He had to get to her place before she did.

Three minutes later, he reached the foyer of her building, panting like a madman. The inner door was just closing behind a large woman with a double baby stroller. Thank

God, the note was still there. He grabbed it, shredding it into bits as he hurriedly exited. He'd try to make the 7:15 train to Pleasantville. Jogging back to the station, he rounded the corner of Meadow Lane. There, five yards in front of him on the sidewalk, a woman leaned over a small black and gray dog. Was it Percy? He'd met the dog once, the year before, but all he could remember was that it had been small. On the phone, Tom had mentioned that Percy was black, gray, and just under eighteen pounds. The dog in front of him fit all three points.

Jack jumped into the bushes, scrambling for cover behind a large oak tree. Trying to catch his breath, he prayed the woman now walking in his direction wouldn't see him.

"What do you see? Is there a squirrel over there?" Her voice was light, melodic. It sounded as if she were humming when she spoke. "Come on, Snuggle Bunny, let's go home. You're not going to catch that squirrel, no matter what you think. Let's go, Snuggle Boy."

He held his breath, in equal measure trying not to be seen and straining to hear what endearments the woman would next lavish on the dog. A strange and irrational longing for a female to speak to him like that stole over him. Embarrassed for more than one reason, he silently asked the oak tree he hid behind not to blow his cover.

HINT TRIED TO hurry Percy past the large tree across the street from the park next to her building. He was barking wildly as if there were a squirrel aiming an acorn at his head. Hopefully, one day Percy would put aside his puppy dreams and figure out he was never going to catch a squirrel.

When she had been a child she had frequently dreamt that she could fly. At some point she conceded it would never happen. Had she felt sad at that moment? She let out a long "hmmm" as she pondered the tragic gap between imagination and reality that occurred for humans. Was it the same for dogs?

"Dream on, boy. Don't let anyone ever tell you you can't catch a squirrel. One day you will, Baby Boy. You'll catch one." She reached down and stroked the Schnoodle's silky ears.

A sound like a low groan seemed to emerge from the oak tree she had just passed. She glanced back at it. Was someone there? She stared intently. The air was suddenly as still as a painting. Had the tree just weighed in on her thoughts? For all she knew, trees had frustrations just as humans and canines did. Perhaps they wanted to walk. She laughed softly at the thought. Walking trees. Human. She would give it some thought, later. Her inspirations for work came from such ideas, the more fantastical the better.

Percy craned his neck then licked her hand.

She picked him up and buried her nose in his soft fur. The dog squirmed in delight, burrowing deeper into her neck. She took pleasure in his happiness. Would the person she was passing him off to tomorrow take such good care of him?

As if in answer, the breeze picked up and ruffled the leaves on the trees.

She shivered and hurried up the front path to her apartment building, still hugging Percy in her arms.

Unbeknownst to her, a stranger watched as she disappeared inside.

THE FOLLOWING EVENING Jack rang Hint's buzzer at 6:15 P.M. He'd dodged a bullet the day before. Sweat rose on his brow just thinking about the woman staring at the tree he'd been hiding behind. Thank God she'd been all wrapped up in the dog and hadn't come closer to investigate.

The door buzzed and he entered the inside hallway, wiping his forehead with the tail of his navy polo shirt.

"Up here on the second floor," a voice sang down to him. If a voice could dance, this one did.

He nimbly took the stairs two at a time to the second floor landing where he was greeted by a barking Percy and the woman he'd seen the evening before.

Up close she was even more attractive than the slim, smallish figure he'd hid from twenty-four hours earlier. Her hair was long and auburn, about six inches below shoulder length. He knew the shade because his sister Bibi used an auburn tint on her hair. When he'd asked her why she had tinted her hair the same color it already was, she had scoffed that he knew nothing about hair shades, then explained that her hair was chestnut brown, whereas auburn brown had hints of red when the light was right.

At that moment, the light was very right. He marveled at the fiery red hues haloing Nicole's friend's face as she swung around, motioning him to come in.

"Percy—calm down. This is your friend. Relax, it's alright."

"Hey, boy. It's me, Uncle Jack." He vaguely recalled meeting the dog the summer before, when Tom had invited him over for a party. He'd been on edge the entire evening, distracted by the argument he'd had in the car on the way there with his ex-girlfriend, who had wanted to attend a fancy event at her club instead. Tightening his jaw, he slammed shut the door on that particular memory. She was now free to attend all the fancy events she cared to with some other clown on her arm.

Percy barked furiously then growled as he stepped over the threshold of the apartment.

"Percy, stop that. This is your new babysitter." The woman scolded the dog as she picked him up and snuggled him against her chest. It appeared that Snuggle Boy had led a charmed life the past five days since Tom and Nicole had left.

Jack surveyed the living room of her apartment, silently approving the mustard-toned couch and faded Oriental carpet patterned in burgundy, navy and gold tones. She had good taste.

"Hi, I'm Hint Daniels." She smiled but didn't extend her hand, busy holding onto the squirming dog.

"Hi. Jack Whitby. How's it going with Percy?"

"He's been mostly a good boy."

He watched as the side of her mouth twitched. What did she mean by 'mostly?' "What's his schedule like? Do you walk him a lot?" he asked.

"I take him out about three times a day. We go out around eight, then midday, then one last walk in the evening."

Jack flashed back to the day before. He'd been lucky not to have been spotted by her. There was no way he could have explained what he was doing outside her building a day before they were scheduled to meet.

"How long do you walk him?" he asked, surreptitiously taking in her features. Finely arched eyebrows framed brown eyes with long lashes. Both were upstaged by a small mouth curved like a Cupid's bow.

"It depends, but usually a good half hour. Sometimes we go to the dog run."

"Do you let him off the leash over there?"

"I have, but you might not want to do that unless you're sure he'll come back to you."

"Do you want to take him for a walk now?" He wanted to spend a few more minutes in the company of this fine-boned, auburn-haired woman who subscribed to *Other Worlds* magazine. And that dancing voice. It was the polar opposite of the matter-of-fact, New York City-accented voices that surrounded him at work all day long.

"I've got to pack for my trip but I'll walk with you over to the train station, so he gets used to you with me around," she agreed.

Jack was impressed with the fact that she hadn't packed yet. Wasn't waiting until the last minute to pack a guy thing to do?

"This is his rabies tag," she continued. She fingered the dog tag on Percy's collar as she clipped on his leash. "It has the name and phone number of his vet on it, so if anything happens, just call him."

"Nothing will happen." He squatted down to examine the tag. As he grasped it, his hand brushed against hers. It was small and warm, the fine bones like a bird's.

Briskly, she stood and handed him the leash then reached for her keys and the bag of dog food and toys sitting on the counter. The instant she opened the door to the hallway, Percy shot out like a cannonball, barking excitedly.

"Whoa, boy. Slow down there." Jack struggled to keep a firm grip on the leash.

"He loves his walk." Hint smiled down at the Schnoodle as she shut the door. A lock of hair curled behind her ear, pointing toward her profile. Her nose was straight and small, like the nose on the American Girl doll he'd given his niece Marguerite for her last birthday.

Outside, the early evening was warm, the air scented with dogwood blossoms. A light breeze fluttered the leaves of the oak tree across the street from her building. Was the tree laughing at him for his missteps of the evening before? They strolled toward Pondfield Road and turned left towards the shops on their way to the railroad station. Percy stopped every few seconds to sniff trees, lampposts and sidewalk smells.

"What do you do when he . . . uh . . . takes care of business?" he asked.

"I bring a bag and clean it up. They're pretty strict around here." Something about her voice didn't sound strict at all. It was filled with different tones that all seemed to be dancing with each other.

Jack looked around, noting flower window boxes and planters, well-trimmed lawns and carefully tended gardens. It wouldn't do to kick doo-doo into the bushes in this town. An alarm would probably go off and a policeman appear out of nowhere with a summons.

"What if you forget to bring a bag?" he followed up.

"You won't forget, because you've got the bag dispenser attached to his leash."

"Is that what this is?" Jack examined the red object in the shape of a fire hydrant hanging from the leash handle. The edge of a small blue plastic bag hung out from one side.

"There are bags rolled up on a roller inside the hydrant. I just put in a refill, so you've got enough bags in there to get you through the next five days." Hint appeared to be scrutinizing him, perhaps unsure whether he would be careful to clean up after Percy or not. "And make sure you pull out only one bag at a time," she added. "If you pull out more than one, you'll have a hard time getting the extras back into the holder."

"Why's he going in circles?" Jack watched as the dog circled a spot on the lawn next to a doctors' office.

"That's the cue that he's getting ready to, um, perform his ablutions."

"Nicely put." He was impressed. She had good syntax.

For the first time, she smiled at him, jolting his senses. Her mouth was shapely. It curved like the lips on a Greek comedy and tragedy mask, portending complexity. Was it just physiognomy, or did it signify something about her personality? He thought the latter, given the nuance of tones in her speaking voice, not to mention her taste in magazines.

Jack studied Percy as the dog circled. "Should I tighten my grip when he does that or loosen it?"

"Keep it loose," Hint advised. "Pretend not to notice what he's up to. If you try to rush him, he'll get nervous. The only way he'll get down to business is if you don't hurry him."

"Is that a metaphor for life?" Jack asked. Her explanation seemed apt for a few other important life processes. He turned his face away so she couldn't see the color he could feel creeping up his neck.

"You tell me. Is it?" Her snicker was faint, the sound of rustling leaves.

Was she laughing at him? She had just put her finger on one of his biggest areas of challenge: not rushing. It seemed women needed to take everything slowly, including the most important things. It looked as if canines needed to take things slowly too.

Percy finally appeared to find the perfect spot over which he squatted and did a ridiculous-looking side to side dance step. Jack tried not to notice.

"What do you do that allows you to walk a dog three times a day? Do you work from home?" he asked.

"Yes." She narrowed her eyes at him until they looked like raisins. "I illustrate children's books, coloring and sticker books."

"Do you work for a publishing house?"

"Yes, but not just one. I'm freelance, so I work for a few different houses on a per project basis," she explained, brushing a strand of fiery-hued hair behind her right ear.

"Wow. That sounds like fun. How do you get ideas for your characters?"

"That's a good question." She paused, putting a slim finger to her chin. "I spend a lot of time looking through art books, old fairytale books, magazines, art exhibits. I get ideas from nature too." She smiled wistfully. "Going on walks and looking at trees helps."

"What kind of trees do you like best?" he asked. His niece and goddaughter, Marguerite, had given names to the three largest trees in his backyard. The maple tree guarding the boundary of his yard was Sky; the chestnut tree in the middle, Monkey; and the tallest of them all was Prayer, an oak. When he'd asked why she'd named it Prayer, she'd said it was because the oak looked like it was praying for the people in his house.

Ever since then he'd had a feeling oak trees were looking out for him.

Just as Hint opened her mouth to reply, Percy finished his exertions.

Jack fumbled to unroll one of the plastic bags from its holder.

Hint reached to help him. As he held the container while she pulled off the bag, Percy spotted a squirrel and took off.

The leash yanked free from the bag dispenser in Jack's hands. Both Hint and Jack called to Percy as he ran from them. The dog paid no mind and disappeared around the corner.

"Percy. Get back here. Come here now," he shouted, chasing after the Schnoodle.

"Don't yell at him. You'll scare him," Hint objected as she raced behind him. "Percy, come back. Come on, boy."

This time her musical voice struck Jack as singsongish and lacking in authority. What dog would pay any attention to someone who called to it like that? She might as well be singing a lullaby.

Rounding the corner, he spotted Percy twenty yards ahead of him, wildly barking at a squirrel halfway up the oak tree he'd hidden behind the evening before. He ran toward the Schnoodle. As he was just at the point of reaching down to grab the dog's leash, the squirrel jumped into a neighboring tree branch, and Percy took off after him.

"Wait. That's not how to catch him," Hint scolded as she caught up. "You have to be gentle. Just wait for him to stop chasing the squirrel. Then he'll come back."

"What if he doesn't? I'm not taking any chances. Percy— get back here now," he boomed out.

At the sound of Jack's voice, people on the sidewalk turned to see who was making all the noise.

"Here, boy." Hint squatted beside Jack, speaking to Percy in a childlike voice. "Come on, boy. Come back to me. Come on, sweetie. Here, Percy."

The dog showed no sign of responding. Instead, he ran across the street as the squirrel leapt from tree branch to telephone pole, then ran across the wire to the next pole.

"Percy, get over here now," Jack shouted, running across the street after the dog.

"Don't chase him. You'll only make it worse," she called after him.

Jack realized the dog was unlikely to come to him, not having had a chance to form a bond. But someone had to do something. He glanced back at Hint on the other side of the street. She was sitting on her heels, her eyes closed. Was she meditating or something? She was in another world apparently. A fairyland, no doubt.

"Hey, what are you doing? We've got a dog to catch. Come on," he yelled, cortisol flooding his body. Turning back in the direction Percy had gone, he couldn't see the dog at all. Meanwhile, the shadows were getting long. Soon it would be dark.

"That's not the way to catch him. Stop scaring him off," she huffed, getting to her feet.

"Then what do you suggest? Sitting there hoping he'll return?" He couldn't believe it. Why was this loon falling to pieces when they needed to catch the dog now?

"I'm not just sitting here, jerk." She glared at him, her eyes blazing. "I'm attracting him back to me when he realizes he isn't going to catch his squirrel."

"Right. While you're sitting there, I'll go chase him down."
He turned on his heel and stormed off, fuming at being called a
jerk. Why couldn't she help him instead of just sitting there . . .
like a jerk?

"You don't understand. You aren't going to catch him that
way," she called after him, her voice indignant. "He doesn't
know you. He won't respond to you yelling at him."

"Yeah? Then why aren't you trying to catch him yourself?
He'll respond to you. Isn't he your Snuggle Bunny? Get off
your duff and find him," he roared.

Hint's face blanched.

Immediately, he regretted his outburst. Why didn't women
play fair? She could call him a jerk but he couldn't yell at her?
It was unfair. Then why did he feel like a heel?

"How do you know that name? Who told you that?" she demanded, outraged.

How had Jack known some of her private nicknames for
Percy? It was almost as if he had spied on them. Standing up,
she put her hands on her hips. He'd blown her best strategy for
catching the dog. Now all she could do was call to Percy and
hope he'd respond. But her neighborhood was not his home
and once he'd turned a few corners, he might not know how to
retrace his steps.

She ran down the street in the direction he'd gone, as much
to find him as to get away from the tall boorish man behind her,
who would only scare the Schnoodle further.

Turning the corner of Meadow Lane and Kraft Avenue, she
peered down the street toward the fire station. A few houses

stood on the other side of the street behind which a small creek meandered down to the dog run. The dense woods, where he'd had gotten away from her the day before, were that way, as well as the railroad tracks. She shuddered to think what might happen if the dog attempted to cross them.

"Percy, come back to me. Come back." Even she could tell her voice sounded stressed and anxious.

She peered over her shoulder to make sure Jack was nowhere within earshot. Finally, she spotted his tall frame at the other end of the street. As she made him out in the burgeoning twilight, he called for the dog in a loud, angry voice—exactly the wrong tone to get the canine to come back.

"Percy, Snuggle Boy, come back to me. Come back, boy," she sang out, trying to counteract the bad karma Tom's friend was sending out behind her.

She checked the cemetery behind the firehouse then jogged down to the dog run. There, a handful of dog owners stood quietly enjoying the remains of the year's final day of spring.

"Have you seen a small black and gray Schnoodle? I'm trying to find my friend's dog," she addressed a man and woman watching a yellow Labrador play with a wheat-colored terrier.

"Haven't seen him."

"Sorry."

Was he in the woods? Or down by the river? Either possibility bode ill. Over the next half hour, she searched both locations. It was dark by the time she made her way back to the dog run by way of the stream. Her heart was heavy, thinking of how poorly she'd looked after her friends' dog. What should she do next? Why had that jerk shown up in the first place with no idea of how to handle a dog, never mind dog sit one? He hadn't even known what the doggy bag dispenser had been and had fumbled trying to get the bag out of it, losing his grip on Percy's leash. What a cretin.

Then she thought back to the day before when she herself had lost her grip on the Schnoodle's leash. It could happen to anyone. The trick was to get the dog to want to come back to her. She'd succeeded earlier, but this time Jack had ruined her chances of luring Percy back with his loud voice and overbearing manner. The dog didn't know him from Adam and wasn't going to respond to a tall, strange male yelling at him.

"Hint, hey, is that you? Any sign of him?" Jack's voice floated down to her from the bridge above, connecting the dog run to the town's soccer field. He no longer sounded harsh, just tired and slightly abashed.

"It's me. No sign of him. I looked in the woods" *where I lost him yesterday,* she didn't say aloud, "and asked down at the dog run, but nobody's seen him."

"We've got to decide what to do. Who do you call for a lost dog? Is there a town dog catcher or something?"

"We should probably call the police."

"Do you know what their number is?"

"Not offhand, but the police station is down by town hall, a block away from my building."

"Let's drop by." He took her arm to help her up the embankment.

She didn't resist. Upon reaching the bridge, she let out a long pent-up sigh. Warm, stinging tears welled up behind her eyes. She blinked quickly, trying to catch herself.

The events of the day had been too much for her. A low sob escaped her as she stared into the dark, gurgling stream below.

"I know how you feel," Jack told her.

"No, you don't," she rebuffed him.

"Yes, I do." He put a tentative hand on her shoulder.

"I don't know what to do next," she whispered.

"I don't either," he whispered back.

"That doesn't help."

"Yes it does." His voice was firm.

"How so?" She brushed his hand from her shoulder.

"We're both in the same boat," he pointed out.

"I don't want to be in your boat." She shook her head, refusing to meet his glance.

"Two people can bail out a boat faster than one. We'll figure this out."

The hand was back on her shoulder, warm and firm. Despite herself, she felt comforted.

"I'm supposed to be packing to get on a plane, not bailing out a boat." She thought bitterly of her scheduled meeting on Thursday with Derek Simpson of Story Tales Press. How could she go to Punta Cana with Percy missing? "What are Nicole and Tom going to say when they find out their dog's missing?" she groaned.

"They're not going to find out. We'll find him," he assured her.

"Sure, we will," she replied without conviction, fresh tears welling up. She brushed them away, angrily wiping her face. "What if we don't?"

"Ye of little faith," he remarked, surprising her. "Come on. Let's go over to the police station and see if they can help."

The hand on her shoulder moved to her upper arm as he propelled her in the direction of town. She wanted to shrug it off, but she knew she would feel even more desolate if she did. Surrendering to the comfort of his strong sure grip, she allowed him to guide her in the dark.

2

DECISIONS

"**S**orry. I can't help you with a lost dog. You'll have to call town hall tomorrow morning and ask for Joe Pritchett. He's the town dog catcher." The sergeant at the desk looked bored. "The dog will probably show up when he gets hungry enough. They usually do."

"Thanks for your help," Hint sighed, her voice as low as her spirits. She turned to Jack as they exited the side door at town hall that housed the police station.

"Now what?" She was out of ideas.

"Do you mind if I come back to your place for a minute?"

"I, uh, I guess not. We need to figure out what to do next."

"Right. And two heads are better than one." Then he paused. "What time is your flight tomorrow?"

"My flight? 2:15 p.m." She looked squarely at him. "I need to be on it."

The illustrators' conference she was attending in Punta Cana included a Thursday meeting with the artistic director of

Story Tales Press, the biggest children's book publisher in the U.K. It was the professional opportunity of a lifetime.

"I'll find him," he told her. "I'm the one who dropped the leash, and I'm the one who's got to get him back."

She hesitated, her conscience twinging at the thought of her own mishap with Percy the day before. "It's not just your fault. I . . . I dropped his leash yesterday in the woods and he ran off. It happens."

"When he ran off, how'd you get him to come back?" Jack asked.

"I sat really still and sang a song to him," she explained. "Then I closed my eyes, and when I opened them, he was standing in front of me."

"Wow. Sounds like a fairy tale." He looked skeptical. "Why didn't you try it again when we lost him?"

"I *was* trying it, but you yelled at me to get off my duff," she shot back angrily, marching ahead.

"Hey." He ran to catch up with her. "I'm sorry. I just thought you weren't doing anything. Like you'd closed up shop or something."

"Wrong. Being still and quiet *is* doing something," she said heatedly. "It's being calm, so the dog will come back to you when he's done chasing his squirrel."

"It didn't really work, did it?"

"It didn't work because you screwed it up, okay?" She crossed her arms in front of her and tried to outpace him.

"I just thought we should do something," he said.

"Men always think they should do something. Then they screw everything up."

"Oh really? And what about not doing anything? What's that accomplishing?"

"Like I said, I *was* doing something, but you didn't have the patience to back off and let me do it." She was angry and disappointed. If only Percy had run off a minute *after* she'd handed him over to Jack, she wouldn't have to feel guilty about flying to Punta Cana the next day where her meeting with Derek Simpson would take place as scheduled and she would get the job of her dreams. Quickly, she brushed aside the ungenerous thought.

"So what do you intend to do now?" he asked, infuriated.

"Go home and think," she snapped back. "And maybe it would be better if you don't come, since you'll get in the way."

"Get in the way of what?" he demanded. "We need to work this out together. Stop being ridiculous."

"Who's being ridiculous? Who didn't even know what a doggy bag dispenser was? You know nothing about dogs."

"You're damned right I don't. I didn't even want to do this," Jack blurted out.

"Then why did you tell Tom you would?" she shot back, disgusted.

"He didn't have anyone else, okay? He said you had to go out of town and there was no one else. So what was I supposed to do?" He glared at her. "And who says you're a big dog expert after babysitting one for four days?"

"I understand them intuitively."

"What use is your intuition if you can't get the dog to come back to you?" he asked angrily.

"Just shut up and drop dead," she shouted, causing several townspeople out on the sidewalk, enjoying the balmy June evening, to turn their heads.

"You can haul your rear end onto the plane and go fry yourself on a beach. I'll handle this my own way," Jack countered fiercely.

"You will not handle this alone until I'm out of here at noon tomorrow." Hint could feel her face getting red. "Percy was in my care when you lost him and I'll help find him."

"Oh, so now it *is* me who lost him. I thought you said it wasn't my fault. Funny how your story changed." He glared at her.

"I . . . you . . . you're provoking me. Just go home and leave me alone so I can think clearly. I can't think with you storming around *doing* things," she fumed. "What good is doing stuff if you don't know what you're doing?"

"It's better than doing nothing, all right?"

The entrance to her building loomed ahead. In five steps, they were there. She pushed in the outer door, with Jack following close behind.

"Don't come in here. Just go home," she ordered.

"I'm not leaving until you calm down and we've come up with a plan."

"Your plan is not my plan," she insisted.

"I don't have a plan yet and neither do you, so we've got the same lack of a plan," he pressed back.

The ludicrous logic of his remark made her want to laugh, but the situation was too grim. How could she focus on her upcoming meeting with Percy lost?

The gray head of her downstairs neighbor, Mrs. Pappalardo, popped out of a first floor apartment. She stared at them for a long moment, then shut her door with a bang.

Hint turned and stomped upstairs, Jack in tow. Opening her apartment door, she fought a strong urge to slam it shut in his face. He was infuriating, but she would be even more miserable trying to figure out what to do about Percy alone than in his company. She stormed across the living room out onto her balcony, yanking the sliding screen door shut behind her. If only closing it could shut out the events of the past few hours. With the dog missing, how could she go to her conference? With the career opportunity of a lifetime awaiting her, how could she not?

MANY ARE THE *plans in the mind of a man, but it is the way of the Lord that will be established.* Odd that the biblical proverb had passed through his head, strangely comforting him. God wouldn't want Percy to remain lost would He? They would somehow find him.

"Do you think I could get something for us to drink?" Jack asked through the screen door to the balcony.

He wasn't going out there for the moment. The petite, auburn-haired woman on the other side looked as if she might toss him over the railing, all one hundred fifteen pounds of her at most, he'd guess.

"I've got water, ginger ale, beer, wine, some tea. What would you like?" she called over her shoulder, her tone still sharp.

"What kind of beer do you have?"

"Something imported I think." Returning to the living room, she avoided his gaze then disappeared into the kitchen. "It's German," she announced a minute later.

"I'll take it."

She took one out, popped the top off, then opened the refrigerator again and took one for herself. It had been a long, hot day.

"I hate to think of Percy out there all by himself tonight." She shook her head as she sank into the brown velveteen couch. Nailheads studded each of its arms, a handsome but curiously masculine touch. "What if he gets eaten by wild animals?" She gazed into space then trained her eyes on Jack.

He shifted, unused to being stared at by a woman, especially one with long, dark eyelashes framing eyes that resembled Bambi's. Self-consciously, he took a swig of beer.

"He'll be fine," he reassured her. "It's a warm night. Besides, it's almost the summer solstice, so dawn will come early. The only animals he might run into are skunk or possums. Maybe a raccoon."

"Skunk? What if he gets sprayed by a skunk?" Hint asked, her eyes huge and round. "And aren't raccoons dangerous? They've got enormous fingernails."

"Claws. They use their claws to go through trash, not get into scrapes with dogs. Believe me, Percy will find a nice place to sleep in the hollow of a tree. He'll make it through the night." As he leaned back in the comfortable brown armchair, the titles in her bookcase caught his eye.

Emma, Sense and Sensibility, and *The Jane Austen Handbook* stood next to *The Little Prince, Turkish Miniatures,* an art book entitled *Matisse, Picasso, Bonnard, Braque,* and another one on Kandinsky. A biography of Audrey Hepburn completed the middle shelf's collection. Suddenly, he knew whose eyes Hint's reminded him of; Audrey Hepburn had the same doe-eyed look, encircled with thick lashes.

"Do you think we should make signs?" she asked.

"Definitely. Too bad we don't have a photo of him."

"A photo? Maybe I do. Let me look." She jumped off the couch and rummaged through a collection of photo albums on the bottom shelf of the bookcase. "I think I've got one that Nicole took of Percy and me last Christmas. Where is it?" she murmured, flipping through the pages of the largest album.

Jack looked over her shoulder. Lots of photos of a young boy stared back at him. He shared Hint's warm brown eyes with long lashes.

"Is that a family member?" he asked, hoping irrationally it wasn't her son.

"That's my nephew Russ. He's seven."

"Good-looking kid," he commented, relieved. "Where does he live?"

"In White Plains with my sister and her husband. I'm his godmother."

"You're the godmother? No wonder you've got so many pictures of him." He didn't think this was the right time to mention his own godfather role, judging by the storm clouds on her face. His heart swelled as he thought about his six-year-old niece and goddaughter, Marguerite. If it were her puppy that was lost, he'd move heaven and earth to find it. At the least, he'd take time off from work to look for it.

"Here it is." She held up a four by six photo.

Jack took it from her. Percy stared out at him, an irregular white spot on his forehead. The dog rested in Hint's arms, looking as if he'd found nirvana. Hint looked unmistakably happy, staring straight into the camera with a radiant smile on her face.

"Nice photo," he remarked casually, feeling goose bumps come out on his arms. No woman had ever smiled at him like that. Ever. A split second of envy streaked through him as he wondered who she was looking at. "Let's use it. Do you have this digitally?"

"No, just the print shot."

"Do you have a scanner on your printer?"

"Yup. I scan illustrations for projects all the time," she told him. "Give me that. I'll crop it, so it's just Percy. I don't want my photo posted on lamp posts all over town."

"Why not? It's a good shot." He glanced at her, hoping to catch a glimpse of the radiant expression she wore in the photo. None was forthcoming.

She made a face, reaching for the photo.

"Okay, I guess I know," he continued. "You'll end up with dozens of messages on your answering machine from guys pretending to have spotted Percy. Except that they'll really be trying to make time with you."

"Huh. I doubt it. But I don't need that kind of hassle, so let me crop just Percy in this shot."

She moved to the alcove of her living room where her studio was located.

He noted the way she was all business now that they had a task to focus on. He could imagine her negotiating with a big New York publishing house to sell one of her elves and fairies projects. He would guess she probably didn't act too fairylike on those occasions.

She sat down at the desk, turning on the printer, then lifted the cover and placed the photo face down on the scanning surface. In a minute, Percy's image on the computer screen appeared before them.

"That's one cute dog alright," he commented, leaning over her shoulder. The unmistakable scent of stargazer lilies wafted off her hair. He knew, only because they'd been his mother's favorite flowers. His heart panged as he inhaled deeply. Feeling dizzy, he watched as Hint carefully zoomed in on Percy's image then cropped it so that not a single hair of the dog's coat was cut from the shot.

The result was almost more intriguing than the original. A lush, reddish-brown forest of hair surrounded Percy's head and upper body, making a tantalizing backdrop against which the dog's image stood out in sharp contrast.

"Alright, we need some text. What do we say?" He backed off, regaining his senses as he moved away from the scent of her hair.

"How about "Lost Dog Named Percy?" she suggested.

"Brilliant. I was about to think of that myself."

She rolled her eyes at him and turned back to the computer to type in the headline. The storm clouds appeared to be lifting.

"Then what?" she asked, busy centering Percy's photo.

"Then we say something like 'Lost: Percy, 18 lb. Schnoodle, black and gray—"

"With star marking on forehead," she added.

"You mean white blob on forehead," he corrected her.

"It's a star," she counter-corrected him.

"That's news to me. I thought it was just some irregular blob. Like someone splashed 'Wite Out' on him when he was nosing around their desk."

"Is that something you would do? Maybe it's just as well he got away from you before you could take him," she commented curtly.

"I . . . uh . . . probably wouldn't do anything like that. It was just an idea."

"You have weird ideas," she told him.

"You have weird taste in magazines," he blurted out, regretting it the moment the words left his mouth.

"What do you know about my taste in magazines?" She looked at him sharply.

He shrugged. "I just noticed the one downstairs."

"I got my mail earlier today. There's no magazine downstairs with my name on it." She gazed at him, her brows knitting together.

"Oh. My mistake." Jack looked away, flustered. He'd better keep his mouth shut. It had been the day before that he'd noticed *Other Worlds* magazine. But as far as she was concerned, he hadn't been to her place the day before. *Watch it, big guy.*

"What magazine are you referring to, anyway?" she asked, looking suspicious.

"Get back to work. We've got a dog to find," he ordered, attempting to get her off the subject. He needed her to turn away so he could take a fast inventory of her living room. Maybe there was a magazine or two lying around.

Searching her end tables and the lower shelf of the coffee table, he spied some fashion magazines as well as the *New York Times Sunday Magazine.* Predictable stuff. He looked towards the bookshelf. On top of the photo albums lay a real estate magazine, *Pinnacle.* The cover featured a mansion on the water that looked like it cost a gazillion dollars.

"Well, what magazine did you mean?" she shot over her shoulder as she typed something on the keyboard.

"I mean your fancy real estate magazines. Are you house shopping?" he asked. *Or husband hunting?* Quickly, he chased away the unfair thought.

"What fancy real estate magazines?" She turned around in her chair and narrowed her eyes at him. "What are you talking about?"

"I mean this one." He walked over to the bookcase and casually picked up the magazine. "Is this your idea of where you'd like to live one day?" The caption identified the mansion's location as Greenwich, Connecticut.

"Why not? If you want to know the truth, I use photos in that magazine as inspiration for fairy castles in my illustrations. There're some beautiful estates in there. Why would I have a problem living in one of them?"

"Dream on. D'you know what one month's heating bill would cost in a place like that?" He tapped the cover of the magazine.

"Why shouldn't I dream on? Using my imagination is a part of my job. And there's nothing wrong with appreciating beauty."

"If you can afford it."

"And if you can't? It hasn't stopped anyone yet. People can dream, can't they? What's wrong with that?" She eyed him critically, with what looked like disdain for his plebeian tastes.

"Hey, nothing wrong with it." He held up his hands, palms toward her, on either side of his body. His ex-girlfriend had dreamed big, too; she had only dated men in finance. Why were there so many women out there who insisted on assets from a guy? Couldn't a guy just offer himself? Apparently not.

He glanced at Hint. She was like some sort of fey fairy creature, with her otherworldly methods to lure back the dog. And that dancing voice. Too bad he didn't believe in fairies. A more practical woman who looked like her would have attracted his interest. But not her. No way. She was as weird as her name. Probably high maintenance too.

"So, does it makes you feel pressure when you see a woman admire a beautiful home that's larger than yours?" she asked, her aim hitting its target.

"Uh . . ." Busted. Why did she have to be so perceptive? "Something like that. It's probably a lot more complicated, but if you want to distill it down to one sentence that'll do."

"I admire beauty. I like fine things. That doesn't mean I'll own an estate one day."

"But do you aspire to?"

"That's a good question." She stood and came over to the bookcase, so close that the stargazer lily scent of her hair overtook his senses once again. Unsteadily, he moved away.

"Sometimes owning something really big, or really beautiful or expensive can be a trap." She gazed at him, her large brown eyes capturing his.

He had a feeling she knew about traps, or at least about setting them. Fairies used magic, didn't they? They had unfair advantages, but he wouldn't be taken advantage of again. Annabel Sanford had already done that. Once burned, twice shy.

"How so?"

"I mean you end up devoting all your time and all your efforts to the house," Hint explained. "Or the art collection. You spend your life on upkeep of Persian rugs, window treatments, antique knickknacks, chandeliers, light fixtures, music and alarm systems, pools, spas, Jacuzzi bathtubs. It's a trap."

"Sounds like you know something about it." His mind wandered to Annabel's parents' home in Larchmont. It had been like a museum. He'd had wicked thoughts of knocking something over or spilling his drink on the carpet whenever he'd visited.

"Maybe I do, maybe I don't," she told him. "But I know it can be a distraction. And I don't want to be distracted from what I do. I create. I'm an artist, not a museum curator."

"So no fancy houses for you."

"Not for the foreseeable future," she said blithely.

"Only in your illustrations, right?"

"Let's get back to dog hunting, shall we?" Briskly, she turned back to the computer.

"Okay, where were we?" He peered over her shoulder, staring at the words she'd typed below the photo of Percy. "Adorable eighteen pound Schnoodle. Answers to the name 'Percy.'

Black and gray with white star marking on forehead. Please contact H. Daniels at 914-669-8286."

"Why don't you say 'friendly' instead of 'adorable'?" he suggested.

"Why? Don't you think he's adorable?" She frowned as if he had just failed to offer the right compliment of her infant child.

"Yes, but that's a matter of opinion," he pointed out. "If you say 'friendly' people will know he's not likely to bite if they approach him."

"I get you. Okay, 'friendly.'" She corrected the line.

"And as far as the star marking goes, you might be the only one who sees that blob on his forehead as a star. Just say 'white mark on forehead.'"

"It's not a blob. how can you say that about Percy?" Again, she frowned, looking more insulted by the minute on behalf of the dog.

"I know. I know. It's a mark. Say 'mark,' not 'star.' If someone finds him and they don't see it as a star they might let him go. Or keep him. Oh. And also," he continued, "put down my phone number. You're flying to the Caribbean tomorrow afternoon, so I'll be the contact person."

"I don't know if I can go if he's still lost." She looked uncertain.

"You'd kick yourself if you didn't go and then he turns up ten minutes after you miss your flight," he reasoned.

"What if he doesn't turn up? What if he's been hit by a car or eaten by an animal?"

"I already told you, raccoons have better things to do, and skunks aren't aggressive enough to do anything other than stink him up. He'll turn up. Just go and do whatever it is you were going to do down there. Drink piña coladas. Pick up men. Get a suntan."

"Who says I was planning to drink piña coladas or pick up men?" Her eyes spit fire at him.

"Let me guess. You're going to the Caribbean to research fairy illustrations. Or to organize your business plan for the fall."

Opening her mouth, she closed it again. Whatever she had been about to say, apparently she had changed her mind. "We can put both our phone numbers down if you like," she finally said. "That way, if one of us isn't available, the other one takes the call."

"How are you going to help if you're not even here?"

"I'll know if it's Percy the caller's found and not some other dog. I know his markings better than you. And I've spent more time with him," her voice rose. "Then I'll call you to let you know if you should follow up or not. I told you, it wasn't just your fault. We both lost him."

She looked as if she blamed him, despite her words. Anger flamed inside him, as he pushed away memories of how his ex-girlfriend had enjoyed confusing him with her push-pull games.

"Let's see, that was before you said it *was* my fault," he snapped back. "Remember the line about not knowing what a doggy doo doo bag dispenser is?"

"Okay. I was mad. But I'm helping you find him, whether I'm here or not. I can take calls and help you brainstorm until he turns up."

Weighing her words, he took a deep breath then exhaled. She was definitely different from his ex. Equally confusing, but willing to make sacrifices, which Annabel most certainly had not been. "You are a trouper," he finally got out, his anger defused.

"What are we going to do if Tom and Nicole call?" She pulled wildly at her hair.

"Hey! Stop that." He grabbed her wrist without thinking. It was a shame to see such gorgeous hair pulled out strand by strand.

Pushing her hand down to her side, he released it. The one beer he had drunk was going directly to his head. She was annoying and confusing with that weird fairy style of hers. No wonder she didn't have a boyfriend. If she had, she would have mentioned it when he suggested she might be picking up men on her Caribbean trip.

"Why would Tom and Nicole call?" He hadn't thought of that.

"Why wouldn't they?" she asked.

"Listen, they'll call me, not you, so let me handle it." He had no idea how he would. "Let's post signs tomorrow morning and maybe someone will call or he'll just show up on your doorstep before you leave for the airport."

"Chances are about nil that he'll just show up here," she said mournfully. "This isn't even his home."

"Let's print out a bunch of signs and I'll post them on my way to the train station," he suggested. "Then I'll come back tomorrow morning and we'll look for him until your cab arrives. We probably need to call the Humane Society and some animal shelters too. Do you know the name of his vet?"

"No," she shook her head with a sigh. "His vet's number is on his dog tag, but I didn't think to write it down. What about your job?"

"I'll call in sick tomorrow."

"Just tell them the truth," she advised. "That the dog you're taking care of is missing."

"You're right. My boss has a dog. He might have some ideas."

He looked away from her. The completely irrational thought had strayed into his head to ask to spend the night. He flicked it away. She needed to pack, and he needed to think. His senses battled with reason as he tried not to inhale the mesmerizing scent of her hair.

"I'll print out ten of these," Hint said, moving to her computer.

"Make it twenty. I'll drop by the dog run on my way to the train station."

As they printed the lost dog ad, the phone rang.

"Oh no. What if that's Nicole and Tom? What do I tell them?" Hint's face crumpled, as her hand shot up to her cheek.

"Just wait to see who it is," he parried. "Maybe the police found him."

After three rings, her answering machine picked up. A male voice spoke into it.

"Hey, Hint. It's Brian O'Connell. Thought I might catch you at home. Give me a call, okay? 769-5120."

"Go ahead, pick up. I'll call you tomorrow morning." Jack headed toward the door. Who was Brian O'Connell? The caller's tone of voice told him it was someone interested in her. It was nothing to him, anyway.

"Here's the copies," she called out behind him, making no attempt to pick up the phone. Her face looked flushed as she moved toward him. "If you call the humane society tomorrow morning, I'll get the number of the nearest animal shelter and call them. What time do you think you'll come over?"

"Early. I'll get here before nine if it's okay with you."

"Fine. Early is better. Percy will probably wake up with the dawn. He'll be so confused." Her face fell.

What did she know about being confused? She should try being a man for a day trying to figure out what a woman was thinking.

"Look, just pack your suitcase, assume your trip is on, and think positively," he told her. "We'll find the dog." Without thinking he put his hands on each of her arms as she stood next to the door, her face a tense mask.

She pulled away, apparently startled. Then she tossed her hair. He knew about hair tossing from his sister. It was a good sign.

"See you tomorrow. Goodnight." She crossed her arms in front of her body. A bad sign.

"Goodnight. Try not to worry yourself too much," he bade her, wishing she would uncross her arms and allow him to comfort her. But that would confuse the picture even more. Besides, she was too weird, with her subscription to *Other Worlds* magazine and meditational dog catching techniques.

It was all he could do to stop himself from reaching out to tuck back the reddish brown lock of hair that had fallen into her face, hiding her expression. Catching himself, he turned and strode off. They had a dog to find.

3

DOG HUNT

The next day Hint woke early. She'd been in an embrace before shaking off the cobwebs of her dreams. The man's face wasn't clear, but he smelled like cedar wood chips. She inhaled deeply. The pleasant scent vanished, and suddenly she remembered.

Percy was gone.

Springing out of bed, she rushed to look at her answering machine. Other than the call of the night before, there were no messages. She flipped on the coffeemaker then looked up the number for town hall. She would call Joe Pritchett, the town dog catcher the police officer had suggested they contact the evening before. She called the number but got a recorded message asking the caller to leave a complete description of the lost animal and a phone number. The message ended with a short piece of advice: "Please be advised that lost pets are most likely to be found in the first twenty-four hours after their disappearance." Great. They'd better find Percy within eighteen hours of his disappearance before her cab arrived at noon to whisk her to the airport.

She put down the phone then picked it up to return her superintendent's call, but before she could, it rang.

"Hello, Hint," a low voice greeted her.

"Jack?"

"Yup. Any news?"

"No news," she sighed.

"I'm on my way to your place. Need coffee?"

"I'm making some now," she told him.

"A bagel?"

"Let's pick some up on our way to the dog run," she suggested. "Or wherever we're going."

"We'll go all over," he said. "I've got my car. See you in a few."

As she hung up, an image of Derek Simpson studying her portfolio flashed into her head. She'd seen photos of him in the trade press: a tall, imposing-looking man with a leonine head of hair. There was no way the clumsy moves of Jack Whitby were going to stand in the way of her meeting him Thursday as planned.

When she'd opened her door to Tom's friend the evening before, she'd been pleased to see Nicole's description of him as not bad looking had been apt. He was tall, with wavy medium brown hair just a tad long for someone in the financial services industry. He'd looked straight at her with dark blue eyes that had reminded her of the North Atlantic Ocean—someplace off the coast of Maine perhaps.

As he stepped into her apartment, she'd noted the inverted vee of his lean build; wide, square shoulders narrowed down to slim, runner's hips, where his navy blue polo shirt hung half-tucked into khaki pants. Nicole had told her he edited equity reports for a financial firm. He looked impressively fit for some-one who probably sat in front of a computer all day long. She'd guess he did other things too—outdoorsy, sporty things. He'd been well spoken and polite. But he hadn't known much about how to handle a dog on a leash, then he'd turned into a raging maniac once Percy had gotten loose.

On the other hand, Hint knew a lot about handling Percy; yet, still, she had lost him in the woods two days earlier. Any-one could lose a dog. But not anyone could lure one back. The thought of Jack trying to find Percy after she'd left on her trip alarmed her. The dog didn't know him and Jack appeared to know zip about dogs. God willing, Percy would show up in the next few hours before her cab arrived to take her to the airport.

She hurriedly dressed then picked up the phone again.

"Brian, it's Hint Daniels. Sorry to bother you so early."

"Well, good mo-o-orning. Did you get my message last night?" His voice, full of innuendo, made her cringe.

She suspected that her superintendent had a crush on her. When her dishwasher had malfunctioned a few months earlier, she'd asked him to take a look at it. He had made a few adjust-ments. Then they had had to wait for the twenty minute cycle to run its course. While they were waiting, he had pulled out a book of D.H. Lawrence poems and read a few to her. She had deliberately refrained from all but the vaguest comments on the poems and put it out of her mind. It wouldn't do to encourage him, but right now she needed all the help she could get.

"I've got a problem," she told him. "I was looking after my friend's dog, and he ran off last night. I need to find him."

"Wow. What kind of dog?"

"He's an eighteen pound Schnoodle."

"A what?"

"A Schnoodle—a cross between a Poodle and a Schnauzer. He's black and gray."

"Where'd you lose him?"

"Right around the corner, on the front lawn of the doctors' offices on Pondfield Road. I was handing him over to the person taking him for the next few days, and he got loose."

"You should put up some signs," Brian suggested.

"We posted around twenty last night."

"Put up more. If you give me some, I'll post them around my buildings." He looked after three buildings in the neighborhood.

"Okay, I'll print some out and get them to you," she told him.

"I'll buzz you in a while to pick them up," he volunteered. "Right now I'm over at Twelve Meadow."

"Okay, Brian. Thanks." She hung up and went to turn on her printer, hoping he wouldn't take her request to help as a sign of interest.

Looking at her description of Percy, she inserted "family pet" at the end of the message. She didn't need to specify that she wasn't the family. Then she thought about a reward. Could she spring for one? She could, but she didn't want to run the risk of having less than altruistic searchers looking for him. It seemed to her that a true dog lover wouldn't be motivated by the thought of a reward. Still, she needed to offer some incentive. She put in "reward," and left it at that.

After calling the local dog shelter and leaving a detailed description with them, she searched online to see if she could gather some tips for looking for a lost dog that she hadn't thought of yet. Ten minutes later, she'd read numerous accounts of scams perpetrated by people pretending to have found a lost dog. Not only did blackmailers ask for rewards, but professional scammers asked for airfare to be wired to them to cover the cost of sending home the dog they pretended to have found. Advice was posted on not going alone to meet anyone who said they'd found a dog. A single woman could end up meeting a bad fate instead.

Thank God Jack was around to help her track down Percy. He didn't seem to know much about dogs, but at least, he could offer his time and effort.

The buzzer rang. She ran to it, relieved that her dog hunting partner had arrived. Hitting the button quickly, she opened her apartment door.

Bounding up the stairs, Brian O'Connell greeted her with a sickening smile.

Her stomach lurched. Why did she have to have a superintendent with a crush on her? It was uncomfortable. She needed him for repairs and maintenance projects, yet every time she called, she worried she was leading him on. She wasn't, but he appeared eager to think as much. Why did some men have to complicate everything? There was no way she could complain to the landlord about him. He was Brian's cousin and an even worse letch than Brian was. Fortunately, he was never around.

Pushing his way into her apartment as if he owned it, he searched her face.

"Hint, sorry to hear about the dog. What does he look like?"

"Here. I printed out a dozen of these for you to post." She hated the way Brian O'Connell wore tight muscle shirts and walked around with a smirk on his face. He always seemed to be implying something no matter what the situation. She'd call him to fix a leaky faucet and by the time he was done he acted like he'd spent the night at her place.

"Why don't you give me more, so I can put them up in more places?"

Why did she think this was just a ruse to stay in her apartment talking with her a while longer? Was he going to pull out another D.H. Lawrence poem to read aloud while he waited for her to print out more flyers? She shuddered.

"Okay, give me a minute." She went to her computer and queued up the printer, hoping to get him out the door before Jack arrived.

As the final page printed out, the buzzer rang again. She rammed the extra ads into Brian's hand and opened her apartment door for him to exit before she responded to the buzzer to open the outside door downstairs.

"Thanks, Hint," Brian said, flashing a smile. "Are you going to be around later, in case I need some more?"

No, not for you. As emphatic as that thought was, she could use all the help she could get. "Just give me a call if you need more," she told him. "Thanks for whatever you can do." She gave a short, firm wave goodbye, and attempted to shut the door in his face.

"I'll do whatever I can, Hint. I really want to help." The superintendent lingered just inside her door, his arm casually supporting his body on the door frame. Behind him footsteps rang out on the stairs.

"Hi, Hint. The downstairs door was open. Am I disturbing you?" Jack approached from the end of the hallway, giving the man in her doorway a level look.

"Not at all, Jack. Good morning." The man blocking her doorway showed no signs of leaving. Why was it that Brian O'Connell came across as more of a pick-up artist than a super-intendent?

"Hey, I forgot my cell phone. How 'bout that?" Brian walked back into her kitchen to pick it up off the counter. He more or less bounced with each step.

She began to boil. Her super had a way of acting propri-etary in her presence, as if the fact that he liked her turned him into her boyfriend or something.

Hurrying in front of him, she grabbed his cell phone and shoved it into his hands. His fingers managed to slide over hers as she gave it to him.

Yuck. Double yuck.

She could feel Jack Whitby's eyes on her, assessing who the stranger might be. Deliberately, she had not introduced him.

Finally she got the superintendent out of her apartment. Slamming shut the door, she braced it with her back.

"Want some coffee?" She gave Jack a faint smile.

"Who was that?" he asked.

"Who?"

"Him. Your boyfriend?"

"No. Lord, no. That was my superintendent. He came over to take some ads for Percy. He's going to post them around the three buildings he manages."

"That was your super?" Jack appeared skeptical. He took a long sip from the mug of coffee she handed him while his eyes studied hers over the rim.

She wasn't going to defend herself further. She had told him who her visitor was. There was nothing more to say about it. Who was Jack Whitby that she had to explain herself to him anyway?

"Did you call the Humane Society?" she countered, sidestepping his question.

"Yes. The closest one is in New Rochelle, about three miles from here. I described Percy to them and they suggested we come over in person and post an ad."

"Good. Let's do it. Should we go down to the dog run?" she asked.

"Yes, for starters. I posted two ads down there last night, but let's print out a whole stack of them and bring duct tape. I want to check if the tape I used last night held up. And I have another idea."

"Which is . . . ?"

"Don't think this is weird or anything," he said, "but do you have any gym clothes you worked out in recently?"

She wrinkled her nose, thinking of the smelly running clothes she'd just hauled down to the laundry room that morning.

"If you wear something with your sweat on it, he'll be able to pick up your scent more easily," he explained.

Hint laughed. "I've got some dirty tee-shirts in the laundry room now. I just brought a load down to the basement but the washers were all full."

"The grosser the better. And if you get all sweaty while we're out looking for him, that might help too."

"I'll go get one now." She nodded, then headed out the door and down the stairs. "Keep an ear out for the phone in case anyone calls about Percy," she called over her shoulder.

In the basement she found a faded orange tee-shirt in her laundry pile and threw it on. A washer had become available, so she tossed the rest of the clothes in the machine then headed upstairs. It seemed strange to wear her grubbiest clothes, especially to spend the morning with a man she didn't know very well. But this was all for Percy's benefit. Jack Whitby wasn't a stalker or a pervert, was he? She shuddered, thinking of her superintendent. He frequently loitered on the sidewalk outside her building, looking up at her window. It was almost enough to make her want to move, but she couldn't beat the low rent.

When she re-entered her apartment, Jack's expression seemed odd.

"What's wrong?" she asked, hoping it wasn't the smell of stale sweat from her shirt that made him screw up his face as if he'd swallowed a lemon slice.

"You got a call," he told her.

"About Percy?" she asked, her heart thudding. He looked grim. Had someone called to say the dog had been found dead by the side of the road?

"It was Nicole. You'd better play the message," he said, looking sheepish.

"Why didn't you pick up?" she cried, running to her answering machine.

"Think about it."

He was right. Barring the obvious bad news he'd have for them, wouldn't Nicole find it strange that he was at her girlfriend's apartment answering her phone?

She hit play. Nicole's cheerful voice filled the room. She sounded happy and relaxed. "Hey, Hint—thought I might catch you before you leave town. How'd the handoff go last night? Tom called Jack but got his voicemail, so I thought I'd check in with you. Hope Percy was a good boy. If you get a chance, call me back on my cell or I'll call yours. We're having a ball, by the way. Bye."

"Whoa. Now what?" Hint looked at Jack, fear mingled with guilt flooding her insides.

"We need to call them back," he said.

"And say?"

His eyes locked onto hers as they stared at each other. It was clear he was at as much of a loss for inspiration as she was.

"I think they call this a moral dilemma," he broke the silence first.

She nodded, impressed he had the guts to say aloud what she already knew.

"We need to state the truth," he continued, looking thoughtful.

"The whole truth or nothing but the truth?" she asked, searching his face.

"Ay, there's the rub," he observed.

"*Hamlet.*" She tried not to giggle at the line he'd quoted from Shakespeare. Her nerves were so on edge, she felt as if she might break out in hysterical laughter any minute.

"He wasn't the only one with problems." Jack's eyes held a glint of levity.

"But he didn't know how to make a decision," she protested, thinking what a poor excuse for a guy she'd always found Hamlet to be. He was one of her least favorite Shakespearean characters. Nothing turned her off more than men who were second-guessers. Perhaps because the only man she'd ever been almost engaged to had been one.

"And we do?" Jack countered, one eyebrow going up as he gave her a quizzical look.

"We've got to tell them something," she mused, tapping her fingers on the kitchen counter as she eyed her cell phone lying inches away. "Nic's going to call any minute."

"Nothing but the truth sounds good to me," he told her, "in limited doses, of course."

She looked at his face carefully. "What truths should we touch upon?"

"You had a great time with Percy, he got lots of exercise and you handed him over to me last night as planned." He returned her gaze with equal intensity, then smiled devilishly. "Maybe you could mention it was nice meeting me too."

"Wouldn't that be sort of lying?"

"You mean it wasn't nice meeting me?" His eyebrows knit together in the middle as he glowered at her.

She couldn't tell if he was teasing or really insulted.

"No, not that. I mean, what about losing Percy? What if we don't find him and we have to tell them everything when they get back? Oh, my God, what is she going to do? She'll never speak to me again." Her stomach tightened as she collapsed onto the arm of the couch.

"Back up a minute," he continued evenly. "You tell Nicole everything that happened up until the moment you handed him off to me, at which point it's my story to tell. I lost the dog, not you. *Capisce?*"

"What's *capisce?*"

"Italian for 'do you understand.'"

"Are you part Italian?" she asked. He didn't look it, more Irish or Scottish with his light brown, wavy hair and dark blue eyes.

"No, but *Godfather II* is my favorite movie."

The completely irrelevant thought crossed her mind that *Godfather II* was also one of her favorite movies. "Wouldn't I be a sort of accomplice to the crime if that's all I say?" she asked.

"Then tell her everything." He flung his hands up, looking decidedly like a *Godfather II* cast member. "That you handed off Percy to me, I lost him less than five minutes later, and you're really sorry but you've got a flight to catch, hope you're having a wonderful time."

"Oh, my God, I can't tell her that. It will ruin their vacation," she cried, her throat closing up at the thought of Tom and Nicole rushing back to look for their dog.

Their friends were on a boat at the moment. How long would it take until it pulled into port somewhere so they could disembark and fly back as soon as possible? While in transit, they'd be in agony.

"Look. We decide together what we tell them, then we stick to it," Jack said, his voice firm. "Does that work for you?"

She nodded. He had no idea how well that worked for her. Jack Whitby didn't appear to be a second-guesser. She applauded his resolve, wishing her former almost-fiancé Tim had had it, instead of getting cold feet which he'd used to backtrack on his plans to propose when his company transferred him to Shanghai. Then again, who would want to be married to a Hamlet? Better to end up with someone who knew how to make a decision.

She jumped at the sound of her cell phone.

"I'll bet it's her. What do I say again?" Panic welled inside, but she willed herself to get up, walk to the kitchen counter and pick up the phone. Sure enough, Nicole's name lit up across the screen.

"That's for you to decide," Jack told her.

She clicked on, bile rising at the back of her throat.

"Nic—Hi!" she greeted her friend, her voice light as air.

She would not ruin her best friend's vacation with news there was nothing Tom and Nic could do about in their present location. By the time they got off the ship and found a flight back to New York, it would be close to their regularly scheduled return date anyway. Better to let them enjoy their holiday while she and Jack spent the time before their return searching for and finding the dog. Her heart lurched as she thought of her own flight scheduled to take off in just a few hours. She'd forgotten all about it.

"Hi, sweetie," Nicole sang into the phone. "Glad I caught you before you fly off to your island. How'd it go with Percy?"

"Great. He's a love bug," Hint choked out. "We took lots of walks together and he slept with me every night." She regretted her choice of words as she caught the look on Jack's face. If she wasn't mistaken, a hint of red had just appeared.

"Did Tom's friend show up on time?" Nicole asked.

"He did. Right on time."

"Pretty cute, huh?"

It was Hint's turn to blush. She averted her eyes from Jack and turned to face the window overlooking her balcony.

"I guess," she told Nicole.

"I'm so glad everything went well. I'd die if anything happened to our little boy. All set for your trip?"

"Yes." Hint's stomach dropped at her friend's words.

"Have a great time and don't forget to bring sunblock," Nicole reminded her.

"Nic?"

"Yes, sweetie?"

"There's something else." Didn't Nicole deserve to know what had happened to her dog? But she felt sick at the thought of ruining her friend's vacation.

"What? I can't hear you very well. They're announcing morning activities over the P.A. system. Can you speak up?"

"I. . . we . . . walked Percy together." Hint's voice faltered as she stepped onto her balcony, out of Jack's earshot. She couldn't bear to look at him. Hadn't they just agreed to decide what to say and then stick to it? Was she in this together with Jack Whitby or not? And what if she wasn't? Wouldn't that make her a second-guesser? She groaned inwardly.

"That's great. Listen, they're announcing signups for on-deck massages," Nicole shouted into the phone. "I've got to run. Yesterday they were sold out in five minutes. Bye, sweetie. Don't do anything I wouldn't do in Punta Cana." A tinkling laugh came through the receiver then the connection cut off.

I'd die if anything happened to our little boy. The words rang in Hint's head as she put down the cell phone. If she and Jack didn't find Percy, it would be like losing her closest friend's child. Could she live with that? And how could she get on a plane in less than five hours with her best friend's "child" missing and the only person left to find him a man who knew next to nothing about dogs and hadn't even wanted to take on dog sitting Percy? Putting up her hands to either side of her head, she pulled her hair in frustration. It was a habit she'd never outgrown from childhood.

"You told her?" Jack asked quietly behind her. She hadn't heard him come out onto the balcony.

She shook her head slowly, then turned to face him.

"No. I couldn't."

"You didn't want to ruin their vacation," he consoled her. "And I don't want to ruin yours."

"I can't go unless we find him."

"You have to go," he ordered her. "It was my fault for losing him and I'll take responsibility for finding him. What time does your cab come?"

"I'm not going." She was impressed with his resolve. For some reason, she wanted to show him hers too. The lack of resolve her former boyfriend had shown by his indecisive waffling between her and another woman had left its mark on her. She didn't want to be someone like that. Ever.

"How many ads do we have printed out now?" Jack asked, ignoring her last comment.

"I queued up fifty on the printer," she answered, deciding to leave the issue alone for the moment. She had two more hours before she needed to cancel her cab and flight. If she was going to second-guess her decision not to go, she'd do so silently. Better to follow Jack's example of making a decision and sticking to it than acting like Hamlet or even worse, her ex-boyfriend. She was worthy of much more, she told herself, including finding a partner who wasn't a weathervane and not being one herself.

"Okay, we'll get started with those," Jack broke into her thoughts. "Let's bring a notebook and some cold drinks," he suggested. "Also, do you have any of Percy's toys?"

"Nicole gave me a few things."

"Anything that squeaks or makes a noise?"

"Umm . . ." she rummaged around in the shopping bag she'd packed for Jack the evening before, with Percy's food and toys in it. A bedraggled red dachshund appeared.

"How's this?" The dachshund squeaked when she squeezed its stomach. She tossed it to Jack.

"Pretty gross," he remarked, catching the small, stuffed animal. One eye was missing. A pungent, wet dog smell emanated from the ratty-looking toy. "But perfect, for our purposes." He stuffed it in his back pocket.

In a minute they were downstairs and out the door, where Jack's forest green Honda Civic stood parked curbside in front of Hint's building. She hopped in, noting the interior was fairly neat for a guy. What did the blue ribbons on his rear view mirror signify? Peering closer, she read "First Place, Ox Ridge Hunt Club, Darien CT."

"Do you ride?" she asked, surprised. Most guys she knew steered clear of horses.

"Do I ride? Ride what?" He followed her gaze to the ribbons. "Oh, no. That's my niece Marguerite's ribbon. She won it for best horsemanship or something in a pony show."

"Wow. How old is she?"

"Six. She's just learning how to ride." His face shone with pride.

"I can't believe she gave you her blue ribbon."

"She's won several. Anyways, she likes to ride around with her uncle in his green car, because I brag about her whenever anyone asks about the ribbon."

"Don't her parents brag about her too?"

"Oh yes. They've got a whole rainbow of ribbons attached to their rear view mirror. She's quite a competitor. She takes her horseshows seriously," he said.

"But she's only six. Is she jumping or posting?"

"I, uh, don't think so. She gets ribbons for all sorts of reasons: for grooming her horse nicely, good sportsmanship, good form—that sort of thing," he explained.

"Cutest horsewoman?"

"You got it." He beamed with pride. Flipping down the sun visor, Jack produced a photo of a sweet-looking girl with short blonde braids and an enormous smile, minus two upper front teeth.

"What a doll." She sighed. "How often do you see her?"

"Pretty often. I'm her godfather, so I get invited to all the family events. Her birthday party's coming up this Saturday."

"So you're a godparent too." She'd never met a guy close to her age who was also a godparent. "Do you ever babysit her?"

"Yup. I'm one of her favorite babysitters. Good old Uncle Jack is a pushover for staying up late, eating junk food and watching TV shows her parents won't let her."

"Where does she live?"

"Scarsdale. My brother and his wife aren't far from Nicole and Tom."

"It's nice to have family nearby," she remarked.

"'Tis." Jack looked wistful. He shifted in his seat as if uncomfortable.

Hint glanced out the window to give him a moment with his thoughts. They were entering the driveway to the dog run. It was a shallow decline, rife with potholes and leftover scars from snow melting and running down from the main road to the stream bordering the dog run. On the other side of the stream stood the woods where she had lost Percy a few days earlier. Already, it seemed like a week ago.

They hopped out and went over to the lamppost where Jack had put up one of the ads the evening before. It was still there. Percy's sweet face looked out expectantly at her. Was he looking for her? Or Nicole or Tom? One thing was certain; he wasn't looking for Jack.

As she watched him move off toward the dog run, she weighed the meeting in Punta Cana with Derek Simpson against staying in New York to find Nicole and Tom's dog. One was a professional opportunity. The other was her best friend's little boy. Nicole had said she would die if something happened to him. If she prioritized a professional opportunity to advance her career over a personal and moral obligation to help find her friend's dog she'd be no better a person than her ex-boyfriend had been.

After one year of dating, Tim had brought up the future over dinner at their favorite Thai restaurant. Hint had been surprised, but pleased. Tim was ambitious, hard-working and dedicated to his job as a management consultant. Although he worked insane hours, with frequent business trips, the combination of his steady, corporate lifestyle blended well with Hint's freelance illustrator career. Sometimes she thought he was a bit too married to his job, but her mother had frequently reminded her that the only kind of man with whom she could share a future would be someone with more job security than she.

"So how shall we celebrate one year together?" he'd asked as they'd sipped champagne cocktails before ordering dinner.

"This is a pretty good way," she'd pointed out, wondering what else he meant.

"Isn't it time to make some plans?"

"Plans?" Hint froze, unsure of where Tim was going. He frequently kept her guessing, mostly about his availability, but she had gotten used to it. She told herself it was one of the reasons dating him was so exciting. Except when it had made her anxious, which had been often.

"Yes. Don't women usually like to make plans?"

Women? She didn't want to talk about women. This was her personally he was speaking to.

"I suppose so." She hesitated, eyeing him distrustfully. Why did she feel so unsure of him after a whole year together? "What do you have in mind?"

"Shouldn't we do something like take things to the next step?" he asked.

"What do you mean?" She wouldn't be the one to put words in her boyfriend's mouth.

"Say, find a place together in the city?"

Wow. That was taking things to the next step alright. But the way he'd worded it had sounded so casual.

"You mean move in together?" Her eyes widened as she studied his face closely. Ideas came and went for him at the speed of light; they were what made him shine professionally. She wanted to make sure this wasn't just another one he was trying on for size.

"That would be the idea," he answered, taking a swig of his cocktail.

Hint hesitated. That would be the idea? He hadn't even used a personal pronoun. Or made any mention of marriage up ahead. She was pleased he'd brought up the future but not as rapturously happy as she thought she'd be at a moment like this.

"Let's think about it and we can talk more next time we see each other," she told him. It wasn't much of an answer, but it hadn't been much of a proposal, had it? If she was going to move in with her boyfriend, she wanted to know there was a plan up ahead that wasn't just having a roommate with sleeping together privileges.

"Sure, darling. When I get back from my trip next week we can firm things up further." He'd winked at her, raising his glass.

She'd clinked glasses with him, wondering why she felt as if they'd just been discussing a business deal.

Then one week later, he'd called midday from his office, a rare occurrence.

"I've got news," he'd practically shouted into the phone.

"What is it?" she'd asked, sensing it was work-related. It usually was with Tim.

"They're putting me in charge of starting up the Shanghai office. It's an amazing opportunity. I've got to get out there before the end of the month so we can get a team in place to move into the new space on the first of September."

"Congratulations," Hint had offered, wondering what that meant for their relationship.

"We'll firm up the plans we talked about when I get back," he continued.

"When will that be?" Once again she felt as if they were discussing some sort of work project.

"By Christmas, darling. We'll spend Christmas together. I'll have something to ask you then."

"That's five months away, Tim." Something to ask her then? Maybe it had finally clicked that his idea of the week before of just moving in together hadn't made her jump for joy.

"I know, darling. It'll fly by. Listen, I've got to run. Can you meet me in Manhattan after work tonight? A few of us are going out to celebrate the new office. I'd love you to join us."

"I'll call you later to let you know. Really excited for you. Bye." She laid down the phone thoughtfully. Had this call been about them or about him?

Two weeks later, he'd left for Shanghai. As summer turned into fall and fall moved toward Christmas holidays, Tim's hurried phone calls and short e-mail messages had become less and less personal, as if he were communicating with a work colleague. It became increasingly clear to Hint that Tim's priority was his career, not their relationship.

Thoughtfully, she pulled out her cell phone, scrolling down until she found the number for the airline she was scheduled to fly on that afternoon. She might be committing professional suicide by canceling her trip to Punta Cana, but finding Percy couldn't wait. Hadn't the town dog catcher's message said the best chance of finding a lost pet was within the first twenty-four hours? There was no way Jack could do it without her help.

What goes around comes around, she told herself, as she cancelled her flight, then the car service. Someone bigger than herself would recognize the decision she was about to make and reward her for it. Wasn't that the way things were supposed to work? Even if they didn't, she had to live with herself.

In a minute her calls were done. She took off over the field after Jack, her heart undivided. For the rest of the week she was now free and clear to look for her friends' dog.

JACK COULDN'T FIGURE out what it was about Hint that was so otherworldly. Were there some tips in *Other Worlds* magazine she was following that made her seem like a visitor from another planet? Glancing towards her now, walking away from him to the side of the dog run bordering the riverbed she'd agreed to take while he took the other side, he saw her screw up her eyes. She looked as if she were in a trance. That was some way to look for a dog. He might as well find a dowser stick for her to carry.

For his part, he moved quickly down the field, calling Percy's name and handing out copies of the lost dog ad to the dog owners he passed. No one had seen the dog. Entering the woods on the other side of the small stream, he wondered how Percy would handle a night out in such a setting. Probably the mutt would do fine.

Suddenly, he recalled his track buddy mentioning a coyote the park service had found in Van Cortlandt Park in the Bronx the summer before. Did coyotes only eat carrion or were they predators themselves?

The only time he'd seen a coyote outside of a zoo had been on a trip to Tucson, Arizona. An animal the size of a medium-large dog had crossed the road about fifty yards in front of his car. Its skulking posture and muscular gait had informed him this was no dog. Vicious-looking yellow eyes flashed at him briefly before the shadowy creature disappeared into the brush.

He hoped there were no coyotes currently in the vicinity of lower Westchester County. His only run-in with one had left a haunting impression; he could only imagine Percy's terror, should the dog come across one.

"Percy. Damn you, mutt, get back here. Come on back, boy. Don't ruin your girl's vacation." He shouted and whistled, occasionally squeaking the filthy red dachshund toy in his pocket.

As he circled back to find Hint, he came across a male of about twenty throwing a stick to a large German shepherd.

"Hey, have you seen this dog?" Jack asked, thrusting a flyer into the stranger's hand.

The younger man took a long moment to study the photo. "He looks familiar."

"He does? Where did you see him?" A shot of adrenalin ran through Jack. Percy might be just on the other side of the field at this moment.

"He belongs to a woman with long, reddish brown hair," the man said.

"Have you seen him recently?"

"Yeah. I have."

"You're kidding. Where? Here?" Jack's heart leaped. Maybe Hint would catch her flight after all. Although he had to admit, he didn't really want her to disappear after everything they'd been through over the past twelve hours.

"She was talking to him in some sort of special way. Like, she called him "Snuggle Stuff" or something."

"Do you mean you saw him with the woman you mentioned?" Jack asked, disappointed.

"She was hot, man. Pale skin and this hair. I never saw hair that color on a woman."

"Okay, but the dog—did you see the dog again later, after you saw him with the woman walking him?"

"No. I just remember the woman. Her voice sort of tinkled when she talked. Like wind chimes or, uh—she's not your girlfriend, is she?" The blond guy looked up from the photo, squinting. A patch of blond stubble was barely visible on his chin, as if he'd gotten his face stuck in a bowl of oatmeal cookie batter.

Jack ignored the question, glancing around for signs of Hint. She was nowhere on the horizon. "Her dog is lost. If you find him, could you call one of these numbers here?"

"Sure. Which one of these numbers is hers?"

"This one." Jack pointed to his own cell phone number. It looked as if Hint attracted male attention whether she wanted to or not.

The young man turned to go, but Jack stopped him. "Listen, I'm not a dog owner, but you are. What would you do if you lost your dog?"

"I'd post signs all over. I'd describe her, but I wouldn't make her sound too great. There are people out there who'd find her and just keep her."

"Good thought. Okay, thanks, man. See you around."

"Yeah and, uh—"

"Yeah?"

"Could you let the red-haired lady know I said hi if you see her?"

"I'll let her husband know when I see him later down at the police station. He's a cop."

"Oh. Uh, skip it, dude," Smudge Chin amended, looking worried.

Jack moved on. Had he scared off the guy from calling if he found Percy? If he had, he had done both the dog and Hint a disservice. But he couldn't help himself. His instinct was to

protect her from predators like pretty much every male they'd
bumped into thus far that day. Some guys were such schmucks.
He hoped he wasn't one of them.

SEVEN HOURS LATER, Hint was exhausted. They'd spent the day
driving around lower Westchester County, stopping by Nicole
and Tom's house, visiting the nearest Humane Society, and
posting flyers at all the area train stations. It had been an edu-
cation, if not a rewarding one.

After canceling her flight she'd felt strangely lighthearted.
As she'd told her cousin Kim on the phone, if Percy showed
up by the next morning, she could get on the same flight the
next afternoon. But she wasn't counting on that happening.
Her cousin had been upset, but that was too bad.

She'd called her while Jack had gone into the New
Rochelle Humane Society. They hadn't been able to find a
parking spot in the heart of downtown New Rochelle, so he'd
pulled over in a loading zone and she'd offered to sit in the
driver's seat and move the car if need be while he went into
the building. It had been a good moment to call Kim, who
had already arrived in Punta Cana the day before with their
friend Nina.

"Kim? It's me, Hint. I've got a problem."

"Tell me you didn't miss your flight."

"Yes. I did. Percy's lost. We're looking for him now. If he
turns up, I'll take the same flight down tomorrow," she told
her.

"What do you mean? Who's Percy?" Kim's voice rose, the
way it did when she was upset.

"Percy's the dog I've been taking care of for Nicole and Tom Mays. I was supposed to hand him off to their friend last night, but the dog got loose and ran off. I can't go anywhere until we find him."

"Hint, what are you talking about? Can't the person you handed him off to take care of this?"

"No. Percy doesn't really know him. He's never dog sat for him before."

"That's his problem, not yours. Aren't you meeting with that big shot art director? You can't just cancel. He'll never give you another chance. You've got to get down here."

"It's an emergency, Kim. I'm really sorry. I can't come unless we find him."

"So look for him today then take tomorrow's flight."

"There's no way I can leave here if the dog's still missing. Can you understand? I've got to help find him."

"Why can't the other person do it?"

"Percy hasn't spent any time with him. He doesn't know him and he won't respond to him if he finds him. Also, Percy might be in the area where I've taken him for walks the past five days. I know where I've taken him, Jack doesn't. There's no way he can handle this by himself."

"Who's Jack?" her cousin asked, her voice bristling with irritation.

"Jack Whitby. Tom's friend who was going to take the dog for the final five days of their trip."

"Have you told your friends yet that he's lost?"

"No. It only happened last night." She didn't mention that Nicole had called. "I'm hoping he'll show up today."

"Promise me you'll be on tomorrow's flight, whatever happens."

"I can't," she said firmly. "You've got Nina for company, Kim. I'm really sorry to do this to you, but there's nothing else I can do."

"What about your big meeting?" her cousin wailed. "Don't you even care about your career? What about me? What if Nina and I meet three hot guys on the beach and you're not there?"

"Listen, I'm getting another call," Hint fibbed. "It might be someone who's found Percy. I'll call you if we find him." She clicked off.

Hours later she mulled over the conversation as Jack drove her back toward Bronxville. Her cousin had thought she was crazy for prioritizing finding her friends' dog over her own career. Was she? Maybe it hadn't been a smart professional move, but it had been the only one she could live with when she thought about the next time she looked into Nicole's eyes. *What goes around comes around* came to mind, reassuring her that good deeds get rewarded. She wanted to believe they did, but who knew? At the moment, she was too tired to think.

"You need a break," Jack said, glancing over while driving.

"Thanks, but I'm not taking one until we find him." The deep blue of his eyes made her think of swimming. She wished she could jump into the ocean at that moment and let the water wash away every problem she faced.

"Then what can we do that will give you some down time but keep us on the trail?" he asked.

She liked the way he'd phrased his question. He must be as exhausted as she, but he'd mentioned her needs, not his.

"I've got an idea." She cocked her head. "We could stop off at the butcher's on our way back to my place. I'll pick up some steaks and we can grill them on my patio out back."

"Great idea," Jack agreed. "The smell might attract Percy. We're sweaty too after being out all day, so maybe he'll pick up our scent."

They dropped by Ollie's, Bronxville's family-owned butcher shop.

"Stay in the car," she told him. "I've got this one. Just come up with an idea for finding our boy."

Jack laughed, his eyes crinkling at each corner.

Why did she feel so carefree, considering the circumstances? They would attract the dog back to them, somehow. She felt sure of it as she stood in front of the counter, watching the butcher weigh two thick steaks.

One hour later, with the sun low on the horizon, she had fired up the grill in her small backyard. Looking up, she spotted Jack rounding the corner from one final walk around the neighborhood. A paper bag under his arm, he had apparently made a stop on the way back. After closing and latching the gate to Hint's backyard, he pulled a bottle of Pinot Noir from the paper bag and set it on the wrought iron patio table. Smart man.

"I'll feel guilty having too good a time with Percy missing," she greeted him hesitantly, her words belying her rapidly rising spirits. Her dog hunting partner had manners, if not subtlety.

"Okay, so let's just have a moderately good time," he mollified her. "Don't forget the power of *in vino veritas*."

"Why should I share my *veritas* with you?" she teased, liking the look of his broad shoulders encased in the red polo shirt he wore, faded almost pink.

"I want you to have a revelation this evening," he said.

"A revelation?" What did he mean?

"You're going to get an intuition about Percy. I can feel it."

"You can?" Was he teasing or did he really believe in the kind of stuff she did?

"My intuition tells me yours is going to come up with something." He smiled. "About the dog," he added.

Of course she had intuition. She just wasn't comfortable sharing that side of herself to someone she'd just met. But didn't she need to put herself on the line in order to find Percy? She ran upstairs to get salad and wineglasses.

The steaks sizzled as Jack opened the bottle of wine. He poured two glasses then held one out to her.

"Here's to finding Percy." She lightly clinked glasses with him and looked up at the sky. *We need Your help up there,* she silently added.

Jack's eyes followed hers upward. "Help us to help each other find him," he said, as if he had heard her silent prayer.

Love does not consist in gazing at each other but in looking outward together in the same direction flashed into her mind. They were the words of Antoine de Saint-Exupéry, the author of one of her most beloved childhood books, *The Little Prince.* Something inside her shifted then sighed. It was a happy sigh, like the sigh of a lost dog who's found a comfortable spot to rest and forgotten its worries for the moment.

Jack's cell phone rang. Hint turned back to the steaks, but not before she saw his face darken as he took in the voice on the other end.

JACK'S STOMACH LURCHED as he moved quickly to the far side of the patio, away from Hint. Annabel Sanford. After all these months. Or was it a year? He wondered what had happened to her hedge fund manager. Maybe his fund had gone belly up. Or had it been a private equities guy? Whoever it had been, she'd dumped him for some big shot financier she'd met in the Hamptons and he'd been relieved to let her go. What did she want now?

"Jack. It's Annabel. I'm so-o-o glad you picked up. I meant to call you months ago. Is this a good time to talk?" Her voice purred like the engine on a Lamborghini. He imagined she was probably driving in one at that moment, talking on her cell phone, daring a state trooper to pull her over, so she could savor the thrill of overcoming his senses in a cloud of perfume.

She had enjoyed winning. And Jack had not minded losing, when it came to finally losing her. He had gotten tired of finding himself at the short end of her frequent power plays. With Annabel, every situation had been a win-lose one. He had often wondered what it might be like to be in a win-win relationship with a woman. Wasn't that what being in love was supposed to be about?

"What's up?" he asked brusquely. It wasn't a good time to talk, but he might as well get it over with and get rid of her. They had nothing left to talk about, having discussed their profound incompatibility repeatedly in the final months of their relationship. His jaw hardened as he steeled himself for whatever she had to say to him.

"Darling, how've you been?" she gushed into Jack's ear. "I've missed you. It's been awhile—I mean, a long time—since things fizzled out with . . . um . . . the East Hampton person. Have you been dating?"

Just because he hadn't hung up on her didn't mean it was okay to call him 'darling.' She had incredible nerve. One of the things he'd found attractive about her. Then. Not now.

"Uh-huh." For all she knew, he was on a date at that very moment. He was grilling steaks with an attractive woman, right? Never mind that they were hunting down a lost dog. Why did the sound of his ex's voice irritate him so much? He felt like ripping out one of the slats of the white picket fence he leaned on as he averted his face from Hint.

"Darling, could we *possibly* get together?" Annabel asked. "I really need to see you again. It's been a long, long time."

"Yeah, I know." *And that's a good thing.* What was he supposed to say? She must really be having a dry spell to be calling good old Jack Whitby, her chump standby, the man without a hedge fund.

He burned, thinking of her sitting around with her girlfriends, downing Cosmopolitans and devouring pictorials in *Quest* magazine in their search for Mr. Gazillionaire without an attention deficit disorder. Dream on. She might as well be on a mission to find a camel without a hump.

"Are you happy, Jack? You seemed so content when we were together. I was silly not to appreciate it at the time . . ." Her voice trailed off.

"You're right. I am." *And you're right that you were silly and still are.* Why was he getting so hot under the collar? He'd been thrilled when she'd done him the favor of tossing him aside. He wasn't interested to be picked up again, like an old blanket that a child leaves out in the backyard over winter and rediscovers in the spring.

It wasn't spring in Jack's heart. It was still wintertime and when the spring thaws came they were not going to be ushered in by Annabel Sanford, no matter how good she looked in a red dress.

"So when can we meet? Can we do our Friday afternoon G & Ts at the Stanhope? I miss our Friday afternoons so-o-o much, Jack-Jack."

"I, uh, can't say right now." He hated being called Jack-Jack. Remembering various circumstances under which she'd used that nickname, he felt a blush crawl up the back of his neck.

"I loved our Friday afternoons, sweetie. Remember how they flowed so smoothly into Friday evenings?" Her laugh trilled suggestively.

"Uh-huh." He would rather not remember those moments right now. He had a dog to catch. And it wasn't polite to stay on the phone with Hint right behind him. Listening to every word he breathed, no doubt. What woman wouldn't? What man wouldn't? He knew he would.

"I want to see you again so much. I can't tell you. Would you promise me we'll do the Stanhope this Friday? Please, Jack-Jack?"

"I'll take it under advisement."

"I'll take you under advisement, Baby Boy. On Friday afternoon I'm putting on my red halter dress—you remember the one—and going over to the Stanhope around half past five. I'll sit at our favorite table. You're advised to show up."

"Mm-hmm . . ."

"Was that a yes?" she whispered.

"No. It wasn't," he enunciated clearly into the phone.

A short pause ensued.

"You're not with someone right now, are you?" Her voice suddenly rose, sharp and screechy. The multi-faceted, lightning fast mood changes of his former girlfriend jolted him once again. Why was he allowing her to get to him? It was time to throw her off before she confused him any further.

"Actually I am." Jack chose not to explain exactly what he meant by 'being with someone right now.' The days of explaining himself to Annabel Sanford were over. Long gone. Over and done like a steak that had sat on the grill too long. It had been a good steak before it had burned.

"Oh. I see." Another pause. She seemed to be remembering for the first time in their conversation that he was no longer actually her boyfriend. "Well, great to hear your voice, darling. I'd better get back to the party." The dulcet tone had returned, all sweetness and sunlight, like tiny purple flowers covering the permafrost in the Arctic Circle.

"Good to hear from you," he lied. *Not. Irritating to hear from you. Confusing. Definitely not good.*

He clicked off. Sweat covered his forehead and pooled in his armpits. She'd probably been drunk dialing. He hoped not, for her sake. But it wasn't his business anymore.

Running nervous fingers through his hair, he steeled himself against the image of the tall, shapely blonde who had been his girlfriend for the better part of two years. Only it had been the worse part. She'd been a fluid, endlessly moving weathervane always ready to change course with the latest prevailing wind.

Apparently he'd been in her target range for a brief few seconds that evening. She would move on in another few. He breathed a sigh of relief at having gotten her off the phone so quickly. Why was it that the only way he'd found out anything about women was to get knocked around by one? Turning to Hint, his eyes met hers; but before he could ask her pardon for his time on the phone, a male voice rang out.

"Hey, is that steak I smell?" a man called over the fence.

"Ugh. My building super." Hint made a face before turning to greet the caller.

"Again? He's pretty ubiquitous, isn't he?" Jack remarked, moving to block the gate in the low fence that separated the patio from the driveway. On the other side, the tall, well-built figure of Brian O'Connell appeared, squeezed into a tight white tee-shirt. Ignoring Jack, the newcomer addressed Hint directly.

"Find the dog yet?"

"No. Not yet." She tried not to grimace while addressing the unwelcome guest.

"Taking a break, huh?" the super asked, leaning on the fence in a way that made the bicep on his right arm ripple.

"We're eating dinner." Would he get the message that this wasn't a good time to visit? Along with any other time, except when she needed a repair.

"Thought I'd pick up some more flyers to post around," Brian said.

"I'll print some more out for you and put them inside your screen door," she told him curtly.

"Great. I can drop by and get them later, if it's easier for you." Brian was now giving Jack a cool stare. Some sort of male power play appeared to be taking place.

"No thanks. I'll drop them by your door tomorrow morning." *Get out of here, you dolt*, she thought, not for the first time.

"Hey, well, have a good time. I mean—have a nice dinner." He finally seemed to pick up on her signals to get lost.

"Thanks. Bye," she dismissed him.

The muscle-bound figure swaggered as he walked away. She breathed a sigh of relief.

"Nice blocking," she commended Jack.

"I kind of guessed you didn't want him coming in the gate."

"He's the type of person who doesn't leave once you give him entry," she explained.

"Finding a dog can mean bumping into some strays along the way," he observed, cocking an eyebrow at her.

Her laugh was strained as she turned back to the steaks. He had no idea what words of truth he'd just spoken about her life. Had that been a stray he'd been speaking with just now on the phone?

The steaks were done.

Transferring them to a platter, she brought them to the table, where she served Jack, then herself. Picking up her fork and knife, she was about to dig in.

"Want to say grace?" he asked.

"Sure. Will you do the honors?" His request was a pleasant surprise. In some ways he showed finesse coupled with strength. He had deflected unwanted intruders such as Brian O'Connell and whoever that had been on the phone. Why couldn't he be more graceful in tracking down a dog?

Before she knew what he was doing, he'd grasped her hand and closed his eyes.

"We lift up our search. Give us inspiration and energy to find our friends' dog. Amen," he prayed.

"Amen, " she echoed. Reaching to serve the salad, she tried not to think of how warm and muscular his hand had been around hers. Who had just called him? And why did she care?

DINNER PROGRESSED QUIETLY. He liked the way Hint didn't rush to fill up empty spaces in their conversation. Or was it because she was thinking about the phone call he'd gotten? He hoped not.

The bones of her hand had felt so fine under his. She was no Amazon. More of a half hidden forest creature. Someone from another world, finer than this one. Brushing the thought from his mind, he took a large bite.

"Umm." He nodded his head. The steak was perfectly done: black on the outside and juicy and rare on the inside.

"Good? I was afraid I'd burned them. We had a few distractions." She took a bite herself. "Umm."

"You did a great job. It's really tender. If this doesn't bring back Percy, nothing will," he told her.

"I hope something will." Her face blanched.

"I was just joking. He'll come back. I bet we'll find him tonight." He hadn't meant to upset her.

"What's our plan?" She looked at him expectantly but with reserve, not jumping in to offer a fully executed plan for him to rubberstamp as Annabel would have done.

His ex hadn't actually cared what any of his plans had been. She'd just wanted him to go along with any and all of her own. It had never occurred to her to wait and see what he might come up with. After a time, he'd no longer even tried to come up with any plans. That was when she'd accused him of attention deficit disorder.

Battlefield fatigue was more like it. He'd gotten fed up with going along with her choices just to keep the peace. Although he'd heard many marriages operated on similar premises, he vowed his never would. The only partnership he was interested in was one in which he was a full partner.

"Our plan is to find him before the trail grows stale," he said to Hint. "Can you come with me after we finish eating?"

"Where are we going?" she asked.

"What do you suggest?" He studied her face. Was there been a sadness there that went beyond looking for her friends' dog? "Is there anywhere you think he might have followed a scent to?"

"Somewhere around Tom and Nicole's home," she said.

"Why don't we drive up to Scarsdale after dinner and see if he's made his way back to his own home?" he asked.

She nodded then took another bite. For the next few minutes they ate in silence. Finally, he put down his napkin and pushed back from the table.

"Are you thinking about lying on the beach in Punta Cana right now?" he asked.

"I . . . I was thinking about something else I was supposed to be doing in Punta Cana," she murmured, her voice muffled.

"Something better than lying on the beach watching the sun go down?" He studied her face. Was there someone down in Punta Cana she'd been going to meet? "Hey, I didn't get in the way of you meeting someone special on a tropical island, did I?"

Her expression became even more enigmatic; clouds chased sunlight, as if she were fighting with herself. Finally, stoic calmness replaced regret as she faced him.

"I, um, had a business meeting I had to cancel, but it's more important that we find Percy."

"Do you think you could catch a flight tomorrow if he shows up?" He would give anything to wipe that look of sadness off her face.

"I'm not thinking about catching a flight," she said, her voice clear and strong. "I'm thinking about finding a dog."

"Okay, let's drive up to Tom and Nicole's place and scope out the area." He was impressed with her resolve. "Are there any favorite spots they take him to nearby?"

"There's a park near their house," she told him.

"Let's go there after we check the house."

"We might need some flashlights. I'll go upstairs and get some," she said.

"Let me help," he offered, rising and scooping up her plate before she could protest.

Within ten minutes he was behind the wheel with Hint next to him. As the stargazer lily scent of her hair filled his senses, they drove through the darkening dusk up the Bronx River Parkway to Scarsdale.

4

NIGHT OF THE SUMMER SOLSTICE

Nighttime had fallen, and an enormous full moon was emerging on the horizon by the time they turned off the parkway to Scarsdale. A sign advertising a Midsummer's Eve party to be held that evening at Heathcote Tavern stood prominently at the side of the exit.

"Is it the summer solstice tonight?" Hint asked.

"I'm not sure," Jack answered, not trusting himself with dates after Monday evening's near fiasco. Mixing up Percy's pickup date had been almost as lame as dropping the dog's leash.

"What's the date today?"

"It's the twenty-first. He checked the date on his watch to make sure.

"That's it, the longest day of the year," she remarked, peering up at the sky. The column of her neck arched like a swan, gleaming pale and white in the moon's glow. He wished he wasn't noticing, but he was.

He pulled into Tom and Nicole's driveway and parked directly behind a large, tarp covered object. Jack recognized the outlines of Tom's Triumph motorcycle. He chuckled, thinking of the times he'd watched Tom impress a girl by pulling up to whatever meeting spot they'd chosen on the English motorbike. But once he'd married, Nicole had persuaded Tom it was too dangerous to continue driving it. The danger that had been part of his charm for her as a single man no longer charmed her as his wife. Jack had seen a similar transformation in values happen to his sister and her husband when his niece had been born.

Tom had refused to sell the bike, preferring to keep it parked permanently in his driveway, a swansong to his single days.

"Whoa. I'd forgotten about Tom's bike. It's usually hidden behind Nicole's car when I come over. Maybe Percy slept under this cover last night," he speculated as he whisked it off, wanting to check out the bike in all its glory by the light of the full moon.

He watched as Hint ran her fingers over the black leather seat, the retro handlebars. She squatted to inspect the lacquered engine covers. It was a classic bike, both stylish and powerful. No wonder Tom hadn't wanted to relinquish it. He sighed. Wasn't this like looking at a three-hundred-pound tiger behind bars at the zoo? What was the point of owning such a thing of beauty and power only to keep it under a tarp in one's driveway?

"It's so . . . so . . . " Her voice drifted off.

"Hot?" He hadn't meant to use that adjective.

"Hah . . ." A sound like a laugh mixed with a sigh escaped her.

"Let me ask you something," he said, a mischievous idea springing to mind.

"What's that?"

Her index finger slid across the top tube of the double layer of chrome silencers running along the side of the bike. She looked as if she knew something about bikes. Idly, he wondered if she'd ever dated a biker.

"If you were married, would you let your husband ride this bike?" he asked.

"Only with me behind him," she answered.

"And if you were married with kids?"

"He wouldn't have time to ride a bike." Her eyes sparkled as she faced him.

"I see. So what do you think Tom does with this beauty?" he asked, thinking of another.

"I know what he does, because Nicole told me his driving days are over. He keeps it here in his driveway and feels good every time he walks by it."

"Don't you think he's more likely a bit frustrated not to ride it anymore?" Jack was puzzled.

"Not really." She looked thoughtful. I think he feels happy to remember all the good times he had on this bike and to know he's got a wife who cares about him enough not to let him have an accident on it."

"Hmmm." Jack digested her words. "Do you think he ever sits on it, just to remember how it felt?"

"Sure I do." Standing, she lithely swung one jeans-clad leg over the seat. Grasping the handlebars, she turned to him, eyes flashing.

"I think he sits on it and I think Nicole also sits on it some-times just to remember how Tom made her feel when she rode with him."

Her smile was sphinxlike, inscrutable. Then her face with-drew into shadows and he couldn't say for sure if he'd seen such an expression or just imagined it. He was used to being baffled by women. Usually, he disliked it.

"That's good to know. I like Nicole better just hearing you say that, and I already liked her a lot." He wanted to hoist himself on the bike behind Hint and circle her waist with his hands. His blood raced at the thought of leaning his face into her hair.

But it would destroy the harmony of their dog hunting partnership. She would bolt. If he turned pursuer, she'd feel harried and wouldn't be able to focus on finding Percy. Quickly, he walked back to the car.

"I'll get the flashlights. Do we need anything else?" he asked.

"Bring some drinks," she called. "We'll be out here a while."

GAZING AT THE large, perfectly round moon, low in the sky, Hint got off the bike. It had felt good. She loved how sleek and beautiful the machine was. But a motorcycle was a dan-gerous thing. Years earlier she'd spent time on the back of one with a summer boyfriend whose silky, blond ponytail had hung slightly below his shoulders.

Two months after they had begun dating, his best friend had been killed in a motorcycle accident. Hint hadn't been able to get back on the bike. It had taken less than two weeks after that to figure out they hadn't had anything in common other than a love of riding the bike together, so they'd broken up.

Staring at the huge bright orb low in the sky, she willed it to keep her secrets. In a minute Jack had come up behind her, flashlights and drinks in hand.

"The moon will help us find him. We'll have light to hunt by and he won't be sleepy with this kind of energy shining down on him," she told him.

"He's probably somewhere near his home right now," Jack replied. Energy shining down on the dog? It sounded way out there, but he had to admit, he felt it too.

"I wish I thought so."

"Let's circle the property," he suggested. "I'll go around back if you take the front. Good?"

"Sure." She moved down the driveway to Tom and Nicole's front sidewalk. A faint sound of flamenco music came from the other side of the street. The Midsummer's Eve party they'd seen advertised appeared to be revving up.

"Percy, where are you?" She quickened her step, her hips swaying ever so slightly to the wild percussive beat. "Come to me, boy. Come." She spoke slowly and deliberately.

She would hypnotize the dog into returning to her. As she strolled up the front walk of her friends' house, her eyes fell on the hanging loveseat on Tom and Nicole's porch. It was one of Percy's favorite perches in the summer months. He'd surely come bounding out to join her if he was anywhere nearby.

As she lowered herself into the loveseat, the music seemed to get louder. She could imagine a sultry Spanish dancer tapping her feet with mathematical precision while the feelings she inspired in her partner were anything but mathematical. Were passion and precision mirror images of the same human urge?

The bushes rustled.

"Percy?" she called.

"It's me."

Jack's shadow appeared on the front walk before he did, the moon lighting him from behind.

"See anything?" she asked, noticing the perfect 'L' and its mirror image the sweep of his broad shoulders to neck formed.

"Not much. But I hear some great music. Someone having a party?"

"Sounds like it." Her shoulders moved back and forth as she saw the muscles of his thigh flex to the percussive handclapping of the flamenco beat. "As much as it's drawing us, the music will keep him away. He'll be scared of the noise."

"And all the people."

"Strangers. Guests whose smells he doesn't recognize." She straightened, telling her shoulders to behave. "Let's go. He's not coming back here with a party going on."

"What about that park you mentioned?"

She nodded. She'd never been there at night, but in Jack's company and with the moonlit sky, she wasn't afraid.

Five minutes later they were at Fox Meadow Park in Scarsdale. When she stepped out of Jack's car, she saw that the fireflies had come out. It seemed as though they were dancing to the flamenco music that still tapped through her head.

Energized by the cool night breeze, Hint picked her way along the path, mindful of her footing in the moonlight.

"Watch out for roots," Jack warned behind her.

A chord from Hint's childhood vibrated in her belly when she heard his pronunciation. He'd said "ruts."

"Spoken like a true New Englander," she teased.

"I'm the seventh generation of them, beginning with my ancestor who sailed from England to Stamford, Connecticut."

"But you're a New Yorker now."

"Westchester County borders New England. I'm close enough." He called for Percy, this time keeping his voice low and inviting.

"It's different though, isn't it? I mean New England and New York cultures."

"You can say that again." He laughed. "One's right in your face and the other turns the other cheek—just so as not to see anything unpleasant—even when it's in your own family."

"I wonder which is better," she mused, focusing on a copse of willow trees up ahead. They looked like ancient wise women with long silvery hair.

"Maybe New England civility combined with New York energy," Jack suggested.

"Sounds right." She liked New England civility but tonight New York energy ran through her veins.

Just then the breeze picked up, making the silvery boughs of the willows shimmy in the moonlight. Alerting her to something. What?

"Percy! Are you there?" She ran ahead of Jack, both to look for the dog and to put some space between them. Midsummer night magic was making her nerve endings dance with possibility. As she fought a strong urge to kick off her shoes and lie down in the fragrant grass beneath the willow trees, her senses came alive in the soft night breeze. The wind caressed her arms and ruffled her hair as fireflies flickered all around.

After a moment, a brook appeared, murmuring in the moonlight. She felt her way carefully down to its edge then dipped her hand into the cold, stinging water. Splashing some on her face, she sat on a nearby large rock, humming for Percy and waiting for Jack.

TREADING SOFTLY BEHIND Hint, Jack sensed something afire in her. He'd swear it wasn't just her zeal to find the dog.

All he could think of was pulling her into his arms and burying his face in her hair. It was insane. He tried to retrain his thoughts on finding the dog. But the memory of the scent of her hair as she sat next to him in the car flooded over him, drowning out rational thought. It had smelled like the stargazer lilies his mother had loved, but something more too, a scent he had never breathed in before.

"Ouch." His face plowed into a small branch. Wiping his forehead, he cursed. It was time to get his priorities straight.

Within a minute a brook came into view. Burbling and humming, it sounded a lot like a woman's voice.

Jack froze. It *was* a woman's voice. Hint was singing or humming. Was she trying to lure the dog to her the way those mermaids in the ancient epic he'd read in ninth grade English class had lured sailors to their death? That had been some story to stoke the imaginations of fourteen-year-old boys.

Stealthily, he moved forward, holding his breath.

"Hmm-umm-hmm-umm." The melody went up and down, wandering around without hurry.

He crept closer until Hint's form came dimly into view.

She sat on a rock next to the stream. One arm supported her weight as she leaned over the water. Moonlight behind her lit up her finely-carved profile. His heart ached at the delicacy of her expression. It would disappear the moment she sensed she wasn't alone.

He crept forward, willing himself not to look directly at her. Instead, he studied the stream. Then inspiration struck.

"Huh-hmm-umm . . ." His baritone joined her mezzo-soprano in duet. He kept his eyes on the stream until he felt the urge to look up towards the sky. When he glanced at her sidelong, she too was looking up at the sky. His body warming, he gazed in the same direction.

"Hmm-mmm-umm . . ." His voice increased in volume now that his head was thrown back. He tried to visualize Percy, but instead a lithe figure with a short, straight nose and small, Cupid's bow mouth danced in front of him under the night sky.

"I see you . . ." Hint sang out.

"I see you too . . ." Jack sang back.

"Where's Percy? . . ." Her melody went up with her question.

"I don't know . . ." he sang back. *And I don't care*, ran subversively through his mind.

"Are you trying to find him as hard as you can?" she warbled back, seemingly having read his thoughts.

How can I, with you here distracting me? he wanted to respond. Women were so perplexing. They befuddled men's senses then accused them of being confusing in their actions. Did they do it on purpose, or was it some sort of biological imperative set up by someone with a sense of humor to aid in continuing the species?

"I'm trying as hard as I can at the moment," he melodically responded, congratulating himself on an honest reply.

"Well, try harder, 'cause he's not here yet." Her singing voice had turned playful. With laughing eyes, she looked directly at him.

"Yes, but we're here, aren't we?" he sang back, opening his arms in an operatic gesture.

"Yes, but that's not enough . . ." She pointed a finger as if reprimanding him. Was that a blush that had crossed her face?

It's enough for me, he didn't sing. He tried to channel the tenor in the last opera he'd seen. It had been years ago on TV.

"What would be enough for you, my dear?" he rang out, extending one hand, palm up, as if asking how he could serve his lady.

"To be reunited with our boy . . ." she trilled sweetly.

"To be reunited with our boy . . ." he echoed her melody.

"With our boy . . . "

His voice climbing higher, he harmonized with hers.

"With our boy . . ." Her voice rang out, hitting a high note on the final syllable. Her arms were now both extended and he tried not to notice the sweet swell of her torso. Listening carefully for the end of her note, he cut off his own at the same instant.

There. It was done. He'd sung the first aria of his life and most likely the last.

Singing in the night air had pumped oxygen into his lungs. He felt exhilarated, as if he'd entered some private club of which only he and she were members.

"Nice singing," she complimented him, laughing softly.

"You inspired me," he told her. She had no idea how much.

"Do you sing in a choir?" she asked.

"I don't sing at all," he answered truthfully.

"But you do." She smiled dreamily. "And well."

Despite himself, his head swelled with pride. It was nice to be praised by a woman instead of being told he had attention deficit disorder or what the plan was for the evening.

"He's coming back to us," she stated calmly, her voice confident. "I can feel him moving in our direction."

He could contain himself no longer. Percy was not the only male compelled to move in her direction. With two quick steps he was at the rock she stood on. Reaching up, he grabbed her by the waist and swung her down.

"With a duet like that in his honor, how could he not come back?" he joked, to distract her from his boldness.

Hint appeared flustered, but stood still, unresistant to his touch.

His fingers encircled her impossibly small waist. Even more maddening was the outward curve of her hips that tempted the little finger of each of his hands. It was as if he were touching red hot tongs. He was about to get burned.

But the dog.

Unable to resist one small press of the pliant landscape beneath his hands, he squeezed then released her. He hoped his message would pass directly from hands to hips, bypassing the brain altogether.

The spark in her soft brown eyes as she turned from him fanned his hopes. But she moved beyond his reach, and when she turned to him again, her eyes were veiled. With the dog still lost, he told himself, now was not the right moment.

Reaching for support from the trunk of the willow tree behind her, Hint caught her breath. It was as if the timeline of her life story had just exponentially sped up. Jack had put his hands on her waist and lifted her off the rock she'd been standing on. Then he hadn't let go for a minute and when he finally did, she'd felt a slight but clearly defined squeeze before he released her. The imprint of his hands lingered just above her hips. Her flesh tingled where he had touched her.

How could she concentrate on finding Percy when something new and totally unexpected was finding its way into their search for him? Wasn't it morally wrong to respond to the touch of Jack's hands when a hungry scared Schnoodle was wandering around out there somewhere? She shouldn't be dwelling on the firmness of those hands, their warmth.

Earlier that evening Jack's hand had taken hers to say grace. Now, he'd lifted her up in the air. Those large, muscular hands needed to encircle Percy's dog collar before they were allowed to go anywhere near her again, she silently vowed.

"Where to next?" she asked briskly, smoothing her shirt over her jeans. Traveling over the same areas he'd just touched, she imagined her hands were his.

"Wh-where else does this park go?" Jack stammered, apparently having as much trouble shifting gears as she was.

"It goes back a ways until you reach a meadow." She pointed deeper into the park, glad for a distraction.

"Oh yeah?" His gaze followed her hand. "How about if we go over there?"

"It's sort of far," she hesitated.

"Let's walk awhile, then turn back if it's too far," he suggested.

They'd already gone too far to turn back. She knew it in her heart. As well as the fact that she couldn't say for sure how much farther they were going. Exhilarated, her pulse raced until she remembered they were there to look for Percy. Mentally, she slapped herself, trying to clear her senses. It didn't work. In a daze, she followed the person befuddling them, careful to keep a distance.

"What's that white object over there?" Jack asked, after a minute.

"Where?" She'd had been in Fox Meadow Park many times, but never at night. She craned her neck in the direction he pointed.

"That white object. Is that a statue?" It looked similar to one he'd seen in Paris the summer he'd roamed around Europe at age twenty-six.

"Yes. It is. There's several here. They're modeled after the ones in that famous park in Paris."

"*Tuileries* Gardens," he filled in for her. "I spent a night there once."

"You did?"

"I thought I recognized it," Jack told her. "It's a Greek warrior, but he's not thinking about war." The sculpture was of a young male, fully armed but with a dreamy expression on his face. He moved off the trail to examine the statue more closely.

"He seems to be looking at someone," she observed.

"If it's the same setup as in *Tuileries*, he's looking at the backside of a goddess." He recalled the second statute in sight-line of the warrior statue in Paris's most famous park; it made for a good joke for all the young male tourists who spotted both works of art. Peering across the meadow, he searched for a second statue.

Hint giggled. "I think I see her." She pointed in the direction of a copse of trees about twenty-five yards ahead. Something white was half hidden in the shadows.

Slowly, they approached, until they could make it out.

"Yup. That's her. It's Diana, goddess of the hunt," he said.

"She hunted when the moon was full, didn't she?" Hint asked. Jack's arm brushed hers as they stood side by side, only inches from the wondrously rounded, gleaming white backside of the marble statue.

"I think she did. Do you think she'll get down off her pedestal tonight?" He stole a sideways glance at Hint.

"I think she only does that privately," she told him.

"It seems pretty private here tonight, don't you think?" He caught her eyes, trapping her in his gaze. His arm remained touching hers, its warmth pouring into her.

"It seems we need to find Percy," she responded levelly.

"And then what happens?" he inquired, his arm coming up around her back, drawing her to him.

"And then we'll see," she said, putting her right hand up to brace itself on the crook of his left arm. She felt a slight squeeze before he released her, similar to the one he'd given her when he'd lifted her off the rock.

"And then we'll see," he repeated, his face coming close to hers.

Quickly she moved away from him, calling for Percy in the moonlit park. She was desperate to find him, not only for obvious reasons but for new ones that were beckoning to her but couldn't possibly be explored unless they found the Schnoodle. If and when that happened, they would see what new adventures lay ahead. *If* and *when.* And if not, guilt over losing him would creep in and eat away at any feelings blossoming between them, like crows in a strawberry patch. She forged ahead, determined to find the dog. For all the right reasons. For a few new ones too.

5

ANNABEL

Hours later Jack awoke refreshed from a deep sleep. He'd dreamt he was nestled somewhere warm and fragrant. Looking down, his heart skipped a beat.

His arms were wrapped around Hint. Her silky auburn hair was spread out over his right shoulder, chest, and arm. Eyes tightly shut, a serene smile lay on her small, finely curved lips.

What had happened? He searched his mind, but all he could remember was that they'd lain down to rest at the base of the statue of Diana and the next thing he knew, a beautiful fairy creature was sleeping in his arms. How could he extricate himself from their embrace without waking her up?

A dozen thoughts rushed through his head at once. Foremost was his desire to protect her from any feelings of guilt. Whatever spell had been cast would be broken the moment she woke up. She would kick herself for succumbing to her own feelings before answering the call of duty. He'd spent enough time with her over the past day and a half not to doubt it for an instant.

He inched his right arm from underneath her head. Replacing his arm with his left hand he couldn't help stroking the curve of her cheek as he supported the back of her head with fingers. Her brow was smooth and her eyebrows beautifully arched, as if ready to be surprised at any moment. With the thumb of his right hand, he traced one.

Her eyelids fluttered and she moaned ever so slightly. Jack remained motionless, his right hand cupping the side of her face. Slowly, her eyes opened, looking up directly into his face.

"Good morning, Princess," he whispered, hoping he wasn't scaring her.

"Good morning," she whispered back, looking peaceful and rested. Then her eyes widened. "Ohhh." With one hand she reached up to his forearm and grasped it. Her forefinger pointed up towards his elbow. He thought he felt it gently stroke his arm.

"Ohhh," he echoed her, leaning down. His instincts told him to follow her lead, wherever it might take them.

"I . . . are we?" she gasped out. Conflicting expressions chased each other across her face.

"You're beautiful in your sleep and, yes, we're still in the park. We fell asleep under the spell of the hunting goddess." He smiled at her mischievously. "She must have shot us with one of her arrows."

"She probably didn't like having her privacy disturbed," she added, as roses sprang into her cheeks.

Watching her complexion deepen from cream to pink, he'd never seen anything more ravishing in his life. Until that minute, he had never completely understood what that term meant. Disappointment shot through him when her fingers slipped off his forearm. She slowly stood, turned around, then stretched as she looked in the direction of the statue of Diana, several yards behind them.

He was spellbound at the sight of Hint's compact back curving into her waist. Now he understood why an Indian prince had built the Taj Mahal in memory of his wife. She'd probably had similar curves that had carved themselves permanently into his brain.

He turned away as Hint disappeared into the bushes. It was time to find some cover in the other direction.

A minute later, they met again in front of the statue of Diana. He glanced at his watch. It was only a quarter past six. A clear, pale blue sky hung overhead. The day promised to be fine. Ravishing, even.

"Shall we get breakfast somewhere?" he suggested.

Her reddish-brown hair framed her face in a wild halo as she gave a slight nod. Was her look sheepish or impish? The strongly defined comedy-tragedy shape of her mouth curved up ever so slightly. Her eyes danced. Dared he believe waking up in his arms had agreed with her?

"Don't you have to get to work?" she asked.

"I do. But we've got time. Let's get some coffee, then I'll drive you home and catch the train from there."

Suddenly, he remembered the plans he'd made for that evening. Today was Marguerite's seventh birthday. Her party would take place Saturday afternoon, but he'd told his sister and brother-in-law he'd join them for dinner that night to celebrate his niece and goddaughter's real birthday and give her her present.

"What's up? You look like you just remembered something," she said.

"I did." He spoke without thinking. "Are you free this evening?"

"I'm free until we find Percy."

"I need to drop by my niece's house. It's her birthday and I told her I'd bring her present over after work today."

"Sure. Why don't you do that, then we can meet up and keep looking?" Her face darkened. "If I haven't found him by the end of the day, I mean."

"I . . . I promised I'd have a quick bite with her family tonight. Birthday cake and all. Do you think you could join me?"

For reasons he couldn't fathom, he had just invited her to a family celebration. His senses on fire, he couldn't wait to find out about as many sides to the auburn-haired woman he'd woken up with as she would allow.

"I don't know. It'll take time away from looking for Percy." She looked hesitant, as if unsure of the right course of action.

"How about if you look for him during the day while I'm at work? Then I'll pick you up, we'll drop by my sister's place for a short while, then resume the hunt." He paused thoughtfully. "You're going to need a break, you know. We can recharge our batteries and maybe my sister and brother-in-law will have some ideas on how to find him."

"Maybe your niece will have an inspiration," she suggested.

"Marguerite? She might. She loves dogs."

"Children understand animals in a way that adults sometimes don't."

"But you do, don't you?" Jack asked. "I mean, you haven't lost the ability, have you?" There was something childlike—or was it fairylike—about her that beguiled him.

"I don't know, Jack. We haven't found him yet, have we?" Her face was sad, masked in self doubt. At the sound of her voice uttering his name, he wanted to reach out and stroke her cheek, just as he'd done less than twenty minutes earlier. But the fairy cobwebs that had entwined them together the night before had vanished. The day was upon them, with its list of demands.

JACK'S EIGHT HOURS at the office flew by like cannon shot. At a quarter to seven that evening he and Hint were in his car on the way to his sister Bibi's home in Scarsdale.

"It's a good thing that Bibi and Matt live near Tom and Nicole. They'll know about places we don't, that Percy may have visited near home."

"That's a thought," Hint responded quietly, her eyes fixed on the road ahead.

She somehow looked different this evening. He couldn't figure out what it was. Her hair was the same, the reddish brown locks flowing over her jacket collar. As he glanced over at her, he caught the curve of her mouth. His heart flopped at the sight of it. Quickly, he returned his eyes to the road.

As he drove, the light melodious tones of her voice washed over him as she described calling around to local vets that day to find out if any lost dogs had recently been found. None had. In a minute, he turned into the driveway of his sister's colonial style house.

A red BMW sat behind his brother-in-law's car. It looked familiar. Checking the license plate number, he gripped the steering wheel.

He stepped out of his vehicle and hurried to the passenger side to open the door for Hint.

"You didn't need to do that," she said, as she slid out.

"I need to let you know that someone's here that I didn't invite and I don't want to see," he said, his voice low and even, belying his agitation.

"Who?" Her eyes widened in surprise. She followed his gaze to the red car. "Someone with a red BMW?"

My ex-girlfriend he was about to say when the front door burst open and Marguerite ran towards them. Two strawberry blonde pigtails flew out on either side of the girl's head.

"Uncle Jack. You came," the child sang out, hurling herself into his arms.

"I'm here." He lifted his niece and goddaughter up in the air, then crushed her to his chest in an enormous bear hug. "And guess who else is here?" He turned to introduce Hint to his niece, but before he could, a well-modulated voice from the direction of the house rang out.

"*And* guess who else is here?" The tall, statuesque form of his ex-girlfriend moved slowly down the front path, coming to a halt in the frame of the garden trellis. One graceful, long arm leaned above her head on the wooden slats as if she were posing. She appeared to slowly take in the auburn-haired woman next to him. He thought of the Statue of Liberty for a moment, struck once again by how dramatic his ex could be. Some things never changed.

"What are you doing here?" he asked, carefully controlling his tone of voice.

"Just dropping off Marguerite's birthday present. Aren't I, darling?" She smiled down at the girl, who turned excitedly to her uncle.

"Annabel is taking me to a Broadway show for my birthday. It's the one about the wicked witch in the Wizard of Oz," she exclaimed breathlessly.

Jack stared at the blank, smooth face of his former girl-friend. She had shown no interest in children the entire time they'd dated. All of a sudden, she was taking his niece to a Broadway show? He would discuss this with his sister later. Something fishy was going on. He would not allow himself to be the sacrificial fall guy for Annabel's momentary lapse in fortune-hunting. Maybe she was having a tough month of June, having attended too many weddings with no nuptial plans of her own. As a well-maintained thirty-five-year old, he guessed she'd probably decided her next five-year plan would be the family one. How taken in his niece Marguerite was by his ex-girlfriend's catalogue-cover smile. He shuddered.

"This is Hint Daniels," he told his niece, ignoring Annabel for the moment.

"That's a nice name," Marguerite remarked, looking up at Hint.

"Thank you. I heard you're seven today," she greeted the little girl, crouching down to meet her at eye level.

"Yes. I'm seven and at Christmas I'll be seven and a half. Then I'm going to be eight," Marguerite informed her. "How old are you?"

The wondrous directness of children, Jack marveled, curious to see how Hint would handle the question. He agreed with his niece. Hint was a nice name. It hinted at something, he didn't know what. It was one of the things he liked about it.

"I'm thirty-two, sweetie. Do you know how many more birthdays you'll have before you're thirty-two?"

"Ooh. Is that a math problem?" Marguerite's eyes lit up with excitement.

"Yes. Because I heard you're very good in math."

Jack was astonished. He hadn't said anything at all about his niece's math skills, but Hint was right on the money. Marguerite loved math problems.

" I, uh, let me see. It's . . . "The little girl counted slowly on her fingers, then tapped her head. Her face contorted as she pondered. "Is it twenty-five?" she finally burst out.

"Yes. You have twenty-five more birthdays to go to get to my age."

"That's awesome. Thanks for bringing your friend, Uncle Jack. Is she your girlfriend?"

Gulp. Darned if he couldn't help loving the pig-tailed wonder even when she was embarrassing the stuffing out of him.

"She's my very special friend, Marguerite."

"Does that mean she's your girlfriend?" Like a dog with a rope knot, she wasn't going to let go until she'd wrenched away every ounce of self-possession he had.

"Maybe, baby," he sassed her, making a silly face. This might be an inspired moment to confuse the enemy. He hoped he wasn't embarrassing Hint, who shifted next to him.

"Yippee zippy!" Marguerite bounced up and down with each syllable. "But wait—what does that mean Annabel is?" His relentless niece looked questioningly from him to Annabel.

He cocked his head and made another face at her.

"Why don't you ask her yourself?" he suggested, hoping he was being exceptionally confusing.

"Annabel, how many more birthdays will I have until I get to your age?"

Woops. Jack admired the way Marguerite chose to skip back to her previous topic, her mind as lively as her merry, mobile face. One day she would be best-in-breed in the dating stakes, confusing suitors both coming and going. He chuckled inwardly as he saw the solar plexus of his ex-girlfriend contract, as if she'd been hit in the gut. Sucker-punched.

"Many more, darling. Many presents far into the future," Annabel replied, pursing her lips as she stared down the small but efficient inquisitor.

"Yes, but how many? Give me a math problem like Jack's girlfriend. I like them. Is it twenty-five again?"

"Um . . . it's not important, darling."

Jack got a kick out of seeing his ex gulp.

"It's important to *me*, Annabel." Marguerite stomped her foot and turned to Hint. "Let's do more math. Want to come in so we can get paper and a pencil?"

Hint nodded enthusiastically. Marguerite took her hand and marched her up the front path, striding past Annabel, who had to move back onto the grass to let them pass.

Jack reached into the car to get Marguerite's present out of the back seat. Compared to Broadway theater tickets to one of the hottest shows of the season, the book of Greek myths he'd gotten her suddenly seemed diminished. He burned, thinking of Annabel's predictable ability to trump anything and everything he did. But the thought of the cool, blonde woman gulping in alarm made him laugh inside. It was good to have a seven-year-old on his side, unwittingly or not.

Slamming the car door behind him, he hurried into his sister's house. Annabel was waiting for him at the front door. He steeled himself for whatever she had to say.

"Oh, Jack. I just wanted to explain—" she began.

"Don't bother," he cut her off. "Just don't ingratiate yourself with my family any further." He stared at her for a brief moment. "You have no reason to. None at all."

She met his gaze, her eyes snapping at him. If not for the circumstances, she would have grabbed him and planted one on him, he guessed. She was good at that sort of gesture. Mixing things up for kicks. Then dropping good old Jack the moment a hotter prospect came along. Those days were done.

"You don't understand. I'm fond of Marguerite. She asked me to come," she responded coolly.

"That's ridiculous. There's no reason for you to even be in touch with my family. Why are you doing this?"

"Whatever you think I'm doing, I'm doing it for you. You know that."

"There's no more 'me' for you. Get it? Done. You've made your splash with Broadway tickets for Marguerite, now say goodbye and go." He had never been so angry with her. Actually, he had, but he wanted to forget those moments, too numerous to count.

"Jack, you take my breath away." Her hands behind her back, she gripped the door frame behind her. "You're so—fierce."

The way she said it made him think of what Hint put up with from her superintendent, Brian Muscle Man. He could imagine Annabel and Brian competing on a game show, twisting every word into nuance as they vied to out-seduce each other. It would be a very tough contest.

Why was this not moving in the direction he had intended? It never did with his ex. He couldn't control the situation. All he could do was control how he handled it.

"Listen. We're done," he told her. "You will not ruin this evening for me."

"Or for your very special friend?" she purred.

"Correct. I want you to leave. Now. But if you choose to stay, you will not rock my boat. Not in the least. Just behave, then be on your merry way."

"Not rock your boat, Jack? What about your—"

"Shut it, Annabel. Go rock-a-bye some other baby." He turned sharply and headed into the hallway. Where was safe haven? And why had Hint popped into his mind as soon as he asked himself?

"Rock-a-bye some other baby," wafted into Hint's ears as she descended the stairs with Marguerite behind. She hadn't heard Jack speak like that before. It sounded as if he was telling the blonde woman to shove off. His choice of words and tone of voice confirmed what Marguerite had already indicated. The two had a history. She didn't like it at all.

She wanted Jack's history to have begun that morning, the moment she'd woken up in his arms. But as usual, life was messier. Facing her demons, she looked straight into the eyes of the tall, cool woman in the doorway.

"I'm sorry you have to leave," she graciously lied, as the woman's eyes flickered uncertainly, then glanced away.

"You're leaving, Annabel? What about dinner? Aren't you staying for my birthday cake?" Marguerite called out behind Hint.

"I . . . I ought to get going," the tall woman said. For the first time, her composure appeared to wilt. She tried to catch Jack's eye, but he'd turned toward the kitchen.

A woman with the same posture and carriage as Jack came into the front hallway.

"You're going so soon?" she addressed Annabel. "I thought you were staying for dinner."

Jack gave his sister a meaningful look.

Bibi's eyes widened as she took in Hint. "Oh . . . hello. I'm Jack's sister, Bibi Crane. You must be—"

"Hint. This is Hint Daniels. She and I are working on a project together," Jack interjected.

"How do you do?" Hint held out her hand to Bibi. She made a mental note not to breathe a word of their dog hunt while the tall, blonde woman remained in the doorway. She had thought to enlist Jack's family's help in finding Percy, but not until she knew she could trust her audience.

Bibi shook her hand warmly. Marguerite's pert nose and heart-shaped face were evident in Jack's sister's features.

A cell phone rang. Annabel picked up an expensive looking, buttery leather handbag and retrieved her phone then disappeared out the front door. Hint could hear her voice clearly as she took the call. "Annabel Sanford."

Meanwhile, Jack took his sister's arm then led her into the dining room. Hint guessed what their whispered conversation might be about. Whatever the woman named Annabel had been to Jack, she was no longer, judging by his cool demeanor towards her.

A minute later, Bibi, looking thoughtful, followed Annabel out the front door.

"What about that pencil and paper, Marguerite? I've got another math problem for you," Hint suggested.

"Goody. I'll get one. Let's go out on the back deck so we can work outside." The girl took her hand with her own sticky, deliciously small one.

Hint's heart warmed. Her instincts told her the blonde woman would not be joining them again that evening.

She was right. An hour and a half later, cake had been served, the candles blown out and Marguerite serenaded with the happy birthday song. It was time to get back to dog hunting.

Jack had couched the story of the missing dog in the most general terms, so as not to detract from the birthday celebration. His sister and brother-in-law, Matt, had suggested that a lost, hungry dog from the neighborhood might be found hanging around the backs of shops and restaurants in downtown Scarsdale, looking for food scraps from garbage dumpsters.

"Sweetie, we've got to go now," Jack told his niece after finishing the last bite of German chocolate cake on his plate.

"But Uncle Jack, I want you guys to stay and play more math games with me." She looked from Jack to Hint imploringly.

"Remember I told you Hint and I are working on a project together?"

The girl nodded.

"We've got a deadline, so we've got to get back to work."

"What's a project, Uncle Jack? What's a deadline?"

"It's boring big people stuff, honey. Like homework."

"Ohh. I don't have homework yet. Just reading."

"Right. You should get ready for bed, then read one of the stories in the book I gave you."

"I need you to read me the story. I can't read all the words by myself, Uncle Jack. Let's read a story together, then you can do your project line."

Hint laughed. Marguerite wouldn't be denied.

"Jack, go read her a story. I'll help with the dishes." She picked up his dessert plate and hers to bring to the kitchen. Suddenly, she remembered the small gift she'd gotten for Marguerite that she'd left in the car. She'd meant to bring it in the house, but the presence of the blonde stranger had startled her and she'd forgotten.

"Don't bother with those dishes." Bibi motioned to her to sit down. "That's Matt's job." She looked at her husband next to her, who showed no sign either of having heard or moving from his deck chair.

"I'll just take these into the kitchen. I've got to go out to the car to get something anyway," she told Jack's sister, who waved a hand as if to say go ahead.

After depositing the plates in the sink, she exited the house through the kitchen door into the driveway, heading for Jack's car to get the small princess jewelry box she'd picked up for Marguerite earlier that day.

Reaching into the front seat on the passenger side, she grabbed the wrapped present then reached for the note she'd scribbled to the little girl on the way over. It was on the dashboard on the driver's side. She didn't remember putting it there, but they had been in a rush to get out of the car.

She reached for the note, and turned it over. Hadn't she written Marguerite's name on the outside? She could have sworn she'd done so, but perhaps she'd mistakenly written it on the inside, instead.

She opened the folded paper and stared in astonishment at the words written there.

Stanhope Hotel terrace half past five tomorrow. Don't disappoint me, Jack-Jack. – Your Girl in Red

Hint re-read the scrawled words, stunned. They were written on a piece of paper from the same small notepad she herself had used to pen a short birthday greeting to Marguerite.

Quickly, she refolded the slip of paper, then replaced it on the dashboard.

What would Jack do when he read it? Her mind raced as she hunted for her own note, identical in size.

What would she herself do tomorrow at half past five? Work on the fairy figure for her latest assignment? Cook up another steak to bring out to the backyard to lure Percy back? Take the train into Manhattan and swing by the Stanhope Hotel incognito to see who might be out on the terrace?

Finally, she found her own note. It had fallen between the seat and the gearbox. She fished it out and tucked it into the fold of the wrapping paper of Marguerite's present.

Once again, her eye fell on the slip of paper on the dashboard. The person who had left it there had just been in Jack's car, and had used his notepad. She had no doubt who it was.

Hint headed back to the house deep in thought. In the kitchen, she found Bibi loading the dishwasher.

"They're up in her bedroom. First door on the right. Go on up," she told her, pointing to the staircase.

Carefully arranging her face to reveal nothing of her discovery, Hint went up to find Jack sitting in a white rocking chair next to his niece's bed. The little girl was tucked away under a pink princess summer coverlet, listening to her uncle wrap up the story of Demeter and Persephone from the book of Greek myths he'd just given her. The girl's eyes widened as Hint entered the pink-walled bedroom.

"Ooh, what's that in your hand? Is that a present?" Marguerite sang out.

Hint nodded. She stifled a giggle at the sight of Jack Whitby in a delicate white rocking chair, his thick-soled shoes sunk into plush, raspberry-pink, wall-to-wall carpet.

"It's something small I picked up for you, she said to Marguerite. "I don't know if you'll like it, but your uncle told me you like princesses."

"Let me see." The child grabbed for the package, decorated with pink and purple bows. Within seconds she'd ripped it open.

"It's a princess box!" She opened the jewelry box and admired the prince and princess figures that danced in a circular movement to a tinkling waltz tune. "Thank you, Hint. Yippee!"

"Yippee zippy, Maggie May." Jack turned from his niece and looked up at Hint as she stood in the doorway. An expression of unadulterated joy lit up his face. She wished she herself had the ability to put it there, but perhaps it was the kind of magical power only children possessed. "We've got to go now, sweetie. Hope you had a great birthday."

"I did, Uncle Jack. But I want you to come to my party on Saturday. Can you bring Hint too? We can play games and stuff."

"Uh," Jack hesitated. "That depends on if we've finished our project, honey. We'll see."

"You don't have to bring another present, you know." The girl looked at her uncle beseechingly. "I mean, unless you want to. I just want you to come to my party." She gave Hint a smile, revealing a gap where her lower middle tooth was missing.

"We'll try, Marguerite. Good night and don't let the bed bugs bite," Jack told her, standing up.

Hint turned and headed downstairs, Jack behind her. Her heart felt light, buoyed by the excitement of the young girl. She'd experienced a similar joyfulness less than twelve hours earlier. But a lost dog and now a tall blonde woman weighed upon her, warning her to keep her heart in check.

Exchanging goodbyes with Bibi and Matt, they headed for the car. Hint fussed with her jacket as she pretended not to notice Jack spot the folded slip of paper on the dashboard. He picked it up without opening it and placed it in the left pocket of his jeans. She guessed he knew exactly what its provenance was. Quite likely, he and Annabel had seen each other for some time if she was taking Marguerite to a Broadway show.

Shall we drive down to Main Street?" he broke into her thoughts.

"Good idea. Let's look around the dumpsters behind the supermarket." She shuddered to think of the types of animals they were likely to encounter scrounging for food under cover of the night sky.

As they drove, she hummed softly. No woman in a red dress was going to destroy her peace of mind. They were on a mission, and apparently whatever mission Jack Whitby had once been on with the woman she'd met earlier that evening had ended.

There was only one way to be sure, however. A plan to visit the Stanhope Hotel the following day began to hatch in her brain. She would go undercover.

They parked next to the largest supermarket in downtown Scarsdale. As Hint got out of the passenger seat, she spotted their remaining lost dog flyers in the back of the car.

"Jack, how about if we post a few more of these? I'll do the train station if you take the message board at the supermarket exit."

"Sure. I'll meet you back here at the car."

"See you in ten." She took six flyers and the scotch tape dispenser they'd left in the car the day before, then hurried off in the direction of the train station. She would post the flyers after taking care of one other piece of business.

As soon as she turned the corner of the nearest building, out of sight of the car, she stopped. With her back to the wall, she peeked around the side of the building to see what Jack was doing.

Flyers under arm, he walked towards the supermarket. After a few seconds, he reached into the left pocket of his jeans.

Hint held her breath as he pulled out the note and read it.

She was too far away to see the expression on his face. But she was gratified to see what he did next. Crumpling the note in his left hand, he tossed it in a trash bin on his way into the store. With his shoulders up and his pace quickened, he looked angry.

At the train station she posted three more flyers then checked to see if anyone had torn off the telephone numbered chads at the bottom of the ones they'd already posted. A few were missing. She looked at her cell phone, then remembered the number posted was Jack's. He hadn't wanted her to give out her own.

"How'd you do in the supermarket?" she asked, back at the car.

"I put up two flyers. Some other lost dog and cat notices were there. One's been missing since March."

"That's three months." She winced. "It's been less than three days since Percy's been gone and it feels like a year."

Jack glanced at her, an unreadable expression on his face. "Is that good or bad?"

"It's both." She looked at him carefully. "How about you? How's your past year been?"

"My real past year or since the dog's been gone?"

"Both."

"The former not so great, the latter good." He looked at her mouth. *"Capisce?"*

She nodded, unable to take her eyes off his mouth too, his well-shaped lips slightly open. It was like yawning—totally infectious—except that looking at him made her feel the opposite of tired. Just standing next to him made the blood race in her veins.

They walked in silence toward the garbage bins. The night was alive with early summer noises. A bullfrog's croak repeated nearby.

"Is there a pond near here?" she asked. She picked her way around a half open box of discarded potatoes. If she were a lost dog, she'd choose to spend time around here.

"The Bronx River is right over there behind those trees." Jack pointed to the dark patch of woods behind the parking lot in the direction of the Bronx River Parkway that led from Scarsdale to Bronxville.

As she glanced toward the woods, something rustled.

"Percy? Is that you? Come out, boy. Come out and get something to eat," she coaxed.

Jack stood back as she moved toward the next bin. He cocked his head as if listening to something.

"Hey. I think there's something there. Hang on a minute." In two strides he caught up to her, catching her arm.

She was startled by his touch. Then she saw what he apparently had heard.

"Ahh!" she screamed as a rat with a long, naked tail scurried out from the bottom of the closest garbage bin then disappeared under the recycling bin next to it.

"Comes with the territory," Jack chortled, his eyes gleaming. He propelled her backward, away from the bins, as she caught her breath. Still holding her arm with his left hand, his right hand came up to brush back the strand of hair that had swung into her face.

"You're right," she gasped out. "I just wasn't expecting that."

"Wasn't expecting what?" he asked after a pause, an odd expression on his face. His hand slipped from her hair down the curve of her ear to her neck.

She inhaled slowly. His question was apt. Many surprises were happening, some at the speed of light.

"A lot of things," she answered. A sense of time slowing down stole over her like a warm lava flow.

"How are you at handling the unexpected?" he asked, his voice lower than before.

"Pretty good, as long as terms are well defined," she breathed out, unable to trace how or why she'd arrived at such an answer.

"I don't think that comes with the territory," he cautioned, his right hand now on her left shoulder, his thumb moving up and down the side of her neck.

"Then I can't go there. No visa." Putting her own hand atop his, she slipped it off her shoulder. Slowly, she guided it down the length of her bare arm, then bade it goodbye.

The length of Jack's body stiffened as he let out a long sigh.

"But you do have a visa," he encouraged.

"Says who?" she demurred.

"I do." His right hand sought her left one.

"I think your territory is occupied," she warned.

"Definitely not."

"Are you sure?"

"No one lives within my borders." His dark blue eyes bored into hers as she allowed her hand to be grasped.

"So you say," she countered, not wanting to ruin the moment with mention of the tall blonde.

"So I do." His gaze intensified as his hand slid warmly into hers, his thumb gliding over the joints and knuckles of her fingers.

She returned the caress, her fingers sliding smoothly over his.

"No ring?" she asked, narrowing her eyes to steel herself for whatever response might come.

"No ring," he breathed back, catching her wrist and encircling it with his thumb and forefinger.

"No ring around your heart?" she probed.

"No ring around my heart," he reassured her. "And you?" He released her wrist and found her hand, his fingers interlacing hers. They were warm and insistent.

"This conversation is about you." She pushed him back, extricating her hand.

"I want to know about you," he persisted.

"I'll tell you. . ." With both hands, she pressed his chest, pushing him back. "Another time."

"When?" His eyes sought hers.

"After."

"After what?"

Slowly and deliberately, she cupped one hand on her mouth and leaned up to his ear to whisper into it. "After we find the dog."

6

QUESTIONS

"Why don't we take a walk behind the restaurants on the next block?" Jack asked. "If he's got good taste in food, he'll be over there." His heart panged as sense trumped sensibility.

He couldn't stop thinking about waking up with Hint in his arms that morning. When her eyes had opened on his, she hadn't looked away. From that moment on, a new story between them had begun.

"What do you think he's doing now?" she asked.

Who? Better to remain silent until he figured out what she meant. He wanted to be a hero for her. Yet he knew he wasn't. But at least, he could try as hard as possible until he blew it.

Then he remembered the dog.

"He's sniffing around for a filet mignon and wondering what happened to the full moon tonight," he ad-libbed, smiling. A different set of muscles than usual contracted at the corners of his mouth. He had a large store of socially appropriate smiles, lust-fueled private smiles, sarcastic and forced smiles in the final months of his last relationship, but this was a new one. He felt an unalloyed lightness of spirit when he was with her, similar to the way Marguerite made him feel, except different. His insides shifted at the thought of where the difference lay.

"So what happened to it?" Hint craned her neck to look up at the sky. It was blanketed with dark, warm, moisture-laden clouds.

"Perchance 'twill rain before dawn," he remarked.

"I guess we'd better not sleep outdoors tonight," she whispered, as if musing to herself.

"'Twas a fine thing, my lady," he said, hiding behind his best old English imitation as he steered them both down a side alley that led to the back of a row of restaurants near the Scarsdale train station.

She cocked her head and narrowed her eyes at him, her mouth twisting into an inscrutable curve. "Will our boy catch cold out in a night rain?" she asked.

"He'll find shelter, my lady."

"You'd better be right. I don't know if it's because he's a Schnoodle or because he's Percy, but he's a total wimp when it comes to rain," she observed. "He'll play in the snow for hours, but rain makes him run for cover." She tossed her hair behind her, the lush fullness of it making him want to bury his face in it. Discreetly, he inhaled, catching its lily-infused scent.

They were outside the back entrance to one of Scarsdale's most well known steakhouses. Jack breathed in the tantalizing smells of garlic mixed with fine cuts of broiled meat.

Hint called for the dog as the night cloaked them in dewy moistness. With the barometric pressure dropping fast, Jack's sailor's instincts told him rain would arrive soon.

"Do you think he'll be able to find a shed or a garage to sleep in?" Hint asked anxiously.

"I do. And if not, it's amazing how much cover a leafy tree can provide," he said. "Especially if there's a dead, hollow log underneath," he added, feeling the opposite of dead or hollow as he tried to focus on the lost dog and not the woman next to him.

"Or a rock ledge with a cave below," she added.

They continued calling, walking to the next set of dumpsters outside a Chinese restaurant a few doors down from the steakhouse. In a minute the first drops of rain began to fall. Quickly, they ran back to the car.

Inside, Hint turned to him. "What about Tom's motorcycle over at the house?"

"What about it?"

"Do you think Percy might take cover under the tarp?"

"If he's anywhere in the neighborhood he might."

"Let's drive by and take a look."

Within five minutes they pulled into the driveway at Tom and Nicole's house. The rain was coming down faster, a fine sheet of cooling drops to counter the warm day.

"Wait a minute. I've got an umbrella in back," he told her. He jumped out, fished in the trunk for his old golf umbrella, then ran around to the passenger side.

She stepped out into his arm around her shoulders. He walked her to the lumpy object parked in front of his car. She squatted then pulled up the tarp to reveal the dim outline of the black and silver bike.

"No Percy," she uttered sadly.

He groaned inwardly. It was clear that until they found the dog, the woman next to him wouldn't allow him to step across her borders. Meeting her worried eyes with his own, his mind shut off and instinct took over. He reached for her and wrapped her into his arms.

In response, her hands closed over his biceps. He flexed them, hoping she'd cling to them as if they were rocks.

"We'll find him." He couldn't think of what else to say, so he pulled her closer, mindful to keep the umbrella over their heads.

"He's getting wet somewhere. He could catch cold and die."

As her hands pressed into his upper arms, years of twenty-minute lunch workouts at the gym suddenly made sense. He was glad she couldn't see his expression above her head. Her own face was buried in the left side of his chest, directly above his heart. He hoped she couldn't hear how loud it was beating.

"I don't think animals die that easily. It would take more than a cold to kill him off," he told her.

"Like maybe a wild animal attacking him?" Her shoulders shook as she leaned into him.

"There's little chance of that happening around here," he reassured her, not wishing to bring up coyotes. There couldn't be too many coyotes around with such a dense human population, could there? Or could crowding drive them to more overt, aggressive behavior? He'd look it up on his way into work the next day.

The rain held them hostage several minutes longer under the large golf umbrella. With Hint's small, fine body molded into his, he felt needed. Perhaps only to help her find the dog. Perhaps just to protect her from the rain and the night. Whatever the reasons, he liked the feeling. Hint woke up new sensations within him. He didn't know who he was anymore when he was with her.

The tinkle of a Bach melody interrupted his train of thoughts. A cell phone was ringing, not his.

Hint hunted in her jacket pocket, then turned away as she answered. The connection appeared to be bad, as her voice rose and she repeated herself.

"Where are you? . . . Playa Luca? . . . He what? . . . You did?"

Trying not to eavesdrop, he walked her back to the car so she could have some privacy while he stood outside in the rain. He didn't want her to experience the same embarrassment he'd felt the day before in her backyard when Annabel had called out of the blue. And then the scene earlier that evening . . . His anger rose as he thought of the brazenness of his former girlfriend's note. No way would he show up at the Stanhope Hotel the following day. He was no one's trained Poodle, least of all his ex-girlfriend's. He'd unwillingly played that role for a time; it had been uncomfortable enough for him to know he never would again.

But what if he didn't show up at the Stanhope? Would she continue to stalk him? Restless, he spotted a tennis ball under a nearby bush and went over to pick it up. Now that she'd seen Hint, the stakes were raised. He knew his ex too well to think she'd drop her interest because someone else might be in the picture. That would only increase the challenge for her. Annabel loved winning. She just got bored with her prizes, once she had claimed them.

Sighing, he walked back to the car and leaned against the drivers' side, tossing the tennis ball up and down with one hand. Who could be on the phone with Hint? Her cousin? Her girlfriends now in the Caribbean waiting for her? Whoever the special person was she'd alluded to the day before?

Had she used that term first or had he? Suddenly, he hated words and the way they confused everything. Better to be an animal and act on instinct. He wanted to get in the car, pull the cell phone out of Hint's hand and toss it out the window, then kiss her into oblivion. Hard and fast, he lobbed the tennis ball into the dark, wet night.

"JACK. YOU CAN get in. I'm done." Hint tapped on the drivers' side windowpane until his body moved away from the car.

The door opened and Jack's tall frame folded into the seat. He looked at her questioningly.

"I ought to get home," she told him.

"Yeah? Business calls?" He was fishing.

He could fish all he wanted. She needed time and space to digest the events and new characters of the past two days. Especially the tall, blonde one. Who was he to question her about her personal life?

"No. Sleep calls." She thought of the moment she'd awakened that morning. She'd been in a bed created by Jack's thick, strong arms. Closing her eyes, she tried to chase away the heady memory, but it wasn't budging.

"I'm beat too," Jack said, his face not matching his words. He shot her another questioning glance as he backed the car out of Tom and Nicole's driveway.

"What's our game plan tomorrow?" he asked, steering the car onto the main road.

What's your game plan, is what I'd like to know. She still hadn't decided what she was going to do about the note, but it wouldn't be nothing. By half past five the following day she would have a plan in place.

"I've got some work to finish by tomorrow afternoon, but I'll make some calls in the morning, go down to the dog run, and then—what do you suggest?" She couldn't help putting him on the spot. Would he say he was busy the following evening?

"I've got to put in a full day at the office tomorrow but I can come over to pick you up as soon as I've gotten back from the city. Would that work?"

"Yes-s-s. I guess so." He wouldn't suggest coming to her place directly after an assignation with his ex-girlfriend would he?

Come to think of it, had he ever said the tall, blonde woman was his ex? She searched her mind. He'd seemed to be on the verge of explaining something about the stranger walking toward them in the driveway of Marguerite's house. Hadn't he said he hadn't invited her and didn't want to see her? But then they'd been interrupted. And he hadn't corrected Marguerite when she'd referred to Hint as his girlfriend. Her skin tingled at the thought.

"That's great. Let's both think of new places to look tomorrow evening. We should have about two good hours before it gets dark," he said.

Hint did some math. If it got dark by nine, that meant he'd be at her place around seven. He couldn't possibly meet Annabel at half past five on the Upper East Side of Manhattan, get down to Grand Central Station to catch a train to Pleasantville, then drive down to Bronxville to meet her all in the space of an hour and a half. Maybe he had no intention of accepting Annabel's invitation to meet at the Stanhope.

"I'll call the veterinarian hospitals in the area tomorrow morning," she told him. She'd also call Kim in Punta Cana to see what her cousin had meant when she said she'd spoken to Derek Simpson earlier that day. Had she pretended to be Hint and substituted herself at the meeting scheduled for that afternoon? She wouldn't put it past her. Kim's voice had been muffled by loud background noise. She guessed she had been bar-side with their girlfriend Nina. All Hint could make out was that Kim had said Derek Simpson was a bit of all right and their meeting had gone great. Raucous laughter had ensued on Kim's end, then the line had gone dead.

Turning her head from Jack to conceal her thoughts, she stifled a snicker at the thought of what Kim might have gotten up to. A top salesperson, her cousin rarely walked away from a meeting without getting what she wanted, or at least some of it. Hint could hardly wait to hear the details of her exchange with Derek Simpson.

Jack's car pulled up outside her apartment building. The rain now came down in sheets. He jumped out and ran around to her side of the car, umbrella unfolded. She got out and together, they dashed into the building.

In the foyer, she paused.

"Thank you for bringing me to meet Marguerite tonight," she told him.

"Thank you for coming."

"See you tomorrow." She turned to fit her key into the outer door.

"Don't you need me to walk you to your door?" he offered.

She looked at him, amused. "I think I can manage."

"But don't you want me to?" he pressed.

"That's another question. How about if I let you know some other time?"

"What other time?" His eyes wandered to her mouth. She could feel his breath, warm on her face.

"The right time," she countered. Opening the door ever so slightly, she slipped through it. Then gently but firmly she shut the outer door in his face.

He leaned against the other side, his face pressing into the glass, like a wet, tired six-year-old boy. The navy blue of his eyes beckoned. Her heart melted. Luckily, the locked door between them shielded her from succumbing to her feelings.

She put her finger up to the glass across from his mouth. With her index finger she traced the line of his lips. They were well-shaped, not too thin.

For the first time in her life, she was deliberately teasing a man. Instead of feeling guilty, elation danced inside her. Her gut told her if she was enjoying this so much, then he was too. Something about him made her spiral closer to herself. Who knew she was so playful, deep inside? Even she herself hadn't known until now.

On the other side of the door, Jack's mouth opened. His hands moved up to either side of his head, pulling his hair. He made a pained face, as if he was suffering.

Her index finger took on a life of its own. With it, she outlined the strong line of his jaw, then slowly crawled down his neck over one broad, horizontal shoulder. She wanted to continue, but minefields lay to the south. Besides, her elderly neighbor was a night owl, most likely poking her head out her front door to see who was there at that very moment.

Remembering the background research on Jack she needed to do the next day, she fluttered the fingers of her right hand, bidding him good night. She couldn't help but laugh as his mouth twisted into the same expression her nephew Russ wore when he couldn't get his way.

She turned and slowly climbed the stairs to her apartment, knowing her audience behind would be rapt at the sight of her. With the locked door between them, she took her time. She was in no rush. No rush at all.

Inside her door, the blinking light of her answering machine greeted her as she entered. Her feelings were so charged, the last thing she wanted to do was return to planet Earth, but she knew someone might have called about Percy. She hit the button.

"Hi, Hint? It's me, Brian. I met someone today who may have spotted your friends' dog. You need to call me as soon as you get this. 769-5120. Bye."

She shuddered. Who was this twit in a tight tee-shirt to order her to call him? He was her *superintendent,* for goodness' sake. She would call him when she felt like it. Which would be never.

Then Percy's sweet face came to her, forlorn and confused. Picking up the receiver, she dialed the number Brian had left. The phone rang several times then a click told her his answering machine message was coming on. About to slam down the phone, she caught herself. Jack Whitby's home number was scrawled on her message board, directly in front of her. She'd written it there over a week ago, when he'd first called to arrange picking up Percy.

"Brian, Hint Daniels," she said at the end of Brian's recorded announcement—cocky as usual. "I got your message. Listen, could you call me at 914-727-1078? If I'm not there, just leave the details with my partner, Jack. Thanks a lot for your help. Bye."

There. She hoped Brian would toss and turn all night wondering what she'd meant by 'partner.' She had no idea herself, but she liked the way it sounded.

Still holding the phone, she tried her cousin in Punta Cana. An announcement clicked on telling her international circuits were busy; she'd have to wait until morning.

Putting down the phone, exhaustion engulfed her. It was as if half the events of her entire life had taken place in the past twenty-four hours. After a long hot shower, she pulled on a pale pink tee-shirt with purple silk boxer shorts, then rubbed lavender on each of her temples. She hoped to fall asleep right away, but the thought of Percy outside in the rain forbade her. Hot tears welled in her eyes when she thought about the dog spending his third night alone, outdoors. She prayed, asking

God to protect him and sharpen her wits with new, inspired ways to find him.

Invading her prayers, a silky web of non-dog related thoughts spun into the corners of her mind. Who was she kidding? All she really wanted to think about was the moment she'd woken up in Jack's arms that morning. How had that happened? And what had happened in the hours before dawn when their bodies had found their way to each other in the cool night air?

Despite her unanswered questions, she didn't feel anxious. As she stared up at the ceiling over her bed, she imagined dark blue eyes looking down at her. Watchful. Waiting. An anticipatory energy rocked her in its arms and whispered to her that whatever had passed in the wee hours of the night before had been aligned with the stars, the full moon, and the summer night. It had been meant to be.

Comforted by that divinely irrational thought, she fell into a deep sleep, hoping that more of what was meant to be was about to reveal itself to her through the man she had bade goodnight on the other side of her locked outer door.

As JACK TURNED into his driveway, he let out a sigh of relief. The two-hundred-year-old former pickle farm he called home had been his oasis from his Manhattan workday ever since he'd bought it three years earlier. From its stucco exterior with a wraparound porch to the three majestic trees in the backyard, everything about the farmhouse breathed comfort and rest. After spending the night before in Fox Meadow Park, he was more than ready to be home.

He desperately needed to sleep. His brain tumbled and churned with new thoughts and sentiments. Running up the steps of the front porch, he headed straight indoors and upstairs to his bedroom where he tossed off his shirt and jeans, then threw himself on his bed.

The phone rang. Who the hell was that? His hand fished around on the night table for the receiver. Studying the caller ID, he clicked on after determining it wasn't Annabel Sanford. He'd heard more than enough from her in the past two days.

"Hello?"

"Yeah, I'm looking for Hint. Hint Daniels?" The voice sounded smarmy.

He wanted to punch out whoever was on the other end of the line just for sullying her sweet name by stating it aloud.

"What do you want?" He was less than polite. "And who is this?" He sat upright on his bed, springing to life again.

"It's . . . a friend. I've got some information about the dog she lost. Do you know where I can find her?"

A friend? What friend? The voice was familiar. He'd heard it recently.

"How did you get my number?" he asked. He didn't want any male friend of Hint's to be calling him at home. He didn't want any male friends of hers to be calling, period. How dare she have male friends?

"She, uh, left a message saying I could reach her at this number. Should I try again later?"

"No. I mean, yes. Just tell me about the dog and I'll let her know."

"Uh . . . I'll try again some other time." The caller clicked off.

Who had that been? And why had he reacted that way? The caller had been trying to offer some information about Percy. Hint would be upset to hear he hadn't even gotten the guy's name.

He leaped off the bed and padded into the kitchen, as jumpy as a month-old kitten. He reached into the cabinet over the wet bar for something to help him sleep.

Why had Hint told whoever had been on the phone that he could reach her at his place? Had she intended to come back to his house that evening? Remembering how firm she'd been in clicking the door shut in his face, he doubted it. Perhaps she'd given his number to someone she didn't want calling her, so he could field the calls.

That was it. She needed him to be her hero. Her champion. She had known he would like hearing that she'd implied to a male friend that she could be found over at his place.

Something in the bottom of Jack's stomach caught fire. It was either from the heroic role Hint had cast him in, or the shot of brandy he had just downed. His final thoughts before falling asleep were of the game they had played earlier that evening when they had said goodbye. This time no door separated them.

7

TEA AT THE STANHOPE

The next morning Hint combed her neighborhood for Percy. She dropped into the local pet store where she'd introduced the Schnoodle the past weekend and had a long conversation with the owner. He'd taken ten flyers and agreed to help search. He'd also offered a few grim suggestions that she and Jack hadn't thought of, so she'd returned home shortly past noon and spent the next three hours calling local and state departments of transportation and animal control agencies to find out if they'd picked up any dead dogs in the past few days.

The task had been gruesome. Each time she'd been put on hold after asking if the body of a dog fitting Percy's description had been found, her stomach had tied up in knots until the answer came back negative. While on the phone, she'd worked on her computer, posting a complete description of Percy on www.findyourpet.com.

By half past three her nerves were shot. It was time for a complete change of pace; a brief expedition to the Stanhope Hotel in Manhattan was what she had in mind. If Jack still had something going on with his ex-girlfriend she wanted to know as soon as possible, before she allowed feelings to take root that had begun even before she'd woken up in his arms.

Her former almost-fiancé had left for Shanghai in August of the year Hint had turned twenty-nine. He'd said he had a question to ask her when he returned at Christmastime. But in the ensuing months, via e-mail he'd told her he thought he knew who he was but Asia had shown him a new side to himself. She'd done some research with colleagues of his who'd also been sent out to start up the Shanghai office and discovered the personal sightseeing guide who'd help Tim discover his new side. A stunning Chinese girl had attached herself like a limpet to whichever side of Tim that had forgotten he'd spoken of a future together with Hint before he'd left.

In November she had confronted him on the phone about the other woman. His response had changed her feelings for him in an instant. He'd said he loved Hint, but had also developed feelings for someone he'd met locally. He'd thought he'd been sure of a future with her but when he'd gotten to Shanghai everything had been different and he didn't know who he was anymore.

The conversation had confused her until it had totally turned her off. At that point the fact that he didn't know who he was anymore helped her figure out exactly who she was. No man with divided affections would ever again cross the threshold of her heart.

"I don't know what to do, Hint," he'd moaned into the phone.

"Are you asking me to tell you?" she'd asked, disgust welling up from somewhere deep in her stomach.

"I don't know what I'm asking," he'd waffled. "Can you give me some more time?"

"Tim, do you remember the plans you said you wanted to make with me before you left?"

"Yes, of course."

She sensed he had no idea what she was talking about.

"What were they?"

"They were . . . they were plans we hadn't made yet," he answered sophistically.

"And what were the actual plans you were planning?"

"I hadn't planned them yet."

"But your company did have plans. Did those plans change yours?"

"I had no choice, Hint. It was a great opportunity."

"I'm sure it was. But what about your own plans for yourself? Wasn't I part of them?"

"Yes, of course," he'd stammered.

"But I'm not now."

"Of course you are. It's just that so much has happened," he whined. "I, uh, need some time to sort it out."

"You need to make a decision," she'd told him. It struck her that this was a man who had room in his heart to entertain two women. If she fought for him and won, all she'd end up with was a fiancé then a husband with a track record of divided affections.

"I can't," he'd moaned, sounding like a cross between Hamlet and a two-year-old.

"Well, I can." Suddenly Hint knew this revelation of Tim's character would help her better define her own. "Let me ask you one thing."

"What's that?" His voice had sounded muffled, thin.

"Were we engaged to be engaged?" She might as well know for the record.

"Yes. Something like that," he'd replied.

"Well, now we're not." She hung up.

At a quarter to four Hint rose from her desk and went into the bedroom. She put on hoop earrings, and her largest pair of sunglasses, then carefully hid every strand of her hair under a black and white checked newspaper boy hat.

Studying herself in the mirror, she decided she vaguely resembled Audrey Hepburn. There was no way she looked like Hint Daniels. Grabbing keys, cell phone, and handbag, she set off for the train station to catch the four fifteen train to Manhattan.

On the walk to the station, she tried calling Kim in Punta Cana again, but international circuits were still busy, as they had been all morning. Perhaps they were having a tropical storm there. She frowned. What had her cousin meant when she'd described Derek Simpson as a bit of all right?

She didn't often go into the city. Occasional contracts, presentations and lunches with editors called her in no more than once every other month. She was perfectly happy not to frequent the big city, as it still retained its exoticism for her. The second the train crossed over the Harlem River that separated the Bronx from Manhattan, a buzz began inside her.

"I'll take Manhattan," she hummed as she adjusted her cap in her reflection from the train window.

She was on her way to the Stanhope, one of New York's finest and most historical hotels. Once there, she was determined not to be outclassed by any other female on site. Lots of ladies who lunched met there, as well as ladies and gentlemen who cocktailed until they turned into men and women of a less refined order.

She stared out the window, seeing nothing while she anticipated the events that might unfold from half past five on. If Jack showed up and responded warmly to his ex, she would quietly slip away. If he had the nerve to show up at her place later, as planned, she'd not be home. Just for fun she'd tape a note to the door in the foyer saying she was out looking for Percy with Brian O'Connell. Had the muscle-bound clod actually called Jack's home number looking for her?

How could life suddenly have gotten so complicated? Thinking back to Jack on the other side of the outer door the night before, she no longer recognized her own behavior. For the first time in her adult life, she realized that when men and women played games with each other, it was not necessarily a bad thing. More accurately, she'd call it an educational process. Wasn't that why children were taught to play games? It was to learn how to play nicely together: share, show good sportsmanship, be gracious in either victory or defeat.

Sure it was. Her hand clenched the armrest of her seat, throttling it.

How gracious would she be if that tall blonde bombshell laid one finger on Jack Whitby's body? And what if he responded? Who would she throw the contents of her drink at first? The blonde or the man whose arms she'd woken up in the morning before?

Succumbing to her inner devil, she thought about what kind of drink she should order while staking out Annabel.

"Something funny?" a man seated next to her inquired.

She'd laughed out loud.

"No. I was just thinking about what kind of drink a person might order if they were planning to toss it into someone's face," she shared before realizing it would have been best not to.

The man moved slightly away from her, not before she detected a glimmer of admiration in his widening eyes.

"Wow. You've got some plans for the afternoon," he remarked.

"No, you don't understand. I'm, uh . . ." She searched for a reason why she might have said something so crazy. "I'm writing a screenplay and my character is confronting her rival. They're at a cocktail party, so she's about to throw a drink in her face."

"Nice. I thought she was going to toss her drink into some guy's face. Phew." He looked relieved. Then his expression brightened. "I've got it."

"What?" Where was she going with this? And why was she discussing an act of violence with a total stranger on the train?

"Have her order a Bloody Mary. She should tell the waiter to make it extra spicy. It'll sting like crazy. Make sure she squeezes the lemon into the drink before she tosses it."

"Ouch." She winced. Was she sitting next to a psycho? Maybe he thought the same of her. She needed to be polite just in case he was some sort of nutcase. "That's a great idea. Thanks so much."

"Hey, will I get a plug in your book? Or play?"

"Umm, sure. I'll thank you on my acknowledgments page. Look for "Guy on the train." She stood as they pulled into Grand Central Station.

"Great. Glad to be of help. Who's the author of this work, by the way?"

"Oh, uh, I go by my pseudonym."

The man looked confused.

"I mean, my pen name."

His expression remained puzzled.

"Um, just look for the latest play by Annabel Boleyn. It should come out in about a year," she ad-libbed.

"What's it called?"

"Uhh . . ." She searched for inspiration. Bingo. Looking straight into his eyes, she spoke firmly.

"Bloody Friday."

"Great title."

"Thanks. Have a nice evening." She stepped forward to get past him and as he moved back, he shot her a look of approval. Apparently her perverse imagination had inspired awe. Funny. She was on her way to a more advanced level of adult womanhood. Whatever happened with Jack Whitby, she had him to thank for transforming her into a sharper, more well-defined version of herself.

THE STANHOPE HOTEL's outdoor terrace in the month of June blended tranquility with sophistication, in one of Manhattan's most exclusive neighborhoods. Located on Fifth Avenue at East 81st Street, it faced the grand front steps of the Metropolitan Museum.

At a quarter past five, Hint entered the hotel and quickly found the café bar. She asked to be seated in a corner, directly inside from the terrace and with an unobstructed view of the entrance. Keeping on her sunglasses, she pretended she was Audrey Hepburn having tea at the Stanhope instead of breakfast at Tiffany's. Batting away wicked thoughts of ordering a Bloody Mary, extra spicy, she settled for a narcissus tea.

She took in the crowd, noting the angular lines of the women seated at tables and at the bar, the strong definition of their jawbones and necklines. Every one of them assumed the same posture, their heads held high in permanent hauteur.

People were different here. She straightened her back, raised her head and thrust out her chin to make like an ice cutter. Was this the world Jack's former girlfriend came from? If so, what was his background?

She glanced at her watch. It was now twenty-five past the hour. A couple entered, the woman exuding waves of floral scent as she glided to the outdoor terrace. The man wore cufflinks and loafers that looked as supple as ballet slippers. Hint's eyes followed them, drinking in their details.

"The terrace please," a regal voice commanded from the direction of the entryway.

Hint's blood froze. Adrenalin surged through her veins. Slowly turning her head, she pretended to study the clock on the wall over the bar.

The tall blonde from the day before was moving in her direction. She sailed, rather than walked. Head held high, with shoulders erect, she took no notice of anyone in the room. Hint was reminded of fashion models whose eyes gaze elsewhere when photographed, as if a better party was forever going on somewhere else.

The red dress was spectacular. Hint wished desperately that it was a tad too flashy or trashy, but it wasn't. It was well constructed, revealing a modest expanse of throat. The halter design artfully showed off well-toned, sun-kissed shoulders and arms. The skirt was flared, the length perfect, ending just below the knees. Annabel looked like a tawny tigress, loping its way through the jungle, lazily contemplating its next meal.

Moving only her eyes to the extreme right, under her sunglasses, Hint observed the woman sit down, give her order to the waiter, then slowly and elegantly cross her legs. Hint crossed her own legs. She would not be outcrossed.

The next ten minutes went by in a zen-like state of total focus, while Hint pretended she was concentrating on nothing at all. It was harder than it looked.

She remembered yoga classes she'd taken, where the instructor would tell everyone to empty their heads of all thoughts. As soon as she'd hear such a command, her head would fill up with to-do lists, analyses of recent dates, plans for the weekend, etc. while she pretended her mind was a perfect blank.

Annabel studied her cell phone out on the patio. Meanwhile, a man at the bar appeared to be taking in Annabel. The woman's foot, attached to one long sleek, perfectly tanned leg, swung lightly up and down as if waiting to be asked to dance by someone else's foot.

The blonde woman's drink arrived. It was a white wine, served in a glass with a stem so impossibly slender, Hint could only guess it was a metaphor for the general shape of the women who frequented the place.

Annabel took a sip, her little finger extended. Hint picked up her tea cup and extended her own pinkie. Instead of leaning over to sip, she kept her back perfectly straight, making it one long journey to bring the tea cup from the table up to her mouth. With her other hand, she held the saucer underneath. There was much detail involved in showing the world how well bred one was.

It was now a quarter to six. The foot had ceased swinging. Annabel had picked up her cell phone and was texting someone.

Hint leaned down, pretending to fish for something in her handbag. Cocking her ear, she smiled when Annabel made a sound like "Hmph" then put down her phone. In another minute the woman looked at it again, her free hand tapping against her thigh.

Who else would she be texting than the person she was waiting for?

Rummaging through her handbag, Hint's hand alighted on her own cell phone. Quickly, she hit the name of the last person who'd called. It had been Jack, at lunchtime, who'd phoned to say he'd heard from someone who'd read their flyer and had found a black and gray dog with a bushy tail. She had reminded him that Percy's tail had been clipped shortly after birth.

"Busy" came up on her cell phone screen. Someone else was calling Jack at that moment. Surreptitiously, she glanced at Annabel. She was speaking into her cell, her hand covering her mouth. Whatever the woman was saying, Hint couldn't hear a thing. It had to be a message because Annabel hadn't paused for a response at the other end. The elegant woman clicked off and returned to her drink, her forefinger drumming up and down on the skirt of her dress, in a sort of overwrought military march.

Hint watched with wicked enjoyment as Annabel's composure slowly melted in the warm June late afternoon sun. It was now ten minutes before six. Suddenly Hint had an inspiration. There was a way to find out if Jack was intending to show up and was just late.

Then it occurred to her that maybe he was here now, about to enter the café lounge. Would he recognize her? Quickly, she got up, accidentally upsetting her cup and spilling tea on her white linen pants. Idiot. She rushed to the ladies room, head down, her sunglasses still on. She needed to call Jack, as well as recover her cool. Annabel wasn't the only one losing it at the moment. Hint would die if he showed up and recognized her under her disguise. What would she say when he asked what she was doing there?

In the powder room, she rubbed desperately at the tea stain on her trousers. Was the universe telling her she didn't belong here? If so, she wasn't the only one. Trying to imagine Jack in such rarefied surroundings, with his rumpled shirts and unruly hair, she choked back laughter as she pressed his number.

"Hint? Is that you?" he answered almost immediately.

"It's me." Relief flooded through every vein in her body. "Just wanted to know when I should expect you." She glanced in the mirror, patting her eyebrows into place. Why did the other women here look as if they'd had their eyebrows perfectly shaped, then glued in place? Probably because they had.

"I'm on the train now. Should be home in twenty minutes. It'll take me another half hour to get to you. Would around seven be okay?" He sounded relaxed, not at all as if he were hiding anything. Hint reminded herself that the proposed assignation had been Annabel's idea, not his own.

"Take your time," she said. "I'm tied up with some errands and I don't think I'll be home before seven fifteen. Why don't you plan on coming by around half past?" She checked her lipstick. It needed refreshing. How did the other women here manage to keep their lipstick on while eating and drinking? There were so many secrets of the rich and privileged she wasn't yet in on. Would she ever be? Glancing down at her white paints, she already knew the answer.

"Oh. Sure. Gives me more time to do a few things around the house. I'll drag my patio furniture out of the garage, in case you want to come up and sit on it," he told her.

A warm bolt shot through her stomach. Was he planning to invite her to his place sometime soon? She'd be curious to see it.

"Good idea. You haven't done that already?" The weather had been warm for at least a month.

"I didn't have any reason to. See you later." He clicked off.

She was elated. Apparently, he hadn't entertained Annabel or anyone else at his home in the weeks before they'd met. And he clearly hadn't responded to the woman's invitation to meet at the Stanhope. He'd passed Hint's secret test.

She hurried back to her table to pay the bill. She needed to get to Grand Central to make the six forty-five train.

On the terrace, Annabel was now draining her wineglass. She looked slightly less fresh than she had when she'd sat down. The man at the bar was once again gazing in her direction.

"Waiter?" Hint overheard her say.

"Yes, Madame."

"Do you have any ice cream?" Annabel asked.

"Of course, Madame."

"You wouldn't have a . . . a hot fudge sundae, would you?"

It was the first time Hint had heard the woman stammer.

"Yes, certainly, Madame."

"Fine. I'll have one."

"May I freshen Madame's glass?"

"No . . . Oh hell . . . Yes, sure. Why not?"

"Very good, Madame." The waiter walked away.

What was wrong with Annabel's glass? Was it dirty, that it needed freshening?

Awareness broke over Hint as she realized what the waiter had meant. The glass wasn't dirty, it was empty. The waiter had asked if she'd like another glass of wine in a way that didn't call attention to the fact that it would be her second drink. Alone.

Hint marveled at the ways of the highborn. So many secret techniques to shield oneself from any hint of impropriety. Suddenly, she didn't feel interested to learn any more of them. She had her own life to live, somewhere in the middle class range; it was highborn enough for her and that was all that mattered.

She stood, wallet in hand and walked over to the bar. Stopping directly next to the man sitting there, she turned and smiled into his eyes, surprising herself.

He smiled back.

Handsome, fortyish, well dressed, with a receding hairline of light brown hair, she took him in. "I hope you don't mind my mentioning something," she said.

"Not at all," he replied, his voice slightly accented. His eyebrows rose as he studied her with apparent interest.

"If I tell you, you mustn't divulge its source," she murmured. The inspired surroundings had raised her vocabulary a notch.

"I have no choice but to obey the orders of a woman as beautiful as yourself." The man was well-bred, someone who could catch and hold the attention of a woman like Annabel.

"Good." She lowered her voice. "Directly behind me, out on the terrace, a woman much more beautiful than I has just been stood up for a date. She would most likely be pleased to be distracted by someone such as you at this moment."

"You're mistaken on one point but I'll follow up on it." The man looked at Hint admiringly. "May I ask why I mustn't reveal my source?"

"You'll be much more appreciated if she thinks you took it upon yourself to speak to her."

"Understood. How do you know her?" His eyes were lively, assessing.

She thought for a moment while the bartender handed her the change. Somewhere she had read that the aristocracy never complain, never explain. What could be a more perfect ethos for the present situation? She lifted her chin at the foreigner, her eyes veiled, in her best Mata Hari imitation.

"I'd rather not say." She gave the dashing stranger the faintest hint of a smile, then turned and glided off.

As she walked past the hotel from the sidewalk, she saw the man come out onto the terrace, then stop in front of the woman in the red dress.

Hint giggled. Annabel Sanford had not been the only femme fatale at the Stanhope café bar that afternoon.

8

BACK IN BRONXVILLE

Jack took the stairs to Hint's apartment two at a time. He'd finally gotten a full night's sleep and had put in a productive day at the office. He had been eager to hop on the 5:20 train to Pleasantville and speed home to projects and people who occupied his heart, rather than succumb to Annabel's invitation to meet her at the Stanhope Hotel. He hadn't even been tempted. No longer was he some pathetic toy for a preppie princess to play with until she got bored. He smiled to himself, remembering how good it felt not to respond to her texts or call to his cell phone on the train ride home.

Then Hint had phoned. Little did she know he was speeding away from his past as they confirmed their plan to meet later.

The only thing not going his way was finding the dog. He had no idea what to do next. But if anyone could make it happen, it would be the person whose door was now opening onto the hallway.

"Hi, Jack."

"Hey. How was your day?" he asked.

She seemed lit from within, her auburn hair flowing in waves over her shoulders.

"Great." A slow smile played across Hint's face. He'd swear it was almost catlike.

Just the day before he had thought she looked different, as if she had a secret. Now, once again, her face wore a new expression. Her mystery intrigued him, something that had never happened with Annabel, the ever obvious drama queen. All-out, drop-dead beauty on display for everyone to see had not melted his heart. He was more interested to explore the subtle shadings of the woman before him.

"How was yours?" Hint asked, her hand flipping a thick mass of hair off her shoulder.

"I got some work done. Poked around some more lost-dog sites, but didn't come up with anything." *And thought of you all day*, he didn't add.

"Come in," she invited him.

He reached for her hand.

She let him take it.

His fingers encircled hers. He hoped she couldn't hear his heart, thumping like a fish at the bottom of a boat.

"I . . . I don't know what else to do," she began.

"So we'll keep doing what we have been doing," he said.

"But what's the point?" Her voice wavered as her expression crumpled.

"The point is, it's working," he assured her, telling himself it was. He shifted closer to her, his other hand moving around to the small of her back.

"Who says it's working?" she whispered.

"I do. I'm saying it and your job is to have the faith to believe it. Got that?" He tucked her slim torso into the curve of his own.

She didn't resist.

"Got what?" she asked, looking as if she was trapped in her own fairy tale illustration.

"Got this?" His hand moved up to the back of her neck, sliding under her hair. He gathered it into a thick, silken pony tail, giving it a slow, deliberate tug, until her head fell back, her face just inches away.

Her eyes locked onto his. They smoldered, waiting.

For the first time in forever, it was the right moment. He leaned down, his lips meeting hers.

Relaxing into his embrace, she returned his kiss. His heart on fire, his hands moved over her back, pressing her shoulder blades, moving down over the inward curve to her waist, then out again to her hips.

If he had been driving a race car over her terrain, he would have crashed. But he wanted to proceed slowly on her roads. As slowly as possible, hugging every wondrous inch. He was on the road between Nice and Monaco. It was the most ravishing drive he had ever taken.

After a long moment, Hint stepped back. Her face was flushed, a confluence of conflicting emotions.

"Are you okay?" he asked, gently.

"Yes. Fine," she said, reaching up to push strands of hair out of her face.

"Very fine," he echoed. Pushing her hand away, he pulled his fingers up through her hair on both sides of her head. He let go, watching it cascade gloriously all over her shoulders, a dark red sheath of tumbling waves.

"You're not helping," she protested, a low laugh escaping her.

"Neither are you." Gathering her hair in his right hand, he couldn't resist one more tug. "Do you like that?" he asked in a low voice.

"I haven't decided," she murmured, her eyes and mouth belying her words.

He tugged harder, enjoying her response. Annabel had been an open book, her wiles as transparent as her blatant ambitions. Not Hint. She was all mystery, all the time. Most mysterious of all was the fact that he liked it. A lot.

"How about that?" he asked, even lower.

She said nothing, but her eyes spoke volumes, glistening in the dim light of her apartment.

His lips locked onto hers.

Her arms came up around his neck. They melted into each other, tasting and nipping; drinking each other in. Finally, taking a deep breath, he released her.

Reaching to embrace her again, she stepped back.

He paused as she groped for something on the desk behind her. Was she searching for a heavy object to knock him out with? If so, he would take the blow willingly. Whatever she did to him next, he would take it like a man. Probably because she made him feel like one.

She brought the object around in front of her, brandishing it like a weapon. Except that it was a sheet of paper. Was she waving the white flag of surrender?

He grabbed for it, taking it from her.

In his hand, a huge color headshot of Percy stared up at him. Jack laughed. Hint Daniels knew how to stay focused.

WHY HAD SHE enjoyed him pulling her hair so much? Wasn't that some sort of violent act? Schoolgirls scolded boys who did that sort of thing in class. Yet unexpected shivers of pleasure and desire had run up and down her spine each time he'd tugged. What was she, a masochist?

She waved Percy's photo in front of him, like a crucifix or a bouquet of garlic. As Jack's laughter increased, she couldn't help but join in.

"Okay, I get your point," he choked out, his eyes twinkling. "Find the dog."

She backed away then sat behind her desk. At least two feet of solid wood was now between them.

"Did anyone ever tell you you would have made a great spy?" he asked.

"Intelligence or counterintelligence?" She didn't know where that question had come from.

"You could have been a double agent, for sure."

"Isn't that a bad thing?" she asked.

"In your case, no. Both sides would have forgiven you for anything you did. Probably thanked you."

"But wasn't Mata Hari hanged?"

"She was shot, but not until she'd lived a life others only dream of."

"Well, I like the life I'm living now and I'm not a spy, so I'll just stay on the amateur side of the fence," she declared, thinking of the scene at the Stanhope earlier that day. No more highborn role-playing for her. One hour of studying how the other half lived had convinced her she was better off just as she was.

"You're no amateur, Beautiful. You're the most naturally sophisticated woman I've ever met." He meant it. Every word. After Annabel Sanford's brand of artful sophistication, he recognized Hint's at the other end of the spectrum where beauty complemented nature, instead of trying to improve upon it.

"More so than what's-her-name?" The words had escaped before she could catch herself.

"Who's what's-her-name?"

"You know who. The one we bumped into at your sister's place."

"Oh. Her." His voice hardened. "I'll try to explain it simply." He paused for a moment, staring into space. Then his eyes swung back to hers, clear and focused. "Which stone do you think is more valuable: a perfect diamond or a perfect emerald? Same size, same cut."

"Umm . . . diamond?"

"No. Everyone thinks diamonds are, because everyone knows about them. But an emerald stone of the same size and cut as a diamond is always considered more valuable by a discerning gems buyer.

"Are you one?"

"I might be."

Hint paused, surprised at his story. Her grandmother had always said when a guy brings up diamonds, it's time to listen. Up until three days earlier, she hadn't particularly liked surprises, but she liked the ones Jack offered. Everything was changing around her at the speed of light.

Everything, except that Percy was still lost.

"Let's find our boy, Jack." She strode to the door, picking up a flashlight on the front hall table along the way. Meanwhile, she longed to fast rewind to ten minutes earlier. Jack had kissed her for the first time. Her heart fluttered like the wings on one of her fairy characters, just thinking about it.

"Where are we going?"

"Your pick. Dog run, Nicole and Tom's place, downtown Scarsdale, somewhere new—"

The phone rang. It was her landline in the living room.

"Aren't you going to pick it up?" Jack asked.

"Let me see who it is." She paused, suspecting it might be Brian O'Connell again. She was fed up with his false leads. He had left a message earlier in the day alluding to something important he needed to tell her in person. She didn't understand why he couldn't just spit it out in the message he'd left.

The outgoing message ended.

"Huge news, Fairy Girl," a female voice announced. "He's coming to New York tomorrow. The Algonquin. You're meeting him in the lobby lounge at seven. I found out he's single, by the way. He saw your—"

"Hello . . . hi. Kim, are you there?" A dial tone sounded in Hint's ears as she finally found the phone receiver she'd left under the coffee table when she'd made calls earlier that day. She'd forgotten where it was and now Kim had hung up.

"Jack, I need to make a call," she told him. "Do you want to start looking for Percy? Just circle around the neighborhood. I'll come find you when I'm done." She needed a moment of privacy to talk with Kim. Even if she went in her bedroom to call, Jack's presence would unnerve her. Their recent kiss hung in the air. She couldn't think about business with him present.

"Sure. I can take a walk." His face looked uncertain, his jawline hard. She would explain everything to him once she spoke with Kim.

Rushing into her bedroom, phone receiver in hand, she closed the door behind her. Seconds later, the front door shut with a bang. She scrambled for the piece of paper on her night table with Kim's cell phone and hotel numbers on it. She called the cell phone first. The wait was interminable. Finally, she hung up and dialed the hotel instead.

"Room 431, please."

After endless clicking, then silence, her cousin's voice sounded at the other end. "Hello?"

"Kim, is that you?"

"Yes," the voice at the other end practically screamed. "Honey—I got him! I got Derek Simpson for you. I went to your scheduled meeting and told him you had an emergency with a lost dog and were devastated not to be there because the dog was missing or something, and he was totally simpatico. Turns out he has two Poodles and said he'd have done the same thing. Then I showed him a few of your drawings that I had on my laptop, and he liked them. He's coming to New York tomorrow, and he wants to meet with you."

"I . . . that's great."

"Can you get to the Algonquin Hotel by seven?"

"I . . . yes. I can be there. Is this a confirmed meeting?"

"Yes. You can't imagine what I had to do to get him to agree to it."

"What do you mean?" What exactly had Kim meant by "I got him"?

"And don't wear some stupid, boring business suit."

"I wasn't planning to." It was annoying the way some family members knew her so well. "What do you suggest I wear—a lampshade?"

"No, darling." Massive giggling sounded from the other end. "That's my style. Just wear one of your wispy, fairy outfits. Be what you draw. He'll love it."

"Does he look like his photos?" Hint had seen Derek Simpson's photos a few times in trade publications. She'd never met him in person.

More giggles. "He's better looking than his photos. Like I told you—I found out he's single."

"What did you do to get him to agree to meet me?" Hint asked.

Tinkling laughter was the only answer she got. "I have to go. Felipe is picking me up for dinner at eight."

"Who's Felipe?" Her cousin was a pistol. At least, it wasn't Derek Simpson taking her out to dinner. There were times when Kim's sense of adventure took her to places Hint didn't dare follow. Or ask about later.

"Gotta' go. Love you, sweetie." Her cousin clicked off.

A million thoughts raced through Hint's head. She needed to pull out her portfolio and review it one more time before showing it to the head of one of the foremost children's book presses in the publishing industry. And she decidedly needed to choose something to wear that would announce to the world and Derek Simpson that she was a talented artist with a signature style.

Then she caught herself. Percy. If she went, she would lose at least several hours in their efforts to find him. Her heart tugged again. Jack. Outside, waiting for her. Probably wondering what that message had been all about. Her future was rushing toward her and she wasn't sure if she was ready for it. Why wasn't it Percy rushing toward her instead? Without him back, she couldn't move forward. But she had to. Life was messy and imperfect. She was a fine artist, as fussy and fastidious as they come. The world outside her was fast colliding with the magical safe one she strove to create around her. Nervous, scared and a teensy bit exhilarated, Hint grabbed a light jacket and her cell phone, straightened her shoulders and headed out the door.

9

SHAKEDOWN

*F*airy Girl. Jack's head spun. He'd circled Hint's block twice, looking for the dog, but his heart was looking for an explanation for the message her cousin had just left. It sounded as if Hint had intended to meet a man in Punta Cana, who was now coming to New York. But it was apparently someone new, not a pre-established boyfriend. The woman on the phone had said, "He saw your—" something. What? Her photo? Was this some sort of first meeting for an online dating match?

Would she go meet this guy the following evening? Did she consider her options to be open or had he closed some of them with the kiss he had just planted on her lips? He would know if she told him she had plans for the following evening. It would be their final one to look for the dog before their friends returned. If they didn't find Percy, would it ruin whatever had begun between them? Or would this new mystery guy get in the way?

He had thought of asking her to his place Saturday evening to join him for a light barbecue on his patio after they'd dropped by Marguerite's party and looked some more for the dog. Now he wasn't so sure.

His cell phone rang.

"Hello?"

"Yeah. I'm calling about a lost dog."

"Did you find one?" Jack sprang to attention.

"Yeah, mon." The caller's accent was lilting. Jamaican, he'd guess. "I found a black and gray yesterday on the side of the road. He's pretty beat up, but I've got him with me now."

Jack shuddered. Hint would be beside herself if Percy was hurt. And so would Tom and Nic. He was beside himself just thinking about what the vet bills might be if the dog had a broken limb or worse.

"How big is he?" Jack asked.

"Not so big."

"How many pounds, would you say?"

"Who knows, mon? He's small. He could fit in my lap if I let him, but he's dirty."

"What's your location?"

"I'm off the Grand Concourse in the Bronx. You want to come by?"

"Yes. I can get there in about forty-five minutes. Give me your address."

"Slow down, mon. What about the reward?"

The reward? Had Hint mentioned something about a reward on their lost dog posters? Jack's scam radar switched on. Suddenly, it was a mon-to-mon conversation.

"We'll discuss the reward when I get there. I don't know if it's my dog yet."

"Well, if it is, how much is it?"

Jack was taken aback. Was this the way a dog lover would return a pet to its owner? His muscles tightened, thinking of what he might be getting into, traveling down to the Bronx to find out if this tough-sounding caller had found Percy.

"It's good enough, okay? What's your address?" he responded gruffly.

"There's a bodega at the corner of 159th and the Grand Concourse. I'll be out front."

"With the dog?"

"Sure, mon. But the dog stays unless you got the reward."

"Yeah, okay. Listen, what's the name of the store? And what's your name?

"Name's Harry. I don't know what the store is called. You'll see it. Lots of people out front. We'll be there."

"Wait. Is it on 159th Street or the Grand Concourse?" Jack knew the general area from his days running with the Van Cortlandt Track Club in the Bronx. But the Grand Concourse was enormous, sort of a Bronx version of Paris's Champs Elysées.

"It's on the side street, to the east of the Concourse. Bring the money or no dog." The caller clicked off.

Almost immediately, the phone rang again.

"Jack?"

"Someone just called about finding a dog," he told Hint excitedly, relieved to hear her voice despite his worries.

"Where? What kind of dog?"

"A small black and gray one. I've got to go down to the Bronx now to check it out."

"I'm coming with you," Hint said without hesitation. "Where are you now?"

"I'm standing in front of the post office. And I don't think it's a good idea for you to come too. It's not the best neighborhood."

She had already hung up. In a minute she was beside him, her face expectant.

"I hope it's him. Did the caller say if the dog was hurt? Where did he find him?" she fired off.

"Slow down." He furrowed his brow. "Don't get your hopes up. The dog was found by the side of the road in the Bronx." He didn't want to tell her the caller had mentioned he was in bad shape.

"The Bronx? Where in the Bronx?"

"The South Bronx. And I don't want you coming with me."

"Why not?" She looked hurt, as if he'd pushed her away.

"You don't understand." He reached for her arm. "It could be dangerous. The caller asked about a reward."

Her eyes widened. "A reward?"

"Did you put something about a reward on the flyer?"

"Yes, I guess I did. I was following a template I found online on a lost dog website."

"Did you put an amount?"

"No. It advised specifically not putting any amount. Just to say 'reward.'"

"Well, this guy seemed pretty interested to know what the amount was."

"Hmm," she said. "If it is Percy, what should we offer him?"

"A hundred?"

"What if he says it's not enough?"

"Two hundred?"

"Sure. But it's strange. Why would someone who cared enough to pick up a lost dog by the side of the road ask about money?"

"That's my question," he told her. "And that's why I can't let you come with me."

"That's ridiculous. You can't go alone. It could be dangerous," Hint argued. "Besides, there's nowhere to park in that neighborhood. You'll need someone to stay in the car while you meet the guy."

"Both good points. But that someone shouldn't be you," Jack reasoned. "It's better if you stay here and keep track of what's happening in case things don't go well."

"I can't just sit home while you're down in the South Bronx possibly walking into a frame-up. Who's going to go with you?" Hint looked distressed, her usually almond-shaped eyes now round.

Across the street, the muscular figure of Hint's superintendent caught Jack's eye. The man looked as if he were hurrying towards Hint's apartment building, coming from Bronxville Village center. For once, he was glad to see the guy. Hint appeared to be too.

"Brian, hey. I got your message," she called to him across the street.

Jack guessed the same thought had occurred to her that had just popped into his head.

"Hey, Hint." Brian crossed the street to join them, nodding to Jack without speaking. It was clear the only person he wished to address was his auburn-haired neighbor.

"Brian, what was that call about?" she asked.

"What call?" He looked puzzled, staring at Hint, to Jack's annoyance. "Oh that. Turned out to be nothing." He shrugged.

"Listen. We've got a lead on Percy. But I need your help." Hint looked up at Brian with imploring eyes.

Jack wanted to throw up. The stuff females had to go through to get things done. But they were on the same track now. Brian would be the perfect sidekick to accompany him down to the South Bronx. The man named Harry would take one look at Brian's muscular build and tough face and drop the price of his anticipated reward on the spot.

"What can I do to help?" The superintendent looked adoringly into Hint's eyes. "Anything, Hint. You name it."

If he used her name again, Jack would haul off and hit him. Why did there have to be so many smarmy characters in the world? And why did they have to come in so handy at times? He was beginning to understand why Hint didn't just blow off Brian O'Connell once and for all. There were times when she needed a muscle man. Like now.

"Brian, Jack has to go down to the South Bronx to check out a lead on Percy. Someone just called to say he's found a black and gray stray."

"Oh yeah? The South Bronx can be a pretty tough neighborhood. You sure this is legit?"

"No. We're not sure. That's why I want you to go with Jack."

"I'm game," Brian said. "But you need to stay here. In case anything goes wrong."

Hint rolled her eyes.

"Okay. I will. And let me make sure you two have all the details about Percy. I don't want you coming back with the wrong dog."

Jack couldn't believe it. All of a sudden, he and Brian were blood brothers on the same mission. Whatever happened, he wasn't planning on coming back with the wrong dog.

"I think we've got Percy's number down," he said.

"Okay, does he have clipped ears or not?" Hint asked.

"Umm. What do you mean by clipped?" He wasn't exactly a dog expert.

"He doesn't. His ears flop over, especially the left one," she said. "And what about his tail?"

"Chopped. I remember that one," he answered.

"Good. What about the spots on his tummy?"

"What spots?" Jack hadn't been that intimately acquainted with Tom and Nicole's dog. And what self-respecting male dog would expose his belly to any male other than his master? Jack wouldn't have, if he'd been a dog.

"He has big spots, like black polka dots on a white dress, on his belly. You should turn him over to check it out before you pay any reward."

"Awesome, Hint. How many spots does he have?" Brian asked.

Jack wanted to shove him into the street, but held off.

"Let me see. Maybe four or five. They're big and sort of faint. Maybe grayish black instead of really black. But you can see them clearly on his tummy if you lift him up," she told him.

"His tummy, huh?" Brian continued, looking as if he was about to drool over her choice of words. Jack was sure Brian would like Hint to stroke his tummy too, if given a chance. Before that ever happened, he would stroke the side of Brian's head. Hard.

"Yes." Hint replied. "And give me the plate number of the car you take. In case I need to call the police."

"We'll take my car," Jack said.

"We can take my car," Brian challenged him. "It's right here in the driveway."

"No. Let's take mine," Jack brushed him off.

Both men looked at Hint.

"Why don't you take Jack's car?" Hint mediated. "That way the person whose number is on the flyer will match the person who owns the car. It makes more sense."

Score. Jack was elated to see Brian's face fall.

"That's right. It's a Honda Civic. NY license plate YXN 463," he told her. "Got that?"

"Hang on. I'm writing it down," she said, pulling out a scrap of paper. They were now outside her building. After she finished, she handed Jack a few dog treats she fished out of her jacket pocket. They smelled like liver. "Here. Take these in case you have trouble getting him to come to you. He'll be confused. Do you know where you're going?"

"Yes," they both said.

Jack wasn't pleased to play Lancelot with competition from Sir Gawaine. but he'd take the help if it meant getting the dog back. Hint wasn't going to let her feelings for him progress until they made progress in other areas. *Find the dog, mon. Just find the dog*, he told himself as he motioned Brian toward his car.

THE DRIVE DOWN to the South Bronx was uneventful. Jack drove fairly fast. He wanted to get the business over with before it got dark. Brian O'Connell had fiddled with the radio the entire way, finally settling on an alternative rock station that played mostly Irish music. It seemed fitting for a trip to the Bronx, with its sizeable Irish-American population.

Once they got onto the Grand Concourse, it was as if they'd joined a Mardi Gras parade. Salsa music played, mingling with accents from all over the world from the crowded sidewalks. After the rain of the night before, the denizens of the neighborhood had taken out their lawn chairs and orange crates and were sitting outside, enjoying the warm, dry June evening.

"There's 159th Street. It's one way, so let's take the next one that goes left," Brian suggested.

"Sure." Jack didn't see any convenience store at the corner of 159th and the Grand Concourse, but it was hard to focus with the busy panoply of shops, double-parked cars and trucks, and people milling about everywhere he looked.

He swung left onto 158th Street. Here there was less confusion, although a similar landscape of double-parked cars and drivers in idling vehicles talking to friends on the street made it difficult to get through. It was a festive atmosphere, practically a block party.

"How's your Spanish?" Brian asked.

"Nonexistent." Jack shrugged. Why hadn't he studied Spanish in school instead of French? His French was pretty nonexistent too, due to lack of any opportunities to practice it. "I think the guy's Jamaican or something. He had a West Indian accent."

"That so?" Brian began toying with something he'd taken out of his pocket. Jack glanced over and spotted what looked like a short piece of two-inch metal link chain. Brian idly slapped it against his leg. Was the super expecting some sort of gang rumble? He hoped not.

Pulling into 159th Street, he cruised down a block filled with crumbling tenement buildings, and a few two-family houses with wire mesh fences surrounding them. Some had barbed wire at the top. Driving slowly, he looked for the convenience store.

"Is that it over there?" Brian pointed out the passenger side of the car. "Bodega Martinez?"

Jack peered in the gathering twilight, looking for a place to pull over. Finding none, he decided to follow the time-honored New York City tradition of double parking.

"I'll go. You stay here." Brian started to get out of the car.

The man was brave. Jack had to hand him that.

"No, wait. I'll go. I know what Percy looks like. You stay here in the driver's seat. Just keep an eye on what's happening. Got it, man?"

"Got it." Brian's arm muscles rippled as he leaned into the window of the passenger side of the car. "I'll come 'round."

Jack hopped out and Brian took his place in the driver's seat.

The sidewalk teemed with life. Kids were everywhere, running and playing while elderly men and women sat in lawn chairs enjoying the remains of the day. Jack craned his neck to look for the man who might be Harry. Several adult males stood in front of the bodega. All of them checked him out as he approached.

"I'm looking for Harry. Anyone know him?" Jack asked the man nearest him.

"Don't know a Harry. He go by another name?" the man asked.

"I don't know. But he found a lost dog. Know anyone here who's found a black and gray stray dog?"

The man conferred with his friends. After a long moment, another adult male addressed Jack. "He's upstairs. Third floor on the right." He pointed to the doorway of the building whose ground floor was occupied by the bodega.

"Thanks." Jack walked to the building entrance then stopped. This could be a setup. Why wasn't Harry downstairs, as he'd said he'd be on the phone? Pulling out his cell, he hit the number for the second most recent incoming call after Hint's.

"Yeah?" a gruff voice answered.

"Harry?"

"Who is this?" the voice demanded.

"Jack Whitby. I'm here outside the store. Can you come down?"

"You the lost dog man?"

"Yes. Can you bring the dog with you?"

"Can't, mon. The dog's taken poorly. He's lying down. You come upstairs. Third floor. Wait on the landing."

"Listen, I can't. My car's double-parked. Can't you carry the dog downstairs?"

"He needs a doctor, man. A vet. You need to come up right away. Bring the reward."

Jack thought for a moment. He wasn't going up there by himself. Not without backup help like Brian O'Connell, ready and willing to get in on any action.

"I'll go park my car. Be up in a minute," he told the man called Harry.

Jack strode back to his car, full of purpose.

"Listen, we may or may not have a situation," he told Brian as he leaned into the driver's side window.

Brian's ears literally perked up. "What's up?"

"The guy's upstairs on the third floor. Says the dog's taken ill. He wants me to go up to meet him. With the reward."

"What reward?"

"I don't know. Hint mentioned a reward on the poster and the guy's been asking about it every other sentence."

"So that's how it is." Brian looked thoughtful. "Jump in. We'll park the car and go up there together."

"You sure?" Jack was relieved, but he still wanted to seem tough in front of Brian O'Connell.

"There's something fishy here. I can smell it."

"Yeah, let's hope not."

"We'll prepare for the worst and, uh, how's that line go?"

"Hope for the best."

"Yeah."

Circling the block, they found a parking spot that didn't look entirely legal, but it was a toss up between partially blocking a driveway or parking next to a hydrant. Jack guessed that the traffic cops around there had better things to do on a Friday evening than ticket him.

He made sure he locked the car after Brian got out. The chain in Brian's right front jeans pocket made a noticeable bulge. A small section of it hung out at the top.

As they approached the cluster of men in front of the bodega, Brian's stride slowed down to a swagger. Taking a cue, Jack imitated him, walking deliberately and solidly, as if he owned the sidewalk.

Pausing just outside the downstairs doorway, he caught Brian's eye. "Ready?" He gave the super a steely-eyed stare.

"Ready."

If the glance Brian returned him was any indication, he had chosen the right accomplice for the task ahead. His opinion of Brian O'Connell was improving by the second. He would hook him up with a nice girl as soon as he had a chance. Maybe Hint knew someone.

Jack entered first, Brian behind.

"Got your back, mate," the superintendent said in a low voice.

"It's my front I'm worried about," Jack shot back over his shoulder as they climbed the dank staircase.

At the third floor landing they stopped. A door stood on either side of the landing. Just as he was about to knock on the one nearest, it opened a crack. He listened as someone removed the inside door chain. A dog barked from inside. It didn't sound like Percy, but he wasn't one hundred percent sure.

"Yeah, mon?" A medium-tall ruggedly built man of about forty stepped out onto the landing. With a surly look on his face and a faint scar running vertically down one cheek, he looked like he hadn't lived an easy life.

"Hi. Jack Whitby. My friend, Brian." He gestured to his sidekick, who stepped forward, arms akimbo. Jack was sure he'd positioned his arms deliberately, to display well-defined biceps and triceps in the dim fluorescent overhead light of the stairwell.

"Yeah. The dog's inside. You come in." The man's eyes widened at the sight of Brian. "You stay here."

Jack caught Brian's eye. "That okay with you?"

"Like I said . . ."

"Okay." Brian had his back.

"You Harry?" Jack asked the stranger, just to make sure.

"That I am," Harry announced himself. He stepped into the apartment to make way for Jack.

Jack walked slowly into the hallway of the apartment. He hoped that behind him Brian had found a way to insert his foot into the doorjamb. To the left was a room with large windows. It was filled almost floor to ceiling with TV sets and stereo equipment, including CD players and speakers. There were dozens of unopened boxes. Then he spotted a large cutout box in one corner. An animal lay in it, covered with a dirty blanket. It's sides heaved in and out as if breathing alone was an effort.

Jack gingerly approached.

"Percy? Is that you, boy?" He hunkered down in front of the box, leaning over the dog. In the dim light, he could barely make out the lines of its body.

The dog growled softly.

Jack wasn't about to put his hand anywhere near the canine. He peered at him closely, trying to remember what Hint had said about ears and the tail.

"That your dog?" Harry asked, behind him.

"I, uh, just a minute." Jack examined the animal as closely as it would allow. It growled again, faintly.

The dog appeared to be more gray than black. It had a long, mangy coat, with what looked like wiry, curly hair. Jack thought it might be a terrier, rather than a Schnoodle. But he wasn't sure. He looked at the ears.

They were intact. Both stood straight up. Hadn't Hint said something about one of Percy's lopping over?

"You don't know your own dog, mon?" Harry sounded annoyed.

"Does this dog have a tail?" Jack asked.

"He's got a tail. It's under there somewhere."

"Can I see it?" Jack asked.

"See for yourself, mon."

Jack wasn't taking any chances on touching the dog. It appeared to be injured and in no mood to be handled by a stranger. He sat back on his heels, thinking a moment. As usual, his mind wandered back to Hint. Then he remembered the liver treats she'd given him. He pulled one out of his pocket.

"Here, boy. Look what I've got for you." He dangled the savory-smelling treat over the dog's head.

The canine perked up instantly, sniffing above him. Jack moved back his hand. The dog's nose stretched toward the treat. Struggling, it got up.

Jack put the treat on the floor, about two feet away from the dog. It slowly limped toward the source of the good smell. A long wiry-haired tail appeared at the hind end of the canine.

"It's not him." Jack stood up, disappointed but relieved.

"You sure?" Harry studied Jack, as if assessing him.

"Yeah. The dog I'm looking for doesn't have a tail."

"So that's it, then?"

"I'm afraid so. This isn't Percy."

"And what am I supposed to do with this one, then?"

"Keep trying to locate its owner. And feed it. It looks really hungry."

"Feed it with what, mon? I can barely feed myself, never mind the dog."

Jack wondered if he should suggest taking the dog to a shelter or animal hospital. Wouldn't they just euthanize an animal as badly injured as this one if no one claimed it? He shuddered.

"Look, you did the right thing to pick him up off the road. You saved his life. See it through, man. Someone is going to be really grateful to you when you hook them up with their dog."

"That's then and this is now. I need help feeding him now. I got no more money to look after him."

Jack reached into his pocket and fished a twenty-dollar bill from his wallet. He was careful not to pull out the wallet itself.

"Here. Use this to buy some baby food to feed him until he feels better." He'd remembered the tip from his childhood, when his neighbor's dog had gotten hit by a car. Jack had helped them spoon-feed the dog from baby food jars of pureed vegetables and meat until it had gotten stronger.

"That won't do it, mon. He needs to go to a vet."

"Listen, this isn't my dog. I wish I could help you, but I can't." Jack's scam radar went off. It was time to go.

"What's going on there?" Brian O'Connell's voice called out. As he had hoped, Brian had had the good sense to plant his foot in the doorway to the apartment while he had checked out the dog.

"It's not Percy, but Harry wants a contribution," Jack announced, his voice gruff.

"You want a contribution? For what?" Brian asked the man.

"For my time," Harry snapped back.

"It's not our dog," Jack protested.

"The dog's going to die, mon, if it don't get help. I can't take care of it no more."

"That's too bad. It's not our dog." Brian repeated Jack's words, glaring. Then he turned to Jack. "Let's get out of here."

Suddenly, two men appeared in the passageway from the kitchen. The shorter one addressed Harry with a question Jack couldn't make out.

Harry's back was to Jack, as he murmured something to them. Both men silently eyed Jack and Brian. Slowly, they began to move down the hallway towards them, the shorter one leading the way.

"Give me something more for the dog," Harry demanded.

"Look, I gave you something already. It's not my dog." Jack edged towards the door, every muscle in his body alert and twitching. He sensed Brian beside him, twitching too. A strange, cloying smell permeated the air around him. Was it the smell of cooking drugs? He didn't really know. But then he smelled something else. It was the smell of his own fear: cortisol, more commonly known as a cold sweat. He was in one now.

In less than the blink of an eye, pandemonium ensued. The shorter man reached for Jack and grabbed him around the neck, slamming him up against the wall. Brian O'Connell's fist shot out, punching Jack's attacker in the face. Enraged, the shorter man released Jack and went after Brian.

Jack didn't really know what happened next. Suddenly, a Fourth of July fireworks display exploded in shades of red and orange inside his head. When he opened his eyes the taller man was pinning back his arms while Harry went for his front jeans pocket. They were clearly about to relieve him of his wallet. Jack kicked out as hard as he could.

"Aargh." The tall man crumpled over in pain.

With a distinctive snap, a switchblade flashed open in Harry's hand. Looking wildly for the door, Jack spotted it and ran. "Run!" he yelled.

Brian shot out behind him and together they sprinted down the stairs and stumbled out onto the street.

"Don't stop. Just get to the car," Brian shouted.

Throngs of people looked on as they raced down the sidewalk. Jack couldn't tell if they were being pursued, but he doubted it, with all the potential witnesses on the street. He fished in his pocket for his car keys, hitting the remote button to unlock the doors.

Jumping in the driver's seat, he rammed the key in the ignition. A second later Brian hopped in and slammed his door shut. Immediately, Jack hit the lockdown button, relief coursing through him as he heard the locks click down.

He gunned the engine and backed up, then peeled away from the curb. Kids playing ball in the street jumped to either side to let them pass. As they sped past the bodega, Harry and his henchmen threw something at the car. It hit the back with a loud thud. No doubt there would be a dent, an impressive souvenir of their adventure that evening.

The light was turning yellow at the corner, but Jack gunned through it, wheels squealing as he took a right up the Grand Concourse. He weaved his way through traffic, changing lanes like a New York City cab driver. Within minutes, they were on the Mosholu Parkway on their way back to Westchester County.

"Close call, man," Brian grunted.

"Shit. That was a shakedown. You okay?" Jack glanced at the super. Thank God for Brian O'Connell.

"Yeah. I got dusted up, but I'm fine." Brian studied the side of Jack's face. "You've got a shiner, man."

"No way." Jack glanced in the rearview mirror. His right eye was swollen shut, with a nasty red and purple bruise underneath it. "Whoa," he exclaimed.

"You need some ice on that right away."

"You got your wallet?" Jack asked.

Brian patted his pockets. "Yup. All here. What were those bastards thinking of?"

Jack patted his front pockets with one hand, locating his wallet. He remembered the slimy feel of Harry's hands on his jeans pocket. Banging on the steering wheel, he imagined it was the man's head. "Thanks again for getting my back, man. I owe you one," he told Brian.

"No worries, mate," the brawny superintendent replied.

They drove the rest of the way back in companionable silence.

HINT TRIED TO make good use of her time while the men checked out the lead in the South Bronx. She wandered down to the dog run, then circled around Bronxville, whistling and calling for Percy, not caring how odd she looked to the passersby on the sidewalk. Fingering the remaining dog treats she had in her pocket, she pulled them out from time to time, hoping the smell would attract the Schnoodle.

The thought that Jack had overheard her cousin's message on her answering machine gnawed at her. She would clear it up with him as soon as he got back. Kim had a way of implying things that rivaled Brian O'Connell.

Once it was dark, she decided to go home. This would be a good time to review her drawings in preparation for the meeting with Derek Simpson the following day.

Back in her apartment, she pulled out the portfolio she had already packed for Punta Cana. Would her choices look as good to her now that the meeting would take place in New York City? She covered her work desk with all twenty illustrations she had chosen to show the head of Story Tales Press. Looking them over, she took out a few, leaving only the best. Now all she needed to do was pick out something to wear.

But her conscience stopped her. Jack was actively looking for Percy at that moment. So was Brian O'Connell. She should be focusing on Percy too. Quickly gathering up her drawings, she stuffed them back into her portfolio. Then she laid out a large blank sheet of drawing paper on her desk and picked up a pen. Perhaps if she could visualize the dog, she could find him.

Humming to herself, she shut her eyes tightly and imagined the Schnoodle. Soon her hand began to move over the sheet. Within five minutes, she had conjured up Percy's affectionate and intelligent personality in the image she'd created. There he sat—bedraggled, forlorn and looking for love. His large, expressive brown eyes stared mournfully at the viewer.

She would add this drawing to the ones she'd show Derek Simpson the following day.

She looked at her watch. It was now half past nine and the men were not yet back. Dialing Jack's cell phone, she got his voicemail.

She stepped out on her balcony, breathing in the summer night sky. Only two hours earlier, Jack had kissed her for the first time. Her body was afire, but guilt reined her in at the thought of the still lost dog.

The buzzer for the downstairs door interrupted her thoughts.

Dashing inside, she pressed it, then went out into the hallway. Brian came up the stairs first. He looked scruffy and sweaty.

"Any luck?" she asked.

"Nope. It wasn't him," Brian replied, giving her a wide smile.

Then Jack came into view.

"Oh, my God. What happened to you?" Rushing to Jack, she brushed past Brian as if he were a dried-up dog treat.

"Just a little dustup," Jack replied. She saw his eyes light up as she put her hand to the side of his face.

"Who punched you? Let's get some ice on it." She hung onto his arm, looking closely for more cuts and bruises.

"We had a scuffle," Brian began, as they trooped into her apartment.

"Harry turned out to have some friends," Jack added, leaning heavily on Hint's kitchen counter.

"I can't believe it. Wasn't this guy a good Samaritan, taking home a lost dog?" She shook her head disbelievingly as she studied Jack's eye.

"He was, more or less, but when he asked for money to help him feed the dog, he didn't like what I gave him."

"You gave him money, then he beat you up?" she asked, astonished.

"I guess he thought a twenty wouldn't do it. The dog was injured. And seemed hungry."

"But he wasn't your dog. What did this guy think you were supposed to do about it?"

"Sweetie, it had nothing to do with the dog. He had no money. I had some. It was more or less a social leveling experiment that didn't work out."

Had he just called her sweetie? Blushing, she moved into the kitchen to retrieve one of the ice packs she kept in the freezer for occasional sore muscles after a jog. Jack had called her 'sweetie.' It had sounded so natural. She hoped Brian O'Connell would start doing some math and figure out that one plus one did not make three. But he had just helped Jack get out of a lot of trouble. She couldn't thank him then bid him goodnight right away, could she?

"Hey, you got anything to drink around here? It's been quite an evening," Brian asked, as if reading her mind.

"Let me look," she said, going over to the cabinet containing her best glassware. She pulled out two brandy snifters. Then she reached into the back of the cabinet, retrieving a small bottle of cognac that someone had gifted her with the Christmas before. "You guys ready for a shot? Or would you prefer a cold beer?"

"Both," Jack and Brian answered simultaneously. They looked like members of a returning army. Thankfully the battle had been victorious.

"I can't believe what happened," she exclaimed, pouring out a small amount in the bottom of each glass then handing them each a snifter. "Tell me everything from the moment you got there."

The next half hour was spent in reliving the entire story, Brian striding up and down Hint's living room, and Jack semi-reclining on her couch, with her holding the ice pack over one side of his face. She liked the feel of Jack's warm arm under her hand as she leaned over him. Something told her he was as mindful of their recent kiss as she was.

Finally, Brian's beer bottle stood empty. He got up and before he could go into the kitchen to look for another, Hint headed him off.

"Sorry, guys, I think that was the last of the beer. Brian, thank you so much for going with Jack." She moved to the door, preparing to open it.

"Thanks for covering my back. Who knows what would have happened if I'd been there alone," Jack added. He looked sincerely grateful.

"You don't go wandering down to the South Bronx alone, mate. We both know that," Brian replied.

"You need to rest," she told Jack. Then she looked Brian O'Connell squarely in the face. "And you need to go home." There were limits to her gratefulness for his heroic services. It was time to make it clear which man was staying and which would be leaving. With someone like her superintendent, it was important to be as direct as possible.

Brian looked begrudged for a moment, then recovered himself.

"Goodnight, Hint. Let me know if you need any more help tomorrow." He glanced at Jack as if he wanted to even up the purplish bruise with another one on the other side of his face.

"I will. Goodnight." Sucking in her breath, she forced herself to touch his arm and literally pull him to the door. There was no other way to get him out of her apartment. With a final light push, she propelled him through the door and into the hallway. About to close the door, she was prevented by his hand resting on the doorjamb. His face conspiratorial, he leaned toward her.

"He's not your boyfriend, is he?" he whispered.

Hint recalled her new axiom: never complain, never explain.

"Good night, Brian." She gave him a tight-lipped smile as she firmly removed his hand from the doorjamb and shut the door in his face.

10

NEW DEVELOPMENTS

Jack heaved a sigh of relief as Hint locked the door behind Brian O'Connell.

"He came in handy, didn't he?" She reached out to touch his face as she sat down on the side of the couch next to him.

"He did. Without him, I would have been dead meat. Or at least minus my wallet." Thank God he'd had his wallet and car keys in the front pocket of his jeans. He reached around her waist with his right hand, sliding her closer to him on the couch.

"You deserve a shower after what you've been through," she told him, tracing the outline of his shiner with her finger.

"What, you don't like smelly guys?" He had to smile at her veiled suggestion.

"It depends on which smelly guy."

"This one?"

"Yes. But I'll like you even more when you're less smelly. Why don't you use my shower?"

"Sure." He was eager to find out what she meant by that remark. He looked down at his blood and dirt stained tee-shirt. Too bad he didn't have a change of clothes with him.

"I'll get you a towel." She disappeared down the hallway to where he guessed her bedroom and bathroom were. "You're all set," she called to him a minute later. "I put a yellow towel on the rack for you."

He heard her pad back into the living room. Looking down he saw maroon, velvet slippers on her feet with soft, feathery pink puffs of fabric on top. He'd never seen anything more sublimely feminine in his life. He hoped she hadn't been wearing them when Brian O'Connell had been there. Then he recalled she'd been barefoot when she'd run out to meet them in the hallway.

"Where do I go?" he asked.

"It's at the end of the hall."

In a minute, he'd found the bathroom, but not before taking a peek into the half-open doorway of Hint's bedroom along the way. Glancing inside, his eyes roamed over a forest of green and purple, before resting on the double bed. Its carved headboard appeared to be mahogany, with posts at either end. Reining in his thoughts, he continued on to the bathroom, where he quickly peeled off his jeans and tee-shirt.

The hot water felt great. He marveled at the bottles, lotions, jars and sea anemone-shaped washcloths in the bathroom. How did women figure out what to do with all these products? His own shower stall contained one bar of green soap and a plastic jug of all-in-one shampoo and conditioner.

Then he noticed a small, black object hanging on the back of the shower stall. A thong. The laciest, smallest, sexiest thong he'd ever seen. His imagination ran wild as he soaped up with pink gel he'd squeezed out of a bottle labeled 'Beauty Rush' in large silver script with sparkles on it. The smell of bubblegum wafted into his nostrils. He would be a regular Barbie doll by the time he re-entered the living room.

"Hey, can I ask one more favor?" he called out, opening the bathroom door a crack.

"Sure. What do you need?" Hint called back.

"Do you have a bathrobe or something I could borrow? I don't want to put on my sweaty clothes again until I leave." He didn't mean to imply anything. But if she thought he did, he hoped she was receptive.

"Hang on. I'll get you something." In a minute she knocked on the bathroom door.

He opened it a crack. Two amused brown eyes met his.

" I've got a pink one or a purple one."

"I see. The princess line."

"Yes. Do you want the one with the fur-trimmed collar or the fluffy pink one?"

"I'll take the one most fit for a prince."

"Good choice. Here's the purple. As she handed the robe through the doorway, she closed her eyes. Deciding to take advantage of the moment, he picked up a glitzy spray scent bottle marked "Cucumber Melon Fresh" on the shelf next to the sink and squirted it at her neck.

"Hey? What was that for?" She blinked in surprise.

"I don't want to be the only one smelling like a teen princess around here," Jack explained as melon fragrance wafted over them. It was fresh, light, a bit exotic. Like her.

"Get dressed and stop playing with my stuff," she ordered, slamming shut the bathroom door.

Judging by the sparkle in her eyes, he didn't think she was too upset.

Quickly, he put on the purple bathrobe. The faux fur trim tickled the hair on his chest as he struggled to stretch the robe over his body. How did women survive femininity? Glancing at himself in the mirror, he winced. The shiner was now purple and black, his left eye red in the far corner of the sclera. Not a pretty sight.

He walked back to the living room to the sounds of Latin music. A female voice was half-singing, half-whispering to a bossa nova beat. Her voice stroked his ears the way he hoped Hint's hand would soon stroke his face.

"Do you want something else to drink?" Hint asked.

"I thought you said you're out of beer."

"I am. But I've got other drinks."

"Like what?"

"Come look." She steered him to her kitchen, where she opened the same glass cabinet from whence she'd retrieved the brandy bottle and snifters. He rifled through its contents.

Jägermeister? The weather was too warm for cold-weather schnapps. Cognac? Too heavy. Amaretto, the drink for lovers? Promising.

"Shall we?" He lifted the bottle of almond liqueur, hoping she'd notice the illustration of the man and woman embracing on the label.

"Oh, I don't think I'll have any."

"I won't have any unless you will."

"Well, only a drop," she relented.

Jack poured a healthy swig of amaretto into one snifter and another for himself. He rummaged through her refrigerator for seltzer. Hint took down two water glasses from the cabinet and dropped in some ice. Jack followed her back to the living room, adjusting the dimmer with his right elbow until the recessed lights gave off only the faintest glow.

She stared at him, examining his bruised eye critically.

"It's a mess, isn't it?" he remarked, pleased to be admired for his battle scars.

"Let's put that ice pack back on," she answered, motioning for him to sit back against the couch cushions.

Soon the ice pack lay on the living room floor, abandoned. Jack had found Hint's mouth again. The almond flavor of amaretto mingled deliciously with her even more tantalizing melon scent. After so many days, his longing for her had reached fever pitch.

Jack adjusted his position on the couch, trying to conceal her effect on him, which was fast becoming obvious. He wanted her like no other woman he had ever known. The way she kissed him back told him she wanted him too. But there was the question of who she was planning to meet in Manhattan the next day and why. He would ask in a moment. But for now, he was enmeshed in a cocoon of warm, mind-blowing bliss.

Hint wove her fingers into the hair on his chest at the top of his bathrobe. Dare he hope she'd order him to take it off?

"I'll be right back," she murmured, disappearing into her bedroom.

He sprinted to the kitchen to refill their glasses and get more ice. Flicking on the overhead light, he couldn't help but notice the words scrawled on a notepad on the counter.

Algonquin lobby lounge, 7 p.m. Sat. Derek Simpson.

He flicked off the light. Who was this guy? As much as he wanted to know he didn't want to spoil the moment.

Returning to the living room with the refilled brandy snifters, he lay down on the couch to wait.

A door shut, followed by light footsteps. Hint turned the corner and stood before him in pink sweat shorts and a sleeveless pink tee-shirt with spaghetti straps. It was sexy. But nowhere near as sexy as the luminous, golden-skinned woman wearing it.

"You're beautiful." He wanted to salute her. If he wasn't careful, he would, without using his hands. Inhaling slowly, he squelched his thoughts.

"How's my pink panther look?" She slid her hands down either side of her shorts. "Thought I'd get comfortable."

"I like you in it." He admired the tight tone of her lightly tanned thighs.

"I like you in purple," she remarked.

"You do? Why?" He couldn't think, dazzled by the gold and pink of her.

"I just do," she answered, stepping closer. She grabbed the fur-trimmed collar of his robe.

He liked assertiveness in a woman. Very much. Even better, her line had been as lame as his. Theirs was a match made in heaven. He reached down, lifting her off her feet. They were now eye to eye.

"Explain yourself, woman," he demanded, his voice low.

Her hands on his shoulders, she said nothing, staring at him with liquid eyes. He pressed his mouth onto hers, as he lowered her feet to the floor. With splayed hands, he encircled her waist, his fingers inching downward over the pink fleece of her shorts, exploring the terra firma of her cello-shaped hinterlands. He'd always wanted to play.

She nestled against him as they dropped down onto the couch, her soft contours melting into his chest. His hands explored the landscape of her slim, sinuous body. First, he traced the right side of her torso up to her warm, smooth armpit. Then he traversed her belly, finding the indent of her navel. Next, he pressed his hand on her hipbone as his thumb rhythmically stroked the crease between torso and leg. She shivered beneath him. The tick of the grandfather clock in the corner of the room marked off seconds, each of which brought him to the edge of a new boundary and Hint to a moment of decision.

His bruised eye forgotten, he entered a world composed entirely of sensation. Hint was clear about where she wanted him to go and what she wanted him to do. He hadn't yet seen this side of her. From fairy girl she had metamorphosed into fairy queen as master of the expedition they were now on. She would call the shots and determine which slopes were ski-able and which were off-piste. He had never been so turned on in his life.

HINT HADN'T THOUGHT of her pink panther sweats and tee-shirt as anything but something comfortable to change into after a long day. She hadn't worn them around a man before, so she wasn't prepared for Jack's reaction. They'd moved in a direction she hadn't anticipated. But now that they were there, inspiration struck.

"Lie back and close your eyes," she ordered. "I'll be right back."

Jack grunted his assent.

She went to the kitchen. Opening the refrigerator freezer, she extracted a slim box wrapped in a sealed bag. From it she took out a tightly folded silk scarf. Holding it up to her nose, she breathed in its lavender scent. She would use her favorite method to rid herself of occasional headaches to take Jack's mind off his injury this evening. She returned to the living room, flicking the cool, scented scarf at her side like a matador's cape.

Reaching Jack, she ran her fingers over his eyelids. He shut them obediently.

"Lift up your head," she whispered.

He complied. Quickly, she wrapped the long scarf just above his nose, making sure she didn't hurt his bruised eye. She tied the ends firmly in back. Then she placed his head back down on the pillows.

"Wow," escaped from his lips.

"Breathe in the lavender. It will help heal your eye," She leaned into his ear, tickling it with her tongue as she spoke. "I promise it will make you feel better."

"What black eye?" His hands reached for her.

She sighed, her body relaxing into his.

"You're right. I feel better," he continued, stroking the length of her back.

"That's nice," she whispered. Then she breathed a large but restrained exhalation of warm air into his ear.

"What's nice?" he asked, his voice barely discernible.

"You are," she murmured into his ear, pressing the entirety of her body against his, her hands on either side of his face. Through the silk she nipped his earlobe.

Jack's body jerked. His arms squeezed her in a viselike grip as he groaned unintelligibly. In a second, he had twisted out from under her and was now over her, his eyes blindfolded, his mouth seeking hers.

"Slow down, Jack."

"You're perfect. Every part of you," he breathed.

"I'm not perfect. And neither are you. I'm not expecting you to be."

"Great. Let's not talk."

"I don't want to talk either, but you need to know something."

"What is it?" His body shifted back.

"It's not what you think."

"Nothing about you has been what I've thought," he said.

"Just lie back and breathe in the lavender," she told him. "Keep your blindfold on."

"What is it I need to know?"

"I need time before we can be together." Relief flooded over her to state the truth.

"I already knew that," he said, surprising her.

"How could you?"

"Because I'm getting to know you," he answered.

"Well, I want you to keep on getting to know me."

"Me too." He hand slid over her throat then downward.

"Going too far, too fast has a way of interfering with people getting to know each other," she observed, stopping his hand.

"You think too much."

"I feel too much too sometimes."

"I really want to be with you," he breathed out.

"I want to be with you, too. But I don't want to be wondering when you're going to call, a week from now," she declared, glad to get her thoughts out in the open while she was still capable of thinking.

"That's not going to happen."

"It happens all the time."

"It won't." His voice was firm, along with his hand, now stroking the skin of her back where it met the underside of her right arm.

"It's better to wait." She gently moved his hand down to her waist. "So when we do really get together we'll know it's for real," she said.

"It's for real, Hint." His voice was muffled, his face buried in her hair.

"Only time will tell. So let's give it some more," she replied. She hoped he wasn't getting the wrong idea. There was no way she wanted to stop. But her gut told her it was too soon to proceed. She didn't want the possibility of love stampeded over by the hastiness of lust. She held her breath as she waited for his reaction to her words.

A deep sigh ensued. Slowly, the entire length of his long, muscular body trembled and shifted.

"Just show me where you want me to touch you," he finally said.

"My pleasure," she replied, guiding his hand with hers.

"Is mine," he added, following her lead.

JACK WOKE UP late the following morning. He was on Hint's couch, a white summer blanket draped over him. Turning over, he spotted something on the floor next to him. He picked it up. The scent of lavender from the long, purple and dark green silk scarf flooded his senses with memories of the night before. He buried his face in it.

Jumping up, he headed to the bathroom. Hint's lacy black thong was nowhere to be seen. Was she wearing it now?

He splashed cold water over his face to douse further speculation then dried off with a towel that smelled of her stargazer lily fragrance, instantly igniting him again.

Shaking his head to clear his thoughts, he exited the bathroom and found her bedroom door. About to knock, he paused. She drank coffee in the morning. He could prove to her how handy it might be to have him around by making a pot now.

Within ten minutes, he returned to Hint's bedroom door, two steaming coffee mugs in hand. He had had some trouble locating the coffee filters under the counter; he hoped she'd give him points for finding them. With his foot, he lightly tapped the door twice. "Room service," he announced.

The handle clicked and the door slowly opened inward. Hint stood before him, fully dressed in jeans and a maroon tee-shirt with ruffles at the top of each sleeve. How was it that the tee-shirts some girls wore looked so unlike those that guys wore? Like the pink one she'd worn the night before.

"You look refreshed, my lady," he told her, gingerly stepping into the bedroom as he tried not to spill coffee on the cream-colored rug.

"I am. I slept well. Did you?" she asked, taking one of the mugs from him and critically looking at his eye. She sat down at her vanity table.

Mysterious unidentifiable objects, bottles, jars and hair ornaments decorated its glass surface. He was at a loss for words, even inside his brain, looking at the collection of feminine paraphernalia. He'd ask his sister Bibi to help him with some basic vocabulary if he ever got a chance to spend more time in this room.

"Great. More than great," he breathed out, unsure of what he was commenting on. Then he remembered she had asked how he'd slept.

She nodded to him, taking a sip from her mug.

"Mmm. Nice and strong. Thanks," she approved. A wisp of a smile curled her mouth into the cupid's bow whose arrows had already found their mark. She reached out and lightly stroked the area around his shiner.

"Methinks my lady looks well in pink," he remarked, folding his fingers around her wrist.

"You looked good in purple and green," she said.

"I did?" He'd been wearing a white tee-shirt the evening before. Then he recalled the lavender-scented scarf. "You liked me in your scarf, huh? Do you think I could wear it again?" He took a sip of coffee, surprised at how well it had turned out.

"We'll see." She gave him a quixotic look. "Let's figure out our plan for today."

She looked like a fresh-faced teenager, sitting across from him. How could the same woman have tied him up with a silk scarf just eight hours earlier?

"So what's our Saturday schedule?" he asked. Suddenly, he recalled the message on her answering machine of the night before. Would she be traveling into Manhattan that evening? Without him? His thoughts turned dark.

"Maybe we should go back to Tom and Nicole's neighborhood and really scour the area," she suggested, breaking into his reverie.

"We can drive over to Scarsdale, spend a few hours, and then—" he remembered their promise to Marguerite, "—drop by my sister's place to catch the end of Marguerite's birthday party."

"What time is the party?" Hint's eyes crinkled at the corners as she smiled.

"It's from two to four." He remembered what his sister had told him about eye crinkling when a woman smiles. It meant the smile was a real one, not a fake one where just the mouth smiles. A good sign.

"I'd love to go, but . . ."

"But what?" Jack waited expectantly.

"Well, I guess I can, if I take a train no later than six. I've got to hop into Manhattan for something early this evening.

Something? What did she mean by something? It was like all of those somethings on her vanity table and in her bathroom. The complete mystery of Hint Daniels shut him out once again.

"Will you be back later?" he asked.

"I . . . I should be back by nine at the latest." Her expression remained neutral.

"Oh." He took another slug of coffee. Was it studiedly neutral? He hoped not. One Annabel Sanford in a lifetime, with her machinations and made-up stories, had been enough. "Can we get together when you get back?"

"We could . . ." Her eyes were averted now, the coffee mug hiding her mouth. A bad sign.

"How about if you give me a call from the train once you're heading home, and I pick you up at the station?" he asked casually.

She looked at him levelly then spoke. "That would be nice." She glanced at her watch. "It's past ten already. Give me five minutes and we'll move out."

"I'll be in the living room." That would be nice, all right. A repeat of the night before would be so nice, he almost couldn't bear to imagine it. He tried not to and failed as he waited for her to get ready for their final full day of dog hunting.

On his way to the living room, he dumped the rest of his coffee in the kitchen sink, glancing again at the notepad on the counter. *Algonquin lobby lounge, 7 p.m. Sat. Derek Simpson.* The words taunted him. He needed to know who and what Derek Simpson was to her, before the day was done.

11

LITTLE GIRL WISDOM

Five hours later, they had combed the area near Tom and Nicole's house then watered their friends' backyard plants and bushes. They were now on their way to Marguerite's house, to catch the end of her birthday party, as promised.

Jack glanced sidelong at Hint as he drove. Would she leave him behind in the dust after tonight's meeting with whoever Derek Simpson was? He was probably the sort of man who wouldn't lose a dog. Gripping the steering wheel, he mentally throttled his rival.

"Whatever you're thinking I'm thinking, I'm not," Hint spoke up, reading his mind.

"You're not? How do you know?" She was a cipher, with a way of saying things that made his heart leap, even when he didn't understand her meaning. He hadn't enjoyed being confused by a woman before. But with Hint, he welcomed the deepening of her mystery. Was it because he trusted her? He hoped he would feel the same way the next day, after her excursion into Manhattan that evening.

"I'm guessing. But I think I'm right."

"Do you mean you aren't going to hate me if we don't find Percy before Tom and Nic get back?" he asked.

"No, Jack, I won't hate you. They're going to be angry with both you and me. We're in this together."

"Aren't you going to secretly blame me?" Women did that, didn't they? Except that Annabel Sanford hadn't been secretive when she'd blamed him for just about everything. Having attention deficit disorder when it came to her, for starters.

"Jack, women secretly blame men for things all the time. There's nothing unusual about that."

"That wasn't exactly the answer I was hoping for." He had to give her points for admitting what he already suspected about her sex.

"That was the real answer. I'll be secretly blaming you for lots of other things too."

"Like what?"

"If I tell you, it won't be a secret anymore."

Suddenly, he understood feminine logic. It was logical, but sort of like fighting dirty. A man never knew what kind of weaponry the other side was using.

"It's better if I don't hear, anyway, right?" How could he defend himself against her? Better to lay down arms, hold out his own and hope she'd walk into them.

"Exactly." The impish smile that lit up her face launched another arrow straight into his heart.

She'd been talking in the present tense. About the future. About the dumb things women do to the men with whom they're involved. It didn't sound like she was planning to disappear from his life.

"Let me ask you something," he said.

"What's that?" Her finger stopped winding the tendril of hair at the side of her face.

Taking a deep breath, he bit the bullet.

"Who is this guy you're going to meet this evening?"

"Oh. Him." Her voice was steady. "He's someone I was supposed to meet in Punta Cana."

Her hair hid her face. Unfair.

"Uh-huh." So far, not reassuring.

"He . . . I . . . I had a meeting set up with him for Thursday, which I couldn't make." She looked over at him. "As you know."

"Yes. I prevented you from making it."

"No. Percy did. But anyway, he's coming to New York today and my cousin has set it up for me to meet him at seven."

"Huh." Was this supposed to be an explanation? Her inarticulateness seemed less charming to him than it had earlier that day.

"I mean—it's business. I've been trying to get his attention for more than a year now."

"You have? What do you mean by business?" He gave her a level look, then locked his eyes back on the road.

"He's seen parts of my portfolio. And he's interested. I need to show him the rest."

"Huh." The car swerved ever so slightly under his unsteady hands on the steering wheel. He'd seen parts of Hint's portfolio too. And he was extremely interested to see the rest. As well as to not let any other guy see it. "What exactly do you mean by your portfolio?" he asked, trying to keep his cool.

"My drawings. You know, my fairy illustrations. Gnomes, elves, fairies—that sort of thing."

"Ohhh . . ." He let out a long exhalation. "Of course."

What a moron he was. She was a professional illustrator. What kind of portfolio had he thought she'd been talking about? There he was, reducing the woman of his interest to a sex object. He was no better than the next guy.

"He's the head of Story Tales Press. It's the biggest children's book publisher in the world. It's based in the UK and I've been trying to get in with them for a long time."

"I get you," he said with relief. "So this is your shot at the big time, right?" He turned into his sister's driveway.

"Right. And I apologize for taking a few hours off from looking for Percy, but I need to catch him before he leaves town. He's British and he almost never comes to New York."

"Don't worry, I'll hunt for the hound. You get your drawings in front of this guy. Once he sees them, he's going to hire you." *And once he sees you, he's going to want you.* But that was ridiculous. Were all men animals? Only some of them, some of the time. He yanked up the sun visor, knocking it ajar.

Shutting off the engine, he turned to her in his seat. Her crestfallen expression startled him. His heart skipped a beat as he took in her sad eyes.

"It'll be our last night to find Percy. Our last chance before Tom and Nicole get back," she sighed dejectedly.

"Don't worry, Hint. We'll find him." He wanted to hug her, but his mind told him to proceed cautiously until after her meeting with the Englishman later that day. He was glad to see she was thinking about the dog instead of the British twit. Then he pushed away further unreasonable thoughts and leapt out of the car to open the passenger door.

"UNCLE JACK, WHAT happened to your eye?" Marguerite shrieked, the moment she saw him.

Hint stepped to one side to make way for Jack to embrace his niece, who had torn herself away from a gaggle of small girls playing musical chairs.

"Sweetie, it's nothing. I just got hit. Happy birthday, Maggie May!" He lifted the little girl up over his head as she giggled and screamed, her gaze fixed on the black and blue shiner on the left side of his face.

"Is that a black eye? Who gave it to you? Did Annabel do that because you yelled at her for canceling our Broadway date?"

Hint couldn't help but laugh. She could well imagine the likes of the patrician blonde she'd studied the day before, hauling off and smacking a man who'd ruffled her feathers. Had his ex ever hit him? She'd guess if she had, it might have been for bringing the wrong color flowers or dressing inappropriately for some society event she had arranged for them to attend. But what had Marguerite meant by Annabel canceling their Broadway show date? She watched Jack raise an eyebrow at his sister before bending down to address his niece.

"No, Peanut, it wasn't a woman who did this to me. It was a—" he paused dramatically"—a bad guy."

"A real life bad guy? Wow. How did you meet him? Did you beat him up?" As Marguerite quizzed her uncle, her parents came out to greet them.

Jack's sister Bibi silently appraised his injury, then greeted Hint. "Hi, how are you? Did my brother get fresh with you?"

"Not exactly." Hint laughed, the heat rising in her face. It hadn't just been Jack who'd gotten out of hand the evening before, thinking of the purple and green scarf. Au contraire.

"Let's put an ice pack on that. Matt?" Bibi turned to her husband, who was studying Jack's face. He looked impressed. "Can you get the ice pack from the freezer?"

Matt returned momentarily with an ice pack in the shape of a bunny rabbit.

"That's my boo boo rabbit," Marguerite told her uncle.

"Thank you, Funny Bunny. Now get back to your games. I want to see who wins musical chairs."

Marguerite turned back to her friends as her father started the music again.

Jack sat down on a folding chair lined up against the wall and motioned to Hint to join him. She sat, automatically taking the ice pack from his hands and pressing it against his left temple. Out of the corner of her eye, she saw Marguerite's mother give her husband a significant look. In a minute, Bibi came over to Jack.

"What's this I hear about Marguerite's date to go see a Broadway show getting canceled?" Hint heard him ask his sister.

"Actually, it's not canceled," Bibi said. "It's just that Annabel can't make the date. She called this morning to say something had come up and she'd be out of town on the date she got the tickets for." She shrugged her shoulders, giving Jack a look as if to say 'what did you expect'?

"Why would she buy tickets for a date she couldn't make?"

"She said something totally unexpected had happened. Or maybe she used another word."

"Let me guess." Jack sounded sour. "Something marvelous?"

"Exactly. How did you know?" Bibi rolled her eyes. "She said something marvelous had happened and an opportunity had come up she couldn't pass on."

Jack snorted derisively. "Of course you asked what it was," he continued, knowing his sister would have pressed for details.

"Well, yes. I did. It was more or less girl talk. You don't care, do you?"

"No. I don't," he said, enunciating each word clearly. "But I'll bet Marguerite does. What did you tell her was the reason she canceled?"

"Well, I didn't exactly say. I just told her someone else would be taking her instead."

"So what *is* the reason?" he asked.

Hint sucked in her breath. Jack seemed a little too interested to know the details of his ex-girlfriend's social life not to care. She steeled herself for whatever lay ahead.

"She said she'd been invited to the Love Heals AIDS benefit in the Hamptons and it was a must-do event," Bibi told him.

"I'm surprised she wasn't already going," he commented.

"She said she'd wanted to, but when she got back from Europe in April, it was already sold out."

"Give me a break." Jack's mouth curled up at the corners, as if laughing at some sort of private joke.

Suddenly, the image of the man at the Stanhope the afternoon before flashed through Hint's head. Was it possible that the man she had steered to the arresting blonde had invited her to the high society event? She pictured Annabel in her red dress, tail feathers drooping, in need of a diversion from just having had her ego crushed. Not only possible, but likely. Careful to keep a neutral expression, she caught Jack's eye.

"Something funny?" she inquired.

"Just history repeating itself," he said.

"Yours?" She couldn't help asking. She needed to know. If it was time to re-route her emotions, she had done it before. But with Jack, already she knew the time it would take to get over him would be far longer than the actual time they had known each other.

"No." He looked directly at her. "Not mine. Some else's who's no longer a part of mine."

His answer was clear. If she'd learned anything from the past, she knew the only way to move forward was not to drag it into the present and lasso it around the neck of a brand new relationship. Loosening the noose, she pulled it off. Then she sat back and took a deep breath. She wanted to hear what Jack had to say and not some chorus line of ghostly Tims drowning out her ability to evaluate his words objectively. Not all men were like her ex-boyfriend with his divided heart. In the next few seconds she'd find out if Jack was or not.

"Marguerite must be disappointed," he remarked, turning back to his sister.

"Actually, she's not too upset," Bibi told him. "Annabel said we're welcome to use the tickets ourselves. She bought three of them for some reason." She narrowed her eyes as she looked at Jack. "We just need to figure out who's going to take her instead of Annabel."

"What are the dates?"

"They're for next Saturday, a matinee. Matt's boss is having a barbecue we can't miss. So we're stuck."

"Looking for a volunteer?"

"Sure, god-daddy." Bibi smiled at her brother, who then turned to Hint.

"You busy next Saturday?" he asked.

"I . . . No. I mean, who knows?" she stammered, blood rushing to her cheeks.

"Will you join us? Marguerite would be happy and it'll be an excuse to spend a summer day in the Big Bad Apple. What do you say?"

Elation filled her heart. Jack was no second-guesser. Not only was it clear he no longer had feelings for his ex, but he was ready to use tickets Annabel had unwittingly made available, to take her to see a Broadway show. She could almost taste the revenge in his mouth. It was sweet, perhaps as sweet as the feeling she now had knowing his heart was whole, with no piece of it still carrying a torch for his former girlfriend.

"Let me check my calendar, and if it's clear, then—yes," she said, trying not to look too excited. She told herself it was only an afternoon date with him and a little girl, but she knew it was more. It was Jack reaching out to let her know he wanted to see her again after Tom and Nicole returned. He'd just put his family on notice that he and Hint weren't just dog hunting partners any more. She kicked herself for feeling so insanely happy with Percy still missing.

"It's decided then," Bibi said. "I'll go upstairs and get the tickets."

Hint caught his sister's quick glance at Jack's hand on the back of Hint's chair before she turned.

In a minute Bibi was back. She handed her brother the tickets as she flashed a smile at Hint.

In another fifteen minutes, the party was over, with the girls' parents arriving every few minutes to take them home. As Bibi distributed the goody bags, Marguerite whispered something to her mother, who put two aside. Excitedly, the little girl ran upstairs.

Hint enjoyed the festive atmosphere. But her mind was now turning to her seven o'clock meeting. Butterflies rose in her stomach at the thought of presenting her best work to Derek Simpson in the informal atmosphere of a hotel lounge. Was it the right setting in which to make a professional impression? Since no other choice had been offered, she'd work with it. Nervously, she glanced at her watch.

"Need to get going?" Jack asked.

"Sort of. I've got to take care of a few things before catching my train." *Decide what to wear. Figure out my hairstyle. Which jewelry. Which shoes.* Did men slave over these details the way women did? It wasn't fair. She wanted to be judged on her work alone. But that wasn't how the world worked. She had only one opportunity to make a first impression. If it wasn't good, it would be her last.

"Okay, Bibi." Jack rose. "We're on our way. Tell the munchkin I enjoyed her party."

"She's getting something for you now." Jack's older sister gestured to the top of the stairs. "She's got a surprise for your goody bag."

"I can pick it up next time I see you. We've got to get going." Jack took Hint's arm to help her up from her chair.

"No, Uncle Jack. You need this now." Marguerite ran down the stairs. Something small and black was scrunched up in one hand.

"What is it?" he asked.

"It's a secret." She stuffed the black object into the goody bag her mother held out to her. "I got it at the Halloween party at school last year. Don't look until you get home." She giggled. "It's something to make you look handsome with your black eye."

"You don't think I look handsome like this, Maggie May?" Jack feigned indignation, pointing to his bruised eye.

"You look like you got beat up. What happened, anyway? Tell me." She bounced up and down on the bottom step of the staircase.

"I'll tell you all about it next time we see each other. Right now, I've got to get Hint home."

Hint reached to take the two goody bags Bibi held out to them. One for Jack, one for herself. She was curious to know what the black object was in Jack's bag, but she would respect the wishes of the adorable girl in front of her.

"How's it going with the dog hunt?" Bibi whispered to Hint as she ushered them to the front door.

"Not so good. We're running out of ideas." Hint's heart dropped at the thought of facing Nicole and Tom the following day without Percy to greet them.

"When are the owners back?"

"Tomorrow." Hint noticed Marguerite listening intently.

"What have you done already?" the little girl asked, suddenly all grown up.

"We've looked all over," Jack cut in. "In Fox Meadow Park and downtown Scarsdale. We grilled a steak in Hint's backyard and wore our sweaty tee-shirts, hoping to attract him to our smell."

"That was a good idea," Marguerite said.

"But it didn't work," Jack pointed out.

"Because you didn't do it in the right place," the little girl told him matter-of-factly.

"What do you mean?" Hint asked.

"I mean you should have grilled the steaks and worn the smelly shirts in the dog's backyard, not yours," Marguerite explained sternly. Her face looked like the face of a biology teacher Hint had had in junior high school who had pointed out to her that she had dissected the wrong side of her frog, when she'd failed to find its gallbladder.

"But we lost him in my neighborhood in Bronxville," Hint said.

"But the dog will try to find his way home. You should hang out in the backyard of *his* home making yummy smells, not at your place. If he likes you a lot, he won't be afraid to come out of the bushes when he smells the steak."

"Sweetie, you are a genius." Jack gave his niece a look of admiration. "That's just what we'll do."

"Do it tomorrow, before they get back."

"Thank you, Maggie May. You're no Peanut Brain, you know."

"I know, Uncle Jack. Now go home and try on the secret surprise I put in your goody bag."

"'Bye, Sweetie Pie."

"'Bye, Blackie Eye. 'Bye, Hint."

IN THE CAR, Hint turned to Jack. "Do you think she's got a point? I mean, about grilling steaks in Percy's own backyard?"

"I do. She's a smart girl."

"What did she give you?" She reached for the bag in his lap.

"Uh-uh. Hands off." He grabbed her wrist and moved her hand back onto her own lap. "She said not to look until I get home."

Hint laughed. "You're superstitious?"

"Not really. But now that we're in our final twenty-four hours of looking for Percy, I'm not taking any chances. If Marguerite's tossing us some luck, I'm following every bit of advice she gives us, word for word."

"Your niece is magical."

"She's not the only one."

Hint warmed. She felt refreshed by the atmosphere Marguerite had created around them. With her adorable unguarded enthusiasm, her secret surprise for Jack, and most of all, her solid advice on finding the dog, the little girl was a genuine pixie fairy.

They rode the rest of the way back to Bronxville in silence. Hint sensed an unspoken question emanating from Jack in her direction. But there was nothing she could do about it. Gathering her focus around her upcoming meeting, she moved into a world far away from him, as well as Percy. But Marguerite stayed in her thoughts. Something about the way the little girl spread magic around her touched her heart.

The car pulled up outside her apartment building. She moved to jump out, but Jack's hand shot around her back and grabbed her shoulder, turning her toward him.

"Hey," he whispered.

"Hey," she whispered back.

"Don't do anything I wouldn't do, okay?"

"Don't worry, I won't. I'll call you from the train on my way back to let you know what time I get in to Bronxville."

"Okay." His voice was husky. He looked as if he wanted to kiss her.

But she pulled away. A new idea was germinating inside her; she needed a few minutes to sketch it out in her head. Without a backward glance, she jumped out of the car.

"See you at the station," Jack yelled out his rolled down window.

Hint quickly went inside. An inspiration for a new drawing had begun to take hold of her. She wouldn't have time to do it before leaving. But the train ride into the city took thirty minutes. She'd sketched some of her best illustrations in less than twenty. She hurried into her home office, adding a blank sketch pad and some charcoal pencils to her bag.

All the decisions she needed to make about what to wear went onto automatic pilot as the idea in her head began to take root and grow. Without a second thought, she put on a black and white print wrap dress and a pair of black and gold, open-toed shoes.

She made it to the train station with ten minutes to spare. On the platform, she pulled out her sketchpad and began work on a new fairy character. Soon she added a second new character—a canine one.

The train pulled into the station and she got on as if in a trance. Her fairy began to take on features recently familiar to her. With a few strokes of her pencil, a young girl's face took shape. Her blonde pigtails and sweet, engaged smile made her look lit from within. The dog at her side was small and bearded, with huge, soulful brown eyes.

Would sketching her characters into reality help her and Jack find Percy? Perhaps she'd picked up on some of the fairy dust Marguerite had tossed their way a few hours earlier. In their final twenty-four hours to find the dog, they needed every resource they could muster, including a dose of magic power. Little girls had it, she mused. Big people, not so much.

Thirty minutes later, the train pulled into Grand Central Station and its occupants spilled out. There were laughing, well-dressed couples; one nervous-looking man who looked as if he were about to meet someone on a first date; and a group of young women in their twenties ready to hit the town.

Hint's adrenalin raced with the excitement of the crowd. She sprang up the stairs of the lower level of Grand Central

Station into the Great Hall. There the energy level increased, with tourists and out-of-towners all strolling towards their evening destinations. Anticipation crackled in the air.

Exiting the station, she breathed in the fine summer evening as she walked west on Forty-Fourth Street toward the West Side.

Within ten minutes she was outside the Algonquin, the hotel that had hosted Dorothy Parker's renowned literary salons of the 1920s. She smiled, thinking what a helpful dress rehearsal her afternoon at the Stanhope had provided for the evening's meeting.

Straightening her posture, she tossed back her hair and breezed through the revolving door. When she came out the other side into the hotel lobby, a vision of Audrey Hepburn danced before her mind's eye, directing her movements. She wove through the lobby, her head held high. Her neck felt at least two inches longer, willed to extension by sheer mental concentration. She would knock the socks off Derek Simpson. And that would be before he'd seen any of her illustrations.

AFTER DROPPING OFF Hint, Jack drove home dejectedly. Leftover wounds from his days with Annabel Sanford were itching, threatening to re-open. She'd bounced him around like a yo-yo. There had been all sorts of business meetings with businessmen who had turned into boyfriends the moment she'd sniffed out sizeable bank accounts. He'd been left behind in the dust more than once, only to be picked up and brushed off after Annabel's latest monkey business had ended badly, and she'd come sniveling back to him. He wasn't playing that game again. He wanted to be a hero, not a chump. But his thoughts were less than heroic at the moment, imagining Hint with some English twit in a hotel. At least she wasn't meeting him in his hotel room. He gritted his teeth at the thought.

At a red light, he glanced down to investigate the contents of Marguerite's goody bag. He pulled out the black cloth object she'd stuffed inside. An elastic string was attached. Holding it up, he laughed out loud. Marguerite had given him an eye patch, probably left over from a Halloween pirate's outfit.

The light changed and he accelerated. There was something about his niece that invariably lifted his spirits. Was that what children did to adults? Or was it just Marguerite? He loved her in a trouble-free, lighthearted way. Was it possible to love an adult woman the same way?

Thoughts of Derek Simpson crossed his mind and blackened his mood again. He was being unreasonable and unfair. Gripping the steering wheel tightly, he imagined the Englishman's head between his hands. Viciously, he twisted it.

By the time he got home, his plan was set. He ripped off his shirt, dropping it on the hallway floor on his way to the bedroom. Rummaging in the depths of his closet, he pulled out a black sports jacket and a black combed cotton shirt, both Italian. He rarely wore either of them, but the occasion warranted it. He was going into Manhattan.

Showered, shaved, and dressed in under twenty minutes, he tried on the eye patch. The effect was exotic, but dashing. If he wore it with confidence, it would be perfect for what he had in mind.

With five minutes to spare, he sat down at his computer, fed a sheet of card stock paper into his printer and typed a few lines, then hit the print button. When the sheet came out, he used a paper cutter to create eight homemade business cards. Glancing at the result, he chuckled, then tucked the cards into his jacket's inside breast pocket.

The drive back to Bronxville passed quickly. Checking the schedule he saw the next Manhattan-bound train would arrive at half past six. He guessed Hint had taken an earlier train, to make her seven o'clock appointment. But he wasn't taking any chances. When the train pulled into the station he slipped into the end car and held an unfolded newspaper up to his face, checking out the other occupants of the car. No Hint, only a large crowd of Manhattan-bound Saturday evening revelers.

Sighing with relief, he fell into a seat, his body relaxing for the first time in hours. He was a man with a plan, not a chump who'd been dumped. Patting the eye patch in his right jacket pocket, he wondered how the rest of the evening would unfold if Hint was true to her word and spent it with him, as planned.

As the train sped through the woods beyond the station, he thought of Percy. Silently apologizing to the Schnoodle, he explained that he was a very close number two priority. Male to male, he knew the dog would understand. Tonight was a big night and he would make his best efforts to ensure nothing stood in his way, not even lost dogs and Englishmen. Just a business contact, right? He gritted his teeth. He'd heard that line before.

1 2

AT THE ALGONQUIN

At Grand Central Station, Jack leapt off the train and quickly weaved through the crowds toward the Vanderbilt Avenue exit on the west side of the station. Coming into Manhattan on the weekend felt far different than on a weekday. People seemed happy and excited, on their way to social events instead of dreary offices. He would invite Hint into the city some Saturday evening, that was, if they were still seeing each other after the events of the weekend transpired.

Surging with adrenalin, he arrived at the Algonquin in less than ten minutes. Slipping into an alleyway to the side of the hotel, he took out the eye patch and carefully pulled the strap over his head. The effect would either be ridiculous or brilliant. It all depended on how he wore it.

He'd been turned away from plenty of Manhattan dance clubs, standing outside trying to talk bouncers into letting him and his friends in. But there had been others he'd gained entrance to. It hadn't been all about slipping the right gatekeeper a bill, either. When he'd been by himself, he'd imagined he had an attractive woman on his arm. Annabel Sanford, or the thought of her, had worked like a charm on those occasions.

His brow furrowed. No more queen of diamonds for him. He wanted a queen of hearts. Not everyone's heart, just his. And definitely not Derek Simpson's heart. The trick was to make the Englishman fall in love with her work, not her.

He strode confidently through the hotel's revolving door entrance. A woman in the lobby glanced at him, taking in the eye patch. She'd quickly looked away, but not before interest had sparked in her gaze.

Straightening his back, he arched his neck and jutted his jaw out. If he was going to wear an eye patch, he might as well wear it well.

Another woman gave him a discreet once-over while the man accompanying her chatted with the reservation clerk. Jack warmed under the beam of her attention. Gaining confidence, he turned to scope out the lobby lounge.

"A table, sir?" a young, blonde hostess approached him. Her eyes passed lightly over the eye patch, a hint of a blush springing to her cheeks. Was there something about an eye patch that exuded sex appeal? Whatever it was, it was working.

"No. Thank you. I'm just looking for someone."

"A man or a woman?"

" A woman and a man. They were supposed to be here at seven."

"Oh. Perhaps the table in the corner?" The hostess discreetly motioned to a couple sitting side by side, deep in conversation and clearly in love or something close.

" No. Not a couple. Just a man and a woman."

He scanned the room. Hint was nowhere to be found. Had they already retired to the Englishman's hotel room? His blood began to boil. Why was he being so ridiculously unreasonable?

"Perhaps your party is at the table near the window?" the hostess asked. She was pretty, in a carefully made up sort of way. Hint's fresh, natural face popped into his mind. Where was she?

Glancing toward the window, he spied an ancient couple sitting across from each other. They looked as bored as they did rich. The woman applied lipstick from a container she held up in front of her face, peering into a mirror attached to it.

"No, that's not them," he told the hostess. "Anywhere else I could look?"

"There's some meeting areas off the Round Table restaurant in the Rose Room." The hostess referred to the room where Dorothy Parker had held her weekly literary salons in the 1920s. Many a *bon mot* had been quipped there.

"Maybe they're there. Could you check?" He gave her a cocky smile as he pressed a bill into her hand.

Her blush was unmistakable this time.

"Yes. Of course. I'll be right back." She turned and hurried through the doors of the Rose Room. Instead of waiting, he followed her. He wanted to see the room where Dorothy Parker had bantered with Alexander Wolcott, F. Scott Fitzgerald, Harpo Marx and others. Maybe he could catch some inspiration for the fast-talk he was about to attempt on Hint's behalf.

He caught more. As the hostess turned around and almost bumped into him, he paused. In an alcove off the Rose Room, the broad back of a man in a navy blue pinstriped suit leaned over a table toward Hint. Animated and radiant, she gestured toward something on the table—her portfolio, perhaps.

Jack's heart lurched when the cherubic curved contours of her mouth smiled dazzlingly, not at him.

"Is this the party you were looking for?" the hostess asked.

"Yes. Thank you."

She turned as if to announce him, but he stopped her with his hand.

"I'll take it from here," he told her, his voice low. He flashed a devilish smile. "Thanks for pointing them out."

"Oh. Certainly." She moved away, shooting a last admiring glance at Jack.

He melted to one side of the entryway to the alcove. Hint hadn't noticed him. She appeared engrossed in her conversation with Derek Pinstripes. Watching closely, Jack admired her slim, shapely arm as she raised it to point out something on the sketch the man was holding. He was certain Derek Pinstripes was admiring it too, as well as her work.

It was almost time to step in. He fingered the business cards in his pocket he had printed out an hour earlier. The moment Hint spotted him, he would make his move.

"Your drawings are delightful. You have a sort of hidden magic in your characters." The Englishman studied a large drawing of a green and purple-robed fairy queen, nodding his head approvingly. "Do you have any drawings of children in your collection?"

"I . . . uh," Hint hesitated. "I've begun work on a new character—a pixie fairy."

"Let me see." Derek Simpson brushed Hint's arm as he turned to the rest of her collection.

Jack balled one hand into a fist and silently punched his thigh. He wanted to rush in and beat the living daylights out of the man.

"This is rough. I've only just begun work on it," Hint said.

Jack held his breath as she tentatively held out a sketch to the Englishman. If she so much as touched any part of the guy, even his suit, Jack would explode.

She didn't.

He exhaled.

"Your pixie fairy is almost as beautiful as you," the Englishman remarked.

Jack's skin crawled. That was it. He was going in.

"What's her name?" Derek Pinstripes continued.

"Marguerite. She's based on my boyfriend's niece. Sort of magical and adorable, combined."

Her boyfriend? Jack stopped in his tracks. Nice. Very nice. Hint had just let Derek Simpson know she had a boyfriend. Even Jack hadn't known she had a boyfriend. Him. He wanted to crush her in his arms. Then crush the Englishman's arms.

At that second, Hint looked up. Her face froze at the sight of him.

Jack put a finger to his lips and wildly shook his head.

Her colleague turned around to see what had caught her attention.

"Hint Daniels," Jack called out as he sailed toward the table. "What a pleasure. I didn't know you frequented the Algonquin."

"Um, I don't actually. Derek, this is—"

"Max Berenboim. Other Worlds Press. How do you do?" He slapped two business cards on the table, then reached out to shake Derek Simpson's hand.

Quickly, Hint picked up one of the cards.

"Derek Simpson. Story Tales Press." The Englishman's eyes swept over Jack's eye patch; grudgingly, he extended his hand then withdrew it after the briefest of handshakes.

"Nice to meet you. I hope you aren't stealing Hint away from her American publishers, are you?" Jack asked.

"Are you connected with *Other Worlds* magazine?" Derek Simpson picked up the remaining business card and scanned it.

"Distantly." Jack turned to Hint, who was also studying the card he had presented her. Amusement twinkled in her eyes as she looked up at him. Was she laughing at the eye patch or the fake business card? He looked forward to finding out later.

"Hint has done some projects for us," he continued, turning back to the Englishman. "And we want her to do more."

He glanced at the sketch of the pixie fairy she'd just shown Derek Simpson. "Is this some of your latest work?" Jack asked her. The heart-shaped face of his niece stared back at him, next to a dog that was a dead ringer for Percy.

The Englishman deftly swept the sketch his way and turned it over before Jack could study it further.

"Good chap, we're just in the midst of a business meeting here. Could you snag Miss Daniels some other time, perhaps?" Fire and ice flashed in Simpson's eyes.

"Ms. Daniels, could you call my office first thing Monday morning? I've got a project you'd be perfect for and I want to catch you before someone else does."

"What's the project about, Max?" She played along, her eyes gleaming.

"Monday morning, Ms. Daniels. Can't give away professional secrets to the competition." He turned to Derek Simpson and made a short bow. "Sir, you are in the company of a most gifted artist."

"Indeed," the pinstriped Englishman replied, his tone cold. "Good evening, sir." He dipped his head as if to say "You're done here."

"I'll call you first thing Monday, Max," Hint said.

"Fantastic. I'll have my secretary draw up a preliminary contract."

"Have her call me first. My rates have gone up," she countered.

Little minx. Smart move. Jack smiled to see the other man's eyebrow shoot up.

"Since you won the Caldecott Award, I can understand why," Jack ad-libbed, hoping he'd gotten right the name of the top award for illustrators of children's picture books.

"I, uh, it was actually another award," Hint demurred.

"You're the best there is and you know it," Jack said, looking her straight in the eye. "Talk to you Monday." He turned to Derek Simpson. "Cheers."

"Cheers," the Englishman curtly replied, giving him a glacial stare that all but shouted, 'Shove off now.'

HINT SAT BACK, stunned. She had wanted to break out laughing the moment she saw Jack in the eye patch. But it wasn't the moment. She had a business deal to seal and Jack Whitby, a.k.a. Max Berenboim, had just raised her stock in the eyes of Derek Simpson. She needed to seize her advantage.

"You aren't intending to sign an exclusive with Other Worlds are you?" Simpson asked, looking worried. She was surprised to see beads of sweat on the Englishman's brow.

"I hadn't intended to, but it depends on the terms," she answered, taking a long sip of her Campari and soda. An irresistible cockiness had seized her, thanks to the bolstering effect of Jack's compliments.

"Well, don't. We'll offer you better terms," he told her, reaching into the inside pocket of his jacket.

"Excuse me?" Had he just said he was making her an offer? He had no idea what terms Max Berenboim intended to offer, never mind that no such person as Max Berenboim of Other Worlds Publishing actually existed.

"I want you for our Pixie World series. It's a new imprint with a ten-book rollout we're launching in the spring of next year."

"Are the stories written yet?" She stared at him, wide-eyed.

"Two of the ten. We're looking for a strong image for our main character. It's a young fairy girl, just like the one you've drawn here. Your character would be perfect."

"I'm delighted," she said, her heart warming to think her character based on Marguerite had made the biggest impression on Derek Simpson of all her drawings.

"Looks like you're busy too," he added.

"My fall schedule will start filling up on Monday," she countered, reminding him of the offer from the man with the eye patch who had just left.

"It'll start filling up now, if you agree. I propose we make a preliminary commitment this evening and fill in the details this week. I'm back in my office Tuesday morning. We can arrange a conference call to hash out the particulars then. Would that work?"

Hint couldn't believe her ears. Suddenly, she was a hot commodity. She needed to think about money, fast. She thought of her existing hourly rate per project. With Jack's effusive compliments ringing in her ears, she doubled it. The she remembered Simpson's promise to beat Other World's rates, whatever they were. She doubled the number again. "It depends on what you're offering," she told him.

"I'm offering a ten-book commitment over a two-year period."

"An advance and percentage of sales?" she asked.

"Yes," he replied.

"My rates are high," she bluffed.

"So I heard."

She named an absurdly high figure.

"Fine," the Englishman replied.

Now she knew she was dreaming. This would all be over in several minutes and she'd be out on the street hustling for her next project, as usual. Only this time she'd have a boyfriend who moonlighted as a pirate. She wanted to burst into laughter.

Derek Simpson began scribbling something on the document he'd pulled out of his jacket pocket. Hint remained silent. Dumbfounded by what was taking place, she had lost her ability to speak. Instead, she took another long sip of her drink.

"There." He pushed the document toward her. With yellow and pink copies attached, it was a one-page initial agreement between Story Tales Press and Hint Daniels. He'd filled in a time period of two years and a per-book figure that was more than her total income for the year before.

"This isn't an exclusive, is it?" she asked.

"No. It's not. But I hope you will give us the majority of your time on this project."

She smiled but refrained from replying while she went through the contract, line by line. *Never complain, never explain* danced through her head as she studied each clause. She would be busy with other commitments, most importantly ones with the man masquerading as Max Berenboim. They wouldn't be work-related either, but Derek Simpson didn't need to know that. "Where do I sign?" she finally asked, after satisfying herself that it wasn't an exclusive and that rights were appropriately assigned.

He indicated the line and she signed with a flourish, after correcting her first name to Hinton. Then, pushing the contract across the table, she gave him a satisfied smile. Not dazzling. Just serenely full of professional confidence.

"Well done, Hint. I'd be pleased to have you join me for dinner, if you're available." He gave her an assessing look, as if testing the temperature of her response.

"I'd love to, but I'm afraid I have plans," she replied, thinking of Jack. She didn't doubt he was waiting outside. "Shall I expect your call on Tuesday?"

"Yes. My assistant will contact you Tuesday morning to set up a conference call," he said. "We'll hash out details then. So sorry you can't join me for dinner."

"Likewise," she fibbed graciously. "But I look forward to working with you on this project."

"As do I."

Hint rose from her chair and he rose with her. They shook hands, then she picked up her portfolio, as well as her chin. Like a luxury cruise liner, she sailed out of the site of the signing of the most significant professional contract of her career. At least two inches taller than when she'd entered the hotel, she breezed through the lobby. As she approached the revolving doors, a doorman opened one of the side entrances for her, shooting her an admiring look.

Out on the sidewalk, she turned toward Grand Central Station. So much had just happened she couldn't even think. Fingering the signed contract in her handbag, she felt as if music played all around her, an otherworldly melody from the land of fairies. Who did she have more to thank for the good luck that had just befallen her? Jack, with his clever ruse, or his niece Marguerite, with the divine pixie fairy inspiration the girl had given her?

Stopping for the light on the corner of Sixth Avenue, she smiled to herself. People she had known for less than one full week had catapulted her into a whole new successful future. She laughed out loud.

"That funny, huh?" Jack Whitby stood next to her, eye patch in place.

"You." She reached out to hug him.

"No. Max Berenboim." He grabbed her arm and steered her rapidly across the street. "Until we get on the train." He smiled wickedly, then whispered in her ear. "I want to make sure your

English friend isn't anywhere nearby. Did you leave him back at the hotel?"

"Yes. He asked me to dinner, but I told him I had plans."

"You do. Let's go left here, so we get off the same street as the hotel. I don't want him seeing us together." He winked at her.

"I feel like a couple of gypsies, pulling off a job," she confessed, giggling.

"That's us. Pirate Man and his sidekick, Ms. Raised-Her-Rates."

"You mean Ms. Dog Whisperer."

"Yes." His expression grew serious. "That's just what I mean."

"Listen, Jack. I've got a signed contract in my bag, and you're the reason why."

"Does that mean you'll be nice to me for the rest of the evening?" he inquired, his eyes sparking.

Hint elbowed him sharply. "That means you're my hero; no guarantees about the evening."

He sighed. "Argh, methinks I've earned a kiss or two, wench."

"That's not how it works, Pirate Man. But I'm impressed." She broke into peals of laughter. "How in the world did you think up that eye patch disguise?"

"I didn't. Marguerite did. That's what was in the goody bag she gave me."

She shook her head in amazement. "Your niece was the inspiration for my pixie fairy. She's the one I really need to thank."

"How about if you give me the kisses for her and I'll pass them on next time I see her?"

"How about if we go back and look for Percy?" She punched his arm playfully.

"How about if we look for Percy then celebrate your new contract?"

She nodded, wishing desperately her sweet Schnoodle friend was in her arms to help celebrate landing such a plum assignment.

And a new man in her life.

But as with Derek Simpson, she wasn't mixing business with pleasure. She might be partially indebted to Jack for the signed contract in her hand, but when it came to personal feelings, his pleasure would have to wait on hers. She had a feeling it would, if the night before had been any indication. If only they could find the dog, she would be ready to focus the entirety of her feelings on the man in the eye patch beside her.

BACK IN BRONXVILLE, they hopped into Jack's car at the train station. Hint's elation was beginning to subside at the thought of not yet finding Percy.

"Jack, this is it—our final night to find him. What should we do?"

"I thought you might be too worked up to do any more dog hunting today. Sure you want to go out looking for him now?"

She glanced at her watch. It was two minutes past nine. Night had fallen. Another long night for Percy, out there alone somewhere.

"Let's spend another hour looking for him," she told him.

"Where to, Dog Whisperer?"

"Why don't we drive up to Scarsdale again and circle around his neighborhood?" she suggested. "Remember what Marguerite said today? Percy is more likely to make his way back home than to my place in Bronxville."

"From the mouths of babes, pearls of wisdom," he intoned, his warm gaze heating her insides.

"And don't forget her idea about grilling steaks in Tom and Nicole's backyard tomorrow," she reminded him.

"Let's check to see what their grill setup looks like. We might need to bring our own equipment, or fill up their propane tank or something."

"Good plan," she agreed, rolling down her window, then leaning back in the seat.

As they drove through the warm night air, electricity rippled through her. She couldn't believe what Jack had pulled off at the Algonquin. Even more amazing was the amount of thought and effort he had put into it. He had tracked her movements just as she had tracked his, the day Annabel Sanford had invited him to the Stanhope. He had wanted to know what the real deal was between her and Derek Simpson, just as she had wanted to know if he was still involved with Annabel. They had both passed muster—one secretly, one openly.

"A penny for your thoughts," Jack spoke up, looking over at her.

"I've got too many at the moment." She shook her head. Her thoughts were miles away from dog hunting. She tried to refocus.

"How about just one of them?" he pressed.

"Well, what exactly do we say to Tom and Nic if we haven't found Percy by the time they arrive tomorrow?"

"We tell them the truth."

"Do you tell them or do I?" she asked.

"I will. You've done enough." He pulled the car to a stop in Percy's owners' driveway for the second time that day.

"You've done just as much as I have," she pointed out.

"We've knocked ourselves out, haven't we?"

Hint nodded. "It doesn't seem fair. And you got beaten up for your troubles." She reached out and traced a line down the left side of his face, along the edge of the bruise. It looked worse than it had the night before, the purple and blue now mixed with yellow.

"I guess we both know life doesn't work that way. Who gets what's fair?" His words were grim, but not his hands when he reached for the arm she'd extended to touch his face.

Hint tried to pull back, but he held tight, pulling her toward him.

"Maybe no one gets what's fair," she said. "But people who use a little magic get a little magic back." Marguerite's sweet face popped into her head. The girl spread magic all around her. Hint could only marvel to think of the woman she would one day become.

"So what kind of magic is on the menu, tonight?" Jack asked, lowering his head to meet her eyes.

"Dog catching magic. Let's go," she ordered, reclaiming her arm. Quickly, she got out of the car before Jack could stop her.

The moon was low in the sky, with a promise of soon-to-be-full magnificence. She breathed in deeply. The summer night air smelled so fragrant, it made her dizzy.

"Let's check out their grill," she proposed.

Jack reached into the open window of the passenger side and clicked open the glove compartment. He grabbed a flashlight.

Together they opened the trellis gate and entered the back patio of their friends' home. As they passed through it, the flowery scent grew stronger. Heavy wisteria vines covered the trellis, the grapelike blossom clusters everywhere.

Jack squatted and lifted the propane tank under the grill standing in one corner. "It's at least half full. Enough for our barbecue tomorrow."

"What about tongs and all the grill tools? Do we need to bring our own?" she asked, relieved.

Jack beamed the flashlight over the contours of Tom and Nic's sizeable outdoor grill. "They've got all that stuff here on the side."

"Fine. But what about smelly clothes?"

"We'll look for them tomorrow," he said. Tom's probably got some old tee-shirts in the tool shed for when he works on his engines."

"Good. Let's take a walk."

"Yes. Let's." Holding the flashlight before him, he put his arm around her shoulders. They walked to the front of the house, calling Percy's name.

After a few minutes, she led the way to the hanging porch swing. She dropped into it, Jack next to her. The sounds and smells of four nights earlier returned to her—Fox Meadow Park, the statue of Diana gleaming white in the moonlight. She remembered the wild, percussive flamenco music. Suddenly, it was in her ears again.

"I hear music," she told him.

"Shut your eyes."

Without answering, she obeyed. His hands covered her eyes. She breathed in the scent of them—woodsy and something more. Relaxing, she leaned back against his chest. In a minute, another vibration joined the flamenco drumbeat. The thump of Jack's heartbeat filled Hint's ear.

"Do you hear it?" he murmured.

"Yes," she whispered back, not meaning the music.

"Then use your magic and listen for Percy. If you heard the music, you'll hear his breathing. He's out there somewhere taking short dog breaths right now."

She sank deeper into Jack's arms, her eyes still shut. Stroking her hair, he slid his fingers over her earlobes and down the back of her neck, each caress a current of electricity cloaked in velvet.

Second by second, she moved beyond the hint of music to a more subtle sound—the sound of Percy's quiet pants. She visualized the Schnoodle lying in tall grass, breathing in the same night air as she, waiting for her to find him.

Then her vision vanished. In its place, a strange noise came from the direction of the meadow behind the house, like the sound of a dog howling, only wilder. She sat up sharply.

"What was that?" she cried.

The noise sounded again. Against a backdrop of whirring crickets, an animal was howling at the moon. The sound rose and fell, each howl lasting for several seconds.

"What is it? That's not a wolf, is it?" She couldn't believe her ears.

They both sat stock-still for a moment, but the howling had stopped.

"It's not a dog," Jack said slowly, concern on his face.

"God, no," she agreed, fearful. "It sounds like something otherworldly. What do you think it was?"

"I don't know," he answered, hesitating.

"You do know." Searching his face, she was sure he was holding back. "What was it?"

"It wasn't a wolf. There are no wolves in this area."

"Then what was it?" *And does it eat dogs?* A lump formed in her throat.

He hopped off the swing and bounded down the four steps of the front porch. "Let's go take a look."

"Where are we going?" she asked, following him down the front path. She had no wish to track the hideous sound to its source, but she wanted to stay close to Jack.

"Let's check around back again. Maybe there's something in the bushes behind the yard."

"Are you crazy?" she protested. "What if it comes after us?"

"It won't. It'll be more scared of us than we are of it," he assured her, heading around the corner.

"How do you know? Are you sure?" She didn't want to sound cowardly, but the strange animal's howl had chilled her.

"I'm sure," he said grimly, striding ahead of her. He swung his flashlight beam from one end of the yard to the other.

Then they heard it.

"Ahh-wooo." It wavered up and down, faintly but clearly.

"Is it coming from over near the river?" she asked.

"It's farther away than that," he told her.

"You think so?" she pressed, doubtful.

"Yes. If an animal was howling like that down by the river, the bullfrogs and crickets would all be still."

"You know what animal is making that sound," she challenged him.

He turned and stared at her. "I have an idea."

"What is it?"

"Maybe a coyote."

"No. A coyote? In this area?" she cried.

"Yup. They've been found down in the Bronx, in Van Cortlandt Park. Last summer one even popped up in Central Park."

"Don't they eat small dogs?" She tried to keep her voice under control.

"They mostly eat dead stuff. Road kill, carrion."

"Mostly?"

"They'll attack a chicken or a small animal, if they're hungry enough," he admitted.

"That's terrible. What about Percy? What if he's listening to the howling now?"

"He is, if he's anywhere near. Dogs' hearing is much keener than their eyesight."

"What can we do to protect him, if he's around here hiding out?" she pressed.

"We can try a few things. Coyotes don't like water sprinklers. But then, the same can be said for dogs. They're not fond of bright lights either."

"Yes, but Percy is used to his own home. Maybe if it's a light that he's seen going on and off before in his own backyard, he won't be scared."

"Let's check if there's a motion sensor light in the drive-way," he suggested.

"I don't remember one." She clambered over the low stone wall of the back patio, walking the length of the flagstone area waving her arms. No light came on.

Jack followed, then took the lead and went out into the driveway. Two steps from his car, a motion sensor light over the garage came on.

"That's good," he said. "A coyote would think twice about walking into the driveway."

"But what about the rest of the property?"

"Do you think Tom and Nic have a water sprinkler?" he asked.

"Let's look in the tool shed."

Flashlight trained in front of him, Jack opened the shed's unlocked door and beamed the light around. No garden hose or sprinkler presented themselves.

"I think I remember them having a sprinkler on when I've come over before. Let's look in the grass, beyond the patio," Hint suggested.

He shut the tool shed door and turned back to the back-yard. She linked her arm in his and together they felt their way across the dark, rich carpet of grass.

"Ow!" Her foot hit something in the dark. She stumbled, as he caught her arm. When he beamed the flashlight onto the ground, a bronze sprinkler attachment shone up at them.

"Good. Is the hose here too?" He knelt down and felt around for the garden hose.

"I think it's over there." She pointed to a dark lump on the low stone wall dividing the patio from the backyard as she rubbed her stubbed toe.

He moved to the spot she'd pointed out.

"You're right. Let's get this connected to the sprinkler, then find the water faucet."

Hint took the end of the hose and knelt down to connect it to the sprinkler. Meanwhile, Jack used the flashlight to search along the side of the house adjoining the patio. In a minute he'd found what he was looking for. Connecting up the other end of the hose with the wall faucet, he waited for her to finish.

"Come over here, so I can turn it on," he called to her. The beam from the flashlight danced as he carefully guided her.

He turned on the faucet and they waited. Within three seconds, the gentle whoosh of the water sprinkler told them they'd been successful. Multiple jets of water rotated slowly from one side of the yard to the other.

"Nice job," she congratulated him.

"Nice job yourself, Fairy Woman," he responded. They stood side by side for a moment, the peripheral spray from the sprinkler misting their faces and arms.

Suddenly, she felt the urge to release all the events of the day pent up inside her. Her emotions had ranged the gamut from elation to fear. She needed to shake it all off. Tearing off her jacket, she tossed it on the back of a patio chair. The thin black and white dress she wore underneath felt silky and cool next to her skin. Kicking off her shoes, she ran toward the sprinkler.

She would celebrate Percy's return before it actually took place. She would show the dog now where he most wanted to be.

"Feels divine," she sang out, running through the stream of the sprinkler jets. The cool, sharp spray bit into her neck and back, soaking through the thin dress.

Within seconds, Jack was beside her, shouting and laughing as the spray hit his body. Together they ran back and forth like kids on a summer evening. Hint thought of Marguerite, wishing she could have been there too.

She ran back onto the patio, out of breath. Jack raced behind, grabbing her around the waist. Turning, she flung her arms around his neck.

"Hey, Pirate Boy," she whispered.

"Dog Whisperer, you're magic." He buried his face in her neck, amidst a tangle of wet, fragrant hair. Then, lifting his head, his mouth came down upon hers.

Tasting salt, cool water, and the biting, tangy smell of male sweat, she inhaled deeply, then slightly opened her mouth.

They clung together for moments that lingered like hours. His hands slid up and down her torso. She allowed him to take the measure of her curves, feeling his body vibrate as he lingered over the steepest ones. She was a vine curling itself around an oak, a damp, night flower unfolding into full bloom.

Finally, she stepped back. "I know what we need to do."

"What's that?" he whispered, reaching for her again.

"We need to go back to my place," she told him, eluding his arms, "get some sleeping bags and come back here."

"No." He groaned, his face less than enthused.

"How can we possibly sleep inside on the final night before Tom and Nic get back, when Percy's out there somewhere, along with a herd of coyotes?"

"That was just one animal we heard. And I don't think they run in herds. Packs, maybe."

"Whatever. We've got to protect him. And who knows? Maybe he'll come to us when we're sleeping. You know how dogs like to snuggle next to a warm body."

"They're not the only ones. But I like to snuggle in a bed. With sheets and a comforter." *And you.* Fire blazed in his questioning eyes.

"Not tonight. We're coming back here, with everything we need to make sure Percy is safe and no coyote even thinks about coming 'round," she admonished him.

"That's very thoughtful of you. But what if he's nowhere near? Then what's the point?" he asked.

"The point is, this is our last night to find him before our friends discover he's lost. And something tells me he's around here. I saw him."

"You saw him? Where?" He looked doubtful.

"In my head." She tapped it, ignoring Jack's skeptical look. "He was lying in tall grass, like a meadow."

"That could be any number of meadows, Dog Girl. He could be in a meadow in the next state for all we know."

"No. He's in the area. I feel it." She looked him squarely in the eye. "Come on. We're going back to my place then coming back here."

"Do you have any bedrolls, perchance?" Jack looked frustrated.

"You mean those pads that wimpy city dwellers put under their sleeping bags because they can't handle sleeping on the ground?" she asked.

"No. I mean those pads people who don't have lots of padding themselves put under their sleeping bags so they can actually sleep."

"Yeah, I've got something like that. Let's go." She walked to the car and waited by the passenger door, shivering in her thin, wet dress. Behind her, he gave a long sigh of resignation. She knew exactly what they had to do tonight. Too bad if Jack had another idea.

13

FINAL PLAN

Within forty-five minutes they were back at Tom and Nic's home in Scarsdale.

Jack wasn't crazy about the idea of sleeping outdoors, but this was their last night to look for the dog. He hoped he'd find Hint in his arms again when they woke up the following morning.

"These yoga pants don't do much for me." He pointed to the hem of the black yoga pants she had lent him. They ended midway down his calves. She had also given him an oversized tee-shirt so he could change out of the black sports jacket and shirt he'd worn into Manhattan.

"Not a problem, since I can't see your legs in the dark anyway," Hint teased.

"Yeah, but what if mosquitoes find my ankles?" he asked.

"They won't, if you tuck your sleeping bag around you tightly enough. Haven't you ever gone camping before?" She rolled her eyes as she spread out a dark green sleeping bag on one of the chaise longues on the patio.

"Yes. A few nights ago, as you'll recall. And I don't remember anyone I ever camped with sleeping on a chaise longue either. Is that some sort of city slicker camping style?"

"I just thought we'd be more comfortable sleeping on some padding. Look at how thick it is." She bounced as she sat on the green and white striped cushion of the chaise longue. He tried not to notice the motion of her curves under the white tee-shirt she wore. Impossible.

"I see. Look at how narrow it is, too." The contours of the night ahead were taking on a different shape from the one he'd envisioned.

"It's wide enough for you. What's your problem?" she asked, busily folding down one corner of the sleeping bag into a neat vee.

It was wide enough for one, not two, he thought as he watched her shake out the second sleeping bag on the other chaise longue. Shouldering her out of the way, he rolled it directly next to the first one. Only two wrought-iron arms now stood in the way of his plans for the night.

"Is this some sort of 1950s TV sitcom arrangement?" he asked.

"What do you mean?" She pushed him aside, dragging the second chaise longue back to its former position, several feet away from the first.

"I mean this is how Lucille Ball and Desi Arnaz's beds were set up in 'I Love Lucy.'"

"This is our last night to find Percy. We're going to do whatever we can to make him feel safe enough to come back here," she told him. With hands on hips, she looked like a school teacher scolding her class.

"Why will he feel safer with twin beds? Do you think he'll be jealous of me because he's been fixed?" The inanity of his question dawned on him too late.

Hint stared at him a moment then doubled over with laughter. "I don't think so."

"Just remember what happened to Desi and Lucy," he warned.

"What do you mean?"

"They got divorced."

"Nine out of ten Hollywood couples get divorced. So what?" She rolled her eyes.

"So it doesn't help if they sleep in twin beds," he explained, exasperated. "Where do you think it leads?"

"Jack, get your mind out of bed and onto Percy," Hint laughed. "We're trying to lure him back. He knows *my* smell. He doesn't know yours."

"Your point?"

"He'll come to me if I'm alone. Over here. He may not come to me if your smell is anywhere near mine," she spelled out.

"Great. So I guess that leaves us telling campfire stories before we fall asleep," he grumbled.

"Why not?"

He watched as she neatly brushed off the soles of her feet, then climbed into her sleeping bag on the chaise longue facing his. They were at least six feet away from each other.

"Dog Whisperer," he called to her in a low voice.

"Yes?"

"You didn't tuck me in."

"Stop it." The school teacher was back.

"Stop what?"

"You're being silly," she reproved him.

"I'm being totally reasonable," he insisted.

"Go to sleep," she ordered.

"I can't until you kiss me goodnight."

"Jack . . ."

"What?" He liked hearing her say his name, even if she was scolding him.

"We're going to find him. I can feel it." Her voice had softened.

"Close your eyes," he told her.

"Already are," she mumbled.

"Keep them that way. And don't talk," he commanded.

Silence answered him.

At her side in three steps, he leaned over and put one hand on her forehead, smoothing back silky tendrils of her hair.

The sigh she gave in response was all he needed to continue.

Lowering himself onto the side of her chaise longue, he lightly touched her face. Feeling no resistance, he began to massage her forehead and temples.

"Uhh . . . feels good." Her head nestled into the cushion she lay on.

"Shh, Dog Girl. You'll wake the fairies," he told her.

"Fairies," she murmured.

"Empty your head," he intoned. "Don't think. Let Percy wander in, in his own time. Don't force him." He was beginning to feel like a dog whisperer himself.

"Hmm . . ."

He continued stroking her face. Beneath his hands, she slid into sleep.

He hadn't gotten a goodnight kiss, but tomorrow was another day. With Hint the tempo would be slow, but steady. Steadiness was something he hadn't experienced with women before. She was unlocking a door inside him that he had previously slammed shut against her sex. But it took time. Perhaps the same kind of time she needed to allow him closer.

Silently rising, he slipped away. There was something he needed to do. He hadn't wanted to scare her earlier, but it had occurred to him that the coyote out there might just as well examine them in the small of the night as any other living creature sleeping on Tom and Nic's patio. He didn't think coyotes attacked human beings, unless they were the size of infants. But as a precaution, he'd ensure no animal visited without them knowing about it tonight. Where Hint's safety was concerned, he would take no chances.

In a minute he was at his car. Opening the trunk, he took out a coil of thin copper wire and his emergency tool kit. Each item in the kit had a hole at one end, so it could be hung on hooks on a wall. Quickly, he strung them together onto the copper wire, fashioning a wire fence of metal objects that would clank together noisily should anything or anyone step into it.

Holding one end, he draped the other over his shoulders, then made his way back to the patio.

As he approached the chaise longue where Hint lay, she stirred in her sleep, murmuring.

"Snull," she mumbled.

What? He thought to himself. *What's a snull?*

"Snull bun," she muttered, turning over.

Snull bun. It didn't sound like a man's name. Why couldn't she have just said his name in her sleep? He roped the wire cord around the patio furniture and through the tiki lamps at two corners of the low stone wall marking the end of the flagstone where the backyard lawn began.

In a minute, he was done. He hopped into his own sleeping bag and lay back, hands crossed under his head, gazing at the stars.

Then it came to him: *snull bun*—snuggle bunny. Looking at the magical woman sleeping across from him, he asked whatever higher powers there were to substitute himself for Percy as the snuggle bunny of her heart. Or at least to direct the dog to move over to make room for him too.

THE NEXT MORNING, Jack awoke to birds singing and a clear sky overhead. He stretched and walked over to where Hint lay. As he studied her smooth, sleeping face, she opened her eyes and smiled up at him.

"Good morning," she murmured sleepily.

"Good morning, Dog Whisperer."

"Your eye is looking better today. Come here," she ordered.

He sat where she pointed. Her slim fingers wandered over the left side of his face, probing his bruise. Breathing in the scent of her skin, he grabbed her wrist and kissed the sensitive pulse point.

Lazily, she smiled. "No coyotes."

"Only a wolf." His eyes locked onto hers. Then his mouth on her lips. She leaned back; her body welcomed his, stretched full length on hers. The sleeping bag covering her did little to hide his ardor.

For a long moment they lay there listening to the noisy chirping of morning birds. Jack sensed an invisible line drawn that couldn't be crossed until the situation with Percy was resolved. He shuddered, thinking of the possibility of the dog never showing up again.

"Our last day to find him," she read his thoughts.

"We will." If he said it with confidence, maybe it would chase away her doubts.

"Yes. We will," she agreed. She stretched her arms overhead, like a gorgeous hothouse flower opening to the day. He reached for her again, but with a languid stretch of her slender arm, she pushed him off the chaise longue.

"I'll be back," he said. "If you need to take care of any business, I promise not to look on that side of the house." He pointed in the opposite direction of the tool shed, where he then headed.

In a minute, they met back on the patio. She looked him up and down.

"You need to go home and change," she said.

"What? The light of day doesn't favor your clothes on me?" he teased.

"You look better in your own clothes." Then she studied his face. "And you need a shave."

"Thanks."

"Let's get going." She folded her sleeping bag into three vertical sections, then sat on it as she tightly rolled it up. Had she been a Girl Scout? It looked as if she knew what she was doing.

They headed down the Bronx River Parkway on their way to her apartment, each caught up in private thoughts. Taking a page from Hint's visualizations, Jack imagined Percy on the patio behind Tom and Nic's house. If the Schnoodle was any-where in the vicinity of his home, the scent of a nice grilled steak should get him onto the property and into their arms.

"Listen, what about if I go pick up the steaks for our barbe-cue while you're getting ready?" he suggested as he pulled up in front of her building. "Then we can go up to my place, so I can change—then head on back to Tom and Nic's."

"When are they due back?" she asked.

"They told me they'd swing by my place around five to pick up Percy."

"That doesn't give us much time." She shuddered then thought a moment. "Is there anywhere to go for a fast run in your neighborhood?"

"There's the high school track at the bottom of the hill near my house."

"Good. While you're doing whatever you need to do at your place, I'll take a run down there."

"You can shower at my place afterwards," he offered.

"No shower. I want to get as sweaty as possible so Percy smells me while we're barbecuing. We've got to try whatever it takes to attract him back to his own backyard."

"Great. I can hardly wait to smell you myself." He tugged on a loose lock of her hair. "Should I also resist cleaning myself up?"

"No. You need to clean up." Her smile was playful. "He doesn't know your smell. He knows mine. So go get the steaks, if you're offering." She pointed towards Bronxville's main street. "The butcher's closed Sundays, but there's a supermarket two blocks in that direction."

"Meet you back here in half an hour."

"Stay in the car. I'll come down." She grabbed the two sleeping bags and hopped out. After watching her enter her building, he drove off. For once, he hoped Brian O'Connell had been spying on her. Maybe he'd add things up and realize Hint was off the market, if she was being delivered home at eight in the morning.

He picked up three large sirloin steaks, and four ears of corn at the store. It was a lot of food, but he was ready to eat a horse. To stave off starvation, he also got bagels and coffee with the Sunday paper, then drove back to Hint's building to wait outside in his car.

In a minute she was next to him, her hair wet and smelling like flowers, something other than stargazer lilies this time. She wore a fresh tee-shirt and running shorts.

"Hey, no fair. You took a shower," he protested.

"Yes, but I'm not taking another one after I run. I just needed to wash my hair."

"It smells great. What did you put on it?"

"Something from one of those magic bottles in my bathroom," she told him.

"Well worth it. I applaud your support of the toiletries industry."

"Drive. And thanks for the coffee." She took a sip from the takeout coffee cup he had handed her. "Mmm. Hazelnut. Delicious."

"Not just any old hazelnut. Hawaiian hazelnut." He'd found that flavor in her cupboard the other morning when he'd made coffee for her.

"I like it. What's in that bag?" She indicated the paper sack lying in his lap.

"A bagel for my lady."

"What's on it?"

"Butter."

"How did you know I liked butter on my bagel?"

"I'm getting to know you." He hadn't had any idea, but had bought one bagel with butter and one with cream cheese, to cover all bases. He handed her the buttered one.

"Hmm." She rolled down her window as he swung out of Meadow Lane onto Bronxville's main road. In a minute they were on the highway heading toward Jack's home.

Suddenly, he worried that he hadn't picked up around the house last time he'd been there. He hoped she'd forgive his lack of domestic skills. What was the point of picking up when there was no one around to notice?

In twenty-five minutes they were in Pleasantville, in Mid-Westchester County. After another five minutes on local roads, Jack took a left at a fork in the road and began to climb a gently sloping hill. Almost at its top, he took a right and pulled into the driveway of a pale yellow clapboard farmhouse.

"It's beautiful," Hint exclaimed, jumping out of the car.

"It's a former pickle farm. The farmhouse had been restored by the previous owners, so it was move-in ready when I bought it."

"When was that?" she asked, looking up at a tall, stately maple tree in his front yard.

"About three years ago."

"I love your trees," she said.

"Wait till you see the ones in the backyard."

Quickly, he led her through the house to the back deck, conscious of the piles of unopened junk mail on the kitchen table and the basket of dirty laundry next to the washer and dryer in the butler's pantry. If he could just get her out to the back, she might maintain her favorable first impression.

"Here's where my favorite trees are."

Hint said nothing, taking in the expanse of the backyard. The breeze ruffled her hair as she leaned over the deck railing. While she surveyed the three tall trees, he studied the myriad shades of red and dark gold shot through her tresses.

"They're so majestic. What kind of trees are they?" she asked.

"That one's a maple, like the one in front." He pointed to the tallest tree directly in front of them. "Then there's a chestnut over here. And that one in the corner is an oak."

"I like the oak the best."

He had hoped she would say the oak. Prayer was his friend and counselor on quiet summer evenings when he sat out in his backyard alone, a cold beer in hand.

"Why?" he couldn't help asking.

"I don't know. It looks almost human, somehow. Like a watchman protecting your property." She paused, studying the oak.

"He is sort of doing that. Or so Marguerite says."

"It's a he, huh? Does he have a name?" She looked at him out of the corner of one eye.

"Yes, as a matter of fact. He does." He wasn't ready to share it with her just yet. Would she think he was nuts to have a tree named Prayer?

"Are you going to tell me what it is?" she pressed.

"No, but maybe Marguerite will."

"I'll ask her next week." A smile flickered across her face. She seemed pleased to remember their plans for next weekend. Would not finding Percy throw a kink in them? He hoped she could separate whatever feelings she had for him from their dog hunt, no matter what it's outcome.

"I'll go for my run now if you show me which way the track is," she said.

"Sure," he agreed, pride washing over him in introducing her to his neighborhood. "It's right down the hill on the other side of the street. Probably less than an eighth of a mile."

"Great. See you in about thirty minutes."

He watched her slight form as she jogged down the hill. Then he went into the house and bounded upstairs, taking them two at a time. If Hint thought they were going to find the dog that day, then so did he. Great minds think alike, it was said. Greatly in-sync minds thought alike too, as far as he was concerned.

In twenty minutes he was showered, shaved and dressed. He'd picked up his Nantucket red shorts, faded almost to pink, from the bedroom floor and fished out a clean yellow polo shirt from a drawer. Checking the fridge he found a container of potato salad with bacon that his sister had made. He slipped it into an ice cooler, along with assorted drinks. Lugging the cooler out to his car to load into the trunk, he spotted Hint slowly jogging up the hill. As he watched her approach, it struck him that she was the first woman visiting his home to guess that his trees had names.

"Sweaty enough?" he greeted her.

"I'm pretty smelly. Great track." Breathing hard, she climbed the porch steps and leaned against one of the white support columns with both hands to stretch her calf muscles.

"Percy will be happy," he declared, telling himself that the dog would be joining them. "Ready for a barbecue?"

"Ready for a cold drink."

He handed her a bottle of ice-cold water and slung a small towel around her neck. Discreetly, he inhaled as he leaned toward her, embracing her sweaty scent.

An hour later, they were back in Tom and Nicole's backyard. Hint had brought a few of Percy's squeaky toys.

"Should we start the grill then take a walk around while its heating up?" she proposed.

"Sure. Let's bring a couple of these while we're looking." He picked out a bedraggled white stuffed cat and handed it to her, then took a red and white ball. Squeezing it, he chuckled at its gasping squeak. He pushed the cooler holding food and drinks under one of the chaise longues, out of the sun, then fired up the grill and closed the top. It would take a few minutes to heat up before they could slap on the steaks.

They started down the driveway.

"Looks different in the daytime, huh?" he observed.

"A little less scary than last night when the coyote was howling."

"A little less exciting too."

"No flamenco music coming from the neighbors' house," Hint remarked.

"Or from inside your head." He smiled at her, remembering her visions from the night before. She had seen Percy lying in long grass. Where could that have been? All around them were well-manicured lawns and tidy sidewalks.

"Why don't we walk through the meadow behind the back-yard?" she suggested.

"The meadow?" Mentally, he went over Tom and Nic's property. Then he remembered the wild, undeveloped piece of land that lay beyond the backyard. "Let's go." He led the way into the tall grass on the other side of the low stone fence that bounded Tom and Nicole's property. From time to time, he squeaked the ball. Each time he did, Hint followed with a squeak from the stuffed cat. Soon, a savory scent wafted over them from the grill, left over from remnants of whatever Tom and Nicole had made last time they had used it.

Hint stopped short. "What's that sound?"

Jack paused. Something was rustling in the grass up ahead to the right.

"Percy?" he mouthed silently to Hint.

"Percy," she called, then squeaked the cat. "Good boy. Come on, boy. Come here."

Silence followed.

Jack wanted to ask her to call for Snuggle Bunny, but he didn't want to embarrass her. It was a hands-off sort of nick-name, like Prayer for his oak tree.

"Hey, buddy. Come over here," he stage-whispered.

A flash of gray zipped past them up ahead.

"Percy," she sang out. She moved in the direction where the animal had gone, but it had disappeared.

"Do you think that was him?" he asked.

"I don't know." She gave him an unexpectedly confident look. "But let's believe it was."

They fanned out, each squeaking a toy, slowly walking through the field. No more creatures crossed their paths. After a few moments, Jack made his way back to Hint. He found her crouched down at the base of a broad maple tree, examining an opening amidst its roots.

"Something in there?"

"Not now. But it looks like some sort of animal's home." She glanced back at him, her face animated. "Do you think he might have slept there at night or to get out of the rain?"

"I don't know. Why don't you rub his squeaky cat around the opening? Then if he comes back, he'll follow its scent to the patio."

"Good idea." She dragged the stuffed animal along the ground and on the tree roots around the hole's opening. Soon the dirty white toy was completely gray. Standing up, she shook it out, then signaled she was ready to go. He caught her studying the banged-up side of his face.

"How'm I doing?" He pointed to his shiner.

"It's turning yellow, which means it's healing. Why don't we slap a steak on your face for a minute before we grill it?"

"What's that supposed to do?" he asked, as they headed back to Tom and Nicole's property.

"They say there are enzymes in the meat that help heal bruises. In any case, it's cold, so it will help reduce the swelling."

"Awesome. You won't be the only one to attract Percy with your smell."

She punched his arm then ran ahead. He jogged behind her to the patio, admiring her cello shape again for non-musical reasons.

"You check the grill. I'll get the steaks," she ordered.

He complied, turning down the temperature slightly on the fully-fired grill. Then he reached into the cooler and pulled out two ginger ales.

"Not for me right now," she said. She was carving something into one of the raw steaks. Peering over her shoulder, he saw a figure like an X on the meat.

I've got beer in here too, if you're in the mood," he offered.

"I'll be in the mood when Percy saunters into range and we've got his leash on."

"I like your confidence."

"Lie back so I can put this on your face," was her only response.

Once he reclined, her fingertips dabbed at his left temple, laying the cold slab of steak on his eye. The sensation was refreshing; the smell unusual, but not unpleasant. He felt a tingling sensation, as if the meat was drawing something out of his skin.

He jumped up after several pleasant minutes, slapping the slab of meat that had just been on his face onto the grill, then grabbing the other two she handed him. "Time for steak."

"The one with the X is for Percy, okay?" she told him.

"I gathered that. But if he doesn't show up, can I eat it?"

"He'll show up." Her voice rang with authority. With deft moves, she unpacked a pale blue, purple and green striped tablecloth, then laid out cutlery, plates and glasses on it, along with the potato salad he'd brought.

Jack watched, marveling at her inner strength. She wasn't falling apart in their final hours to find the dog. Instead, she had articulated that the Schnoodle would be joining them. Her confidence fired his own. Perhaps it wasn't based on terra firma, but on her own special brand of magic. He was beginning to see that the magic that both Hint and Marguerite wove around them was something he was familiar with, but had always thought of by a different name. Both woman and girl had a way of seeing things that others didn't, that made them real. He'd always called it faith, not fully comprehending what the concept meant. He was beginning to get a sense of it, the more he got to know Hint.

In less than fifteen minutes, the steaks were done. Jack piled two onto a serving plate, leaving the third one on the grill, which he turned off. The scent of the grilled meat was out of this world. Even a rock would work up an appetite. He certainly had.

Salivating madly, he joined Hint at the patio table. "Here's to Percy," he toasted the Schnoodle, raising his can of ginger ale.

"Here's to Percy with us." Her voice was calm, but he noted her hand tremble ever so slightly as she picked up her drink.

"Here's to us," he rejoined.

Hint's eyes met his as she clinked his soda can. Then she cut a large piece of steak and forked it into her mouth.

"Nice. You can cook," she approved.

"I can grill. And I have access to the best potato salad in the universe." He served her his sister's potato salad.

"This is great. What's in it?" she asked, after taking a bite.

"Bacon. And horseradish to give it some edge. One of my sister's best dishes."

"Umm. Your sister is gifted. Percy will gobble this up when he gets here."

"He will, won't he," he agreed. Then a thought came to him like the whisper of a breeze: *He's already here.*

Picking up one of the less dirty squeaky toys, Jack squeezed it.

Several minutes later, Hint pushed back her seat with a sigh. The steaks were gone, except for the one left on the grill. Large, white, puffy clouds lounged overhead, dotting a china blue sky. In the quiet fullness of the moment, neither of them spoke.

"Do you think we should put the last steak down on the ground on the edge of the patio?" Hint broke their companionable silence.

"Let's cut it up and put part of it down," he suggested. "That way, if an animal other than Percy shows up, we'll still have something left for him." He cut the remaining steak into several pieces, put some on a paper plate, then walked to the edge of the patio, where he placed the plate on the ground.

Minutes passed. For Jack, they weren't empty, but full of being there with Hint.

He hoped she felt the same, but he knew what was foremost on her mind.

Again the thought seized him: *He's already here.* Taking hold of it, he wrapped his heart and mind around it, as if it were a fact. Silently, he gave thanks for Percy's return. Except that the Schnoodle wasn't there. *Pay that thought no mind*, he told himself. *So glad you're back, boy. So glad you decided to join us.*

"I think I'm ready for a beer," Hint broke into his thoughts.

"With pleasure, my lady." Hiding his surprise, he opened the cooler, extracting two bottles of ice cold Pilsners. With a practiced touch, he held them both in one hand, twisting off the tops with the other. He handed her one.

She took a sip. "Ahhh. That tastes good. And I usually don't drink beer." She slowly swung back her head, her neck arched, as she searched the sky.

"That good, huh?" he asked. Hadn't she just said she wouldn't have a beer until Percy was within range? He couldn't figure her out. Ever.

"I'm celebrating Percy's return," she told him.

"You are? That's funny, because I don't see him anywhere." He caught himself as the thought took hold of him again: *He's already here.*

"Ye of little faith," Hint admonished him, echoing his words of a few days earlier. "Didn't you say that to me recently?"

"I might have," Jack admitted, suddenly feeling like Peter denying Christ.

"Faith is the substance of things hoped for, the evidence of . . ."

"Things not seen," he finished for her. The verse, from Hebrews in the New Testament, was one of his favorites, probably because it was a complete mystery to him. On both counts, a lot like the woman next to him.

"So drink your beer and believe," Hint said simply.

"Good call." Taking a long draught, he relished the sting of the cold, foamy liquid as it went down his throat. While he drank, he told himself to let go of his disbelief. If Hint could believe the dog was there, so could he. "Ahh, there's something about a warm day and a cold beer that goes together," he finally remarked.

"You can say that again," she agreed.

"There's something about—" Jack stopped short. A movement just beyond the patio had caught his eye. Something was out there in the brush.

She looked to see why he hadn't finished his sentence, then glanced in the same direction.

Frozen, he held the beer bottle midair, unable to move. Something gray was coming out of the bushes, creeping toward the paper plate on the ground.

Jack lightly squeaked the red and white ball he held. If it was Percy, he'd respond. If it wasn't, the noise would scare off whatever creature it was.

The small animal stopped, its ears perking up.

"It's him," Hint whispered, not moving a muscle.

Together they stared as Percy found his way to the plate and gobbled up the steak.

Stealthily, Jack moved to the grill and slid the other pieces of steak onto a second plate. Out of the corner of his eye, he saw Hint fish out a blue leash from the same bag that had held the dog's toys.

The sound of the rustling paper bag caught the Schnoodle's attention. Warily, the dog looked up.

"Percy," Hint murmured, motioning to Jack for the plate.

He handed it to her. The dog didn't seem ready to bolt, but he wasn't rushing into her arms either. Jack noted the matted, bedraggled condition of his coat. Apparently, he hadn't had an easy time of it out there.

"Come here, boy. Here, Snuggle Bunny. Some more steak for you." She put the dish down in front of her, crouching behind it.

Percy sniffed. He moved forward two steps then stopped. Jack remained motionless. He knew he'd bungle it if he made a big, sweeping man-sized move. He'd wait to see what Hint did, then help her, if it looked like she couldn't collar the Schnoodle.

"Good, Percy. Good boy. Come on, Snuggle Boy. This steak's for you." She noiselessly moved the plate another foot in his direction, then retreated, still crouching.

The dog didn't take his eyes off the steak. Slowly, he inched forward. Finally, he reached his goal and gobbled down the meat.

Leash in hand, Hint sprang forward. In one smooth move, she grabbed the dog's collar. He twitched at her touch, but continued to devour the bits on the plate. Quickly, she snapped the leash onto his collar, then backed off, to give him space.

Jack marveled. Who knew what kind of psychological state the dog was in? Most likely he was fearful of strangers, and perhaps viewing he and Hint as such. He picked up Percy's filthy cat toy and lightly squeaked it.

Percy's ears went up as he looked at it. Cautiously, Jack bent down and dropped the stuffed animal on the ground. The Schnoodle hesitated then went over to sniff it.

For one long moment neither Hint nor Jack moved. Their persistence had paid off, with a dose of magic tossed in—or had it been faith? The dog was back. Inside, Jack was on fire. He hoped Hint was, too.

SHE COULDN'T FATHOM it. She had repeatedly told Jack it would happen, but now that it had—she almost couldn't believe their good fortune. Relief flooded every cell of her body, mingled with anticipation. Finally, she could allow her focus to shift— but the direction it would move in was uncharted territory. Trembling inside, she stole a glance at Jack. He looked amazed, staring at the dirt-encrusted dog in front of them.

"I can't believe it," she exclaimed.

"You should believe it. You kept saying he was nearby. Your confidence pulled him back to us," he praised her.

"I wasn't confident at all. I was just saying that."

"Sometimes just saying something gives it credence," he said. "You breathed hope into reality with your words."

"Thanks, but this is a miracle." The confident pose she'd learnt from Jack just the day before, as he'd convinced Derek Simpson of her high professional value, had worked to lure Percy back. That wasn't all she'd learned since meeting Jack less than one week earlier. With her heart expanding more fully every moment she spent with him, she'd also learned she was no longer prisoner to past hurts. Now, with the dog back, she could finally act upon her feelings.

"It is," he agreed.

"Percy, can I hold you?" She eyed the Schnoodle nuzzling his dirty cat. As she moved quietly toward the dog, he paid her no mind. His original leash was missing, a short, jagged remnant of it still hanging from his collar. She wondered how and by what it had been torn off.

Jack, beside her, put a plate of his sister's potato salad on the ground.

The Schnoodle rose, took two steps to the plate and devoured its contents in less than three seconds.

"Hungry," Jack commented.

"And dirty," she added.

"Should we hose him down?" he asked.

"We should give him a nice, warm bath."

"Your place or mine?"

She stood, looking at Jack. "I'd say mine, but if we go there first, will you have enough time to get him back to your place by five?" Her practical words belied her joy. There was a lot to celebrate; Percy's return was just the start of it.

"Will *we* have enough time, you mean. And no, not really. Let's take him to my place. Believe it or not, I have not only shampoo, but conditioner in my bathroom, all-in-one."

"Okay, Jack." She was glad she'd visited his home earlier that day. Maybe now he'd tell her the name of the oak tree in his backyard.

She dipped her finger in the serving bowl of potato salad and crept toward the dog. She wouldn't initiate touch, but would wait for Percy to respond. Sure enough, the Schnoodle sniffed her hand, then licked it. In a minute, she was stroking his tangled, dusty coat. Soon Percy raised his head to lick her face. She lifted him into her lap, petting and snuggling him.

"You two look very happy together," Jack noted, as he gathered up the remains of their barbecue.

"I just can't believe it."

"You should believe it. You were born under a lucky star," he told her.

"We always like to think so," she said, "but it's rare that something this lucky happens." Yet his statement felt right. For the first time in her life, luck and skill had converged in the space of a few days. Perhaps faith had been the glue that had brought them together.

"Not for you, Dog Whisperer," he assured her. "You landed a big, fat professional contract yesterday, and found Percy today. Your stars lined up this weekend."

"Yours too," she declared, thinking of how she would personally help line them up further, now that Percy was found. Inside, she danced on air.

"They're still aligning," he remarked, reaching down to pick up a paper plate. Was he hiding his face deliberately?

A blush worked its way up from the pit of her stomach to her neck. Quickly, she turned away, fishing in her bag for the dog treat she'd brought, in the hopes they would find him.

"Shall we go?" Jack asked, a minute later.

While she'd snuggled with Percy, he'd cleaned the grill, packed everything in the ice cooler, and even folded her tablecloth. She was Mary to Jack's Martha. The dog looked happy, his tail wagging and his liquid brown eyes making contact with hers.

"Sure. I'm ready. She stood up, holding the leash tightly. As she walked toward the car, the Schnoodle followed easily. He seemed ready to go wherever her hugs and caresses led him.

In twenty minutes they were back at Jack's place in Pleasantville. Hint's adrenalin raced as she got out of the car. For the past six days, all of her emotions had been tempered by worry at Percy's disappearance. But, now, the weight dragging her down was finally gone and reality itself had lightened her mood. Bounding onto Jack's front porch, she danced a few steps from sheer joy. Percy jumped at her heels, sensing her exuberance. A moment later, strong, warm arms stole around her.

"Finally," Jack murmured into her hair.

"Finally." She turned around, straight into his arms. Tension melted off her into an invisible pool of relief at her feet.

Percy barked at their ankles, and the leash tightened. He had spotted a squirrel scrambling up the side of the giant maple in the front yard.

"Not now, boy. It's time for your bath." Hint scooped him into her arms and followed Jack inside.

He led the way upstairs.

At the head of the landing stood a large bathroom. A skylight overhead let in light and framed a leafy panorama of trees. She was impressed. She knelt at the side of the bathtub, motioning to Jack to close the door. He did so, leaning against it on the inside.

Finally, finally, finally. She ran water from both faucets until the temperature was pleasantly warm, but not hot. Then she realized she hadn't showered after her run. An idea dawned on her—naughty, but nice, at the same time.

"Jack, would you go downstairs and get me something cold to drink?" she asked, looking at him through half-lidded eyes.

"My lady, your wish is my command. What would you like?"

"Some ice-cold water would be good." She turned back to Percy, unsnapping the collar from around his neck. His coat was filthy, covered with crusted dirt. Quickly, she lifted the Schnoodle into the bathtub.

Once the door closed behind Jack, she reached over and locked it. She would rinse off Percy first, to remove the initial layer of dirt, then soak him in the bath.

Within seconds, her sweaty running clothes lay in a heap on the floor. She stepped into the bathtub then pulled the shower nozzle out of its holder on the wall. Carefully picking up the dog, she sat on the side of the tub then turned on the shower spray.

Percy didn't seem to mind at all. Hint sensed his joy in having a warm human being with which to snuggle. Evidently, it trumped whatever discomfort he felt in getting wet. She sprayed the length of his body with warm water then reached for the shampoo bottle. Opening the top, she squirted a quarter-sized glob onto the Schnoodle.

Two knocks sounded at the door.

"Hey. Can I come in?" Jack called from the other side.

"No. I'm busy."

"I've got your drink here."

"Thanks. Just leave it outside the door," she ordered.

"Okay. I'll be downstairs. There are fresh towels in the cupboard next to the sink. Help yourself," he offered.

"I will. Bye." She didn't mean to sound dismissive, but she had a job to do. After lathering and rinsing Percy twice, she was finished. With limpid eyes locked onto hers, the dog licked her arm; he seemed overjoyed with the double massage he'd been given. Quickly, she took her own shower, with the Schnoodle behind her in the tub, avoiding the spray of water.

She stepped out, grabbed the large white bathrobe hanging on the back of the door and wrapped herself in it. Then she found a fluffy towel to dry off Percy. Now it was time for the fun part. She always got a kick out of seeing dogs shake themselves dry after a bath or swim.

Percy didn't fail her expectations. Drops of water flew in every direction as the Schnoodle shook himself vigorously. She giggled.

Another knock came at the door.

"Everything okay in there?" Jack's voice called.

"Yes. We're fine."

"You didn't take your drink. It's here waiting for you," he pressed.

Okay, Pirate Boy. I get the message. Then, inspiration struck. The dust, dirt and tension of the past six days had all been washed away in the shower. With one graceful motion, she swung the bathroom door open and gave the man waiting on the other side a smile straight from her heart.

"What's here waiting for me?" she asked.

"Umm. Your drink, my lady." He handed it to her. His eyes were warm as they looked into hers with perfect understanding. Then they danced over her form, wrapped in his white bathrobe, letting her know she belonged inside it. "And if I might add . . ."

"Yes?" Hint lifted an eyebrow, waiting for him to finish his sentence.

"Your future."

ACKNOWLEDGMENTS

My deepest thanks to Terri Valentine, Diana Cecil, Bill, Ava, Grey, and the magical Marguerite Daniels. Most of all, thank you, Percy. You are a good boy.

ROZSA GASTON writes about men and women who follow their hearts as well as their bliss. Her motto? Stay playful.

She studied European history at Yale, and received her master's degree in international affairs from Columbia. In between she worked as a singer/pianist all over the world. She lives in Bronxville, NY with her family, including their Schnoodle Percy.

Post an online review of *Dog Sitters* and she will thank you with a complimentary e-book edition of your choice of any of her other books at **http://bit.ly/RozsaGastonbooks**.

Find her on Facebook at https://www.facebook.com/rozsagastonauthor. Follow her on Twitter at @RozsaGaston or on Instagram at rozsagastonauthor. For special offers and news of upcoming releases, sign up for her newsletter at **www.rozsagaston.com**. She is always happy to hear from her readers.

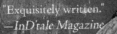

"Exquisitely written."
—InD'tale Magazine

SENSE of TOUCH

LOVE AND DUTY AT
ANNE OF BRITTANY'S COURT

ROZSA GASTON

An excerpt from Rozsa Gaston's captivating medieval historical romance, a 2017 RONE Award finalist

SENSE of TOUCH

1

THE COURT OF ANNE OF BRITTANY

"WHAT DO MEN KNOW of what we endure?" Nicole raged as she hurried down the hallway from the queen's bedchamber. Better to be angry than sad. The latest was beyond unbearable.

She slipped into the outer room of the king's quarters, catching the eye of Hubert de St. Bonnet, the king's head chamber valet. Quickly she shook her head and glanced away. He would understand. Silence spoke volumes. It always did at these moments.

Hubert hurried to Charles VIII at the far end of the room. Nicole watched as the men conferred, their backs to her. By the time her monarch turned to her she told herself he would be ready to receive whatever fortune had to deliver.

"The queen?"

"Fine, Sire. She is resting." Nicole couldn't bear to go on.

"And the dauphin Francis?" King Charles' posture held erect. His fourth son had been born three hours earlier. He had briefly seen him and given him the name Francis for his wife's father, Francis II, Duke of Brittany.

Nicole opened her mouth but nothing came out. The thought came to her that if she didn't say the words, they wouldn't be true. Finally, she spoke.

"The doctors would like a word with you if you can come."

"Does my son live?" the king thundered.

Perhaps he was less ready for the answer than she had thought. He had had plenty of practice receiving similar news in times past, but who could be prepared to hear it yet again?

"He—I cannot say, Sire. The doctor has asked only that you come," Nicole stammered. Better to let those more senior than she deliver the blow.

A tinge of gray passed over the young king's face before he turned from Nicole to his valet. At the age of twenty-seven he had already sired four sons and two daughters. All rested under the Earth save the one who had just arrived.

Hubert de St. Bonnet nodded, almost imperceptibly. "I'm sure they are doing everything they can for—"

"Silence!" The king smashed both hands down on the wood table next to him. Then he overturned it. Courtiers scattered out of the way, the youngest running toward Nicole.

"Go now. The king will come when he is—when he is ready," he whispered, giving her a small push toward the door. The contact was comforting.

"Of course." She bowed her head but looked up through her eyelashes. For the briefest moment before Charles covered his long angular face with one large hand, she saw abject anguish there, a look of misery that made her heart drop. No such expression should cross the face of a man so hale, so fit and full of life as her monarch.

She backed out of the room, then turned and ran down the hallway to the queen's rooms. She could only imagine how the queen felt if the king's grief was that evident. Pray God Anne of Brittany was asleep, drugged with the sleeping draught the doctor had been preparing when Nicole had left. What comfort would the queen have when she woke up and found no small warm being snuggling at her side?

Oh God, how could You be so cruel? Nicole crossed herself.

Who knew what was in the mind of the Master Creator? What point for a woman to hope, to suffer, then finally to labor in unbearable pain at the end of the better part of a year only to deliver a child to die just hours after being born? No doubt God was a man with such faulty designs for womankind. She hoped one day she would get a chance to ask Him why he'd come up with this particular one. Catching herself, she crossed herself again and told herself to stop questioning what was beyond her ken.

❖ ❖ ❖

THE STALLION HAD arrived the week before from one of the royal estates near Toulouse, in the region of Aquitaine in southwestern France. The queen was due to see the stunning new horse the king had gifted her with after the loss of their latest child. Six weeks had passed since the dauphin Francis had died and Anne of Brittany, Queen of France, had seemed on the road to recovery.

But over the past week the queen had been out of sorts. Nicole hoped the combination of the glorious early September weather and the arrival the day before of the groomsman from Agen who would train the new horse would put her in better spirits.

"I am not in the mood today. Someone must go in my place," the queen said, looking sourly toward the cluster of maids of honor at her side. Her expression looked out of place on her young, fair face. Heart-shaped, with a charmingly pointed chin and rosy cheeks, such a face seemed ill-suited to wear such a world-weary expression. Losing six children by the age of twenty had had its effect.

Nicole discreetly scrutinized her royal employer. Her broad forehead glowed with health despite the downward curve of her mouth. Either all was not well or perhaps it was the best of all possible news. Whichever it was, she couldn't bear sitting around trying to coax the queen out of her doldrums any longer.

"Your Majesty, I will go," Nicole and Marie de Volonté offered simultaneously. Nicole looked at the younger girl next to her. The newest addition to the queen's ladies, Marie's head of lush, dark brown curls was beginning to be matched by the promise of an equally lush figure. At age fourteen, she would soon be a candidate for the queen's considerable matchmaking skills, if she showed promise at court.

"Whoever." The queen raised a limp hand, and let it drop again in her lap. She breathed deeply, then leaned back in her chair, closing her eyes. One of her attending ladies stepped forward and held a vial of violet musk perfume under her delicately upturned nose. It was the queen's favorite scent.

Nicole's heart leapt. She had seen that bone-tired attitude before. She would wager it heralded the first weeks of a pregnancy; a time when no one dared breathe a word but when all of the court ladies included the queen in their evening prayers and petitioned God for the child to grasp hold of its mother's womb and refuse to let go until the full time had come to enter the world. Later, the even harder work of keeping the newborn infant alive would begin.

Only once had the queen succeeded: she had given birth to Charles Orland almost five years earlier. The following year, Charles Orland's brother Francis had been delivered prematurely, stillborn. Twice since, the queen had been pregnant, but delivered stillborn daughters. Then the worst had happened.

Just after his third birthday, the young dauphin, Charles Orland, had succumbed to measles. Almost nine months to the day after that terrible event, the queen had delivered a new dauphin, again named Charles. The boy lasted several weeks before a sudden high fever sent him back to Heaven. After that, the latest delivery; again a son, again named Francis like his stillborn brother. The new Francis lived a mere three hours.

Some wondered if perhaps the queen had begun breeding too early, producing Charles Orland just ten months after her marriage at age fourteen to the king. Most didn't though, since it was common practice for royals to marry as soon as they reached puberty; especially if the marriage was one to cement an alliance for reasons of state. In Anne's case, she had agreed to marry Charles VIII in order to win her country's independence after the Franco-Breton war of 1491. The best way for her to secure her position was to produce a dauphin for France. If only one of them had lived.

SENSE of TOUCH

Available wherever books are sold or at
http://lrd.to/Sense_of_Touch

BOOKS BY ROZSA GASTON

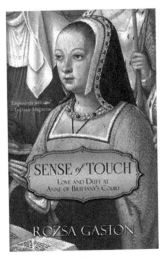

"A striking story."

—Historical Novel Society

A "thoughtful romance."

—Publishers Weekly

Available wherever books are sold or at
http://bit.ly/RozsaGastonbooks

THE AVA SERIES

BOOK 1

"With vivid detail and humor, *Paris Adieu* takes readers straight into the heart of Paris."

—Wild River Review

BOOK 2

"A compelling, entertaining, and deftly crated read from first page to last."

—Midwest Book Review

Available wherever books are sold or at
http://bit.ly/RozsaGastonbooks

Printed in Great Britain
by Amazon